Is there salvation in truth?

Kitten is pregnant and torn between the idea of being both
mommy and sex slave. With the help of her master, Lord Fyre,
she makes the hardest decision of all...infuriating Garret, her
second master. This revisits the question: can one woman truly
serve two masters?

Lord Fyre is torn between blood and ménage. When his twin
brother arrives shot and strung out, Fyre's world of bdsm
suddenly collides with his past. Disappearing with his twin
seems the only answer. But how can the ménage survive if he
isn't there to hold it together?

Garrett faces uncertainty, knowing he has lost control of
Kitten. He knows he must embrace his inner-Dom, known as
Lord Ice, if he is ever to come out of the shadow of Lord Fyre
and gain full control of Kitten. But is another man the answer?

The bonds of love and commitment is further tested when
Lord Fyre pulls his lovers into his dark and dangerous world
of intrigue in this fourth installment of the Chronicles of
Surrender series.

ECHO OF REDEMPTION

Chronicles of Surrender

Book Four

ROXY HARTE

Lyrical Press, Inc.

New York

LYRICAL PRESS, INCORPORATED

Echo of Redemption

13 Digit ISBN: 978-1-61650-185-3

Copyright © 2010 Roxy Harte

Edited by Pamela Tyner

Book design by Renee Rocco

Cover Art by Renee Rocco

Lyrical Press, Incorporated

337 Katan Avenue

Staten Island, New York 10308

http://www.lyricalpress.com

PUBLISHER'S NOTE:

This book is a work of fiction. The names, characters, places, and incidents are products of the writer's imagination or have been used fictitiously and are not to be construed as real. Any resemblance to persons, living or dead, actual events, locale or organizations is entirely coincidental.

The publisher does not have any control over and does not assume any responsibility for author or third-party Web sites or their content.

Published in the United States of America by Lyrical Press, Incorporated

First Lyrical Press, Inc electronic publication: May 2010

First Lyrical Press, Inc print publication: August 2010

DEDICATION

For Mom and Dad, I miss you every moment of every day.

"For it was not into my ear you whispered, but into my heart. It was not my lips you kissed but my soul."

Judy Garland

CHAPTER 1

KITTEN

San Francisco, CA

January 21

Sitting cross-legged on the sofa, a man on my left, a man on my right, I have no idea who to look at, so I stare straight ahead. Garrett. Thomas. *My men.* Known to me as Master and Lord Fyre. Our ménage is still intact. I sigh heavily and both men squeeze a hand. I hadn't noticed before that they are each holding one of my hands. Across the room, I can see their faces reflected in the darkened floor to ceiling bank of windows, framing the inky night sky. I try to read their expressions, but it is impossible. They aren't looking at me. They are staring at each other, increasing tension already so thick in the room I could choke on it. I wait for the war to begin imminently. All because I'm pregnant. No, that isn't the *all.*

I tried to tell Thomas first and considered not telling Master. Ever.

Master saw it as me choosing Thomas over him, but I wasn't. I was choosing the ménage over a baby. *Bloody hell, this is impossible.* It certainly doesn't help that Garrett believes the child is Thomas's. Every parent wants to see a bit of themselves in their child's face. Garrett will never have that opportunity. He will look at this child and see Thomas. Every. Single. Time. I am an idiot. I am surprised he is even *here*.

Without meaning to, my gaze focuses on the reflected image of Thomas, and I try to imagine him as a child. The thought makes me smirk as I visualize his face beardless, his eyes and mouth younger…younger still. I imagine his long dark hair as short dark curls. Bright pink, pudgy cheeks. I snort, the face I have conjured in my mind could be boy or girl. A beautiful child. Their reflected faces are suddenly looking at me, both demanding answers to unasked questions. I force myself to look at neither and both.

I am not choosing sides!

This child could as easily be Garrett's. An equally beautiful child.

It is hopeless. I love both men.

I can't help remembering the night Master collared me, the same night he bought me at auction. We stood in a storeroom and he was explaining the rules of the member's only area of Lewd Larry's, his BDSM nightclub. Feline. Canine. Pet play. It all seemed so foreign, but then the collar closed around my neck and he commanded me to meow.

"Merroww." I'd done the best imitation I was capable of doing of Monet, my luxurious Maine-Coon cat, and suddenly *everything* fell in place for me. I was collared, owned, but I could also be a more base being than my mundane-human counterpart could ever be. Animals have no morality. Animals have no sin. I cried, unashamed, and became Kitten in that moment. Garrett Lawrence had claimed my heart the instant he became *Master*.

But feeling that way, I also feel if Master owns my heart, Lord

Fyre owns my soul. I felt it the first time our eyes locked, even though at the time I was comparing him to the one most evil. I felt it then, I still feel it now, every time he looks at me, he sees my darkest needs...and I know his.

I am no longer collared, a matching brand on each of our left arms makes us each others. In the beginning, our ménage was perfect. We took turns playing with each other but as time has marched on, I think Master has become jealous of the time I spend with Lord Fyre.

I don't understand jealousy.

Garrett has private play dates with Lord Fyre, and I don't get all moody and sullen. If anything I'm happy for them both because there is a difference in both of them after a scene, one that is hard to explain but I know is a good thing for them because they are so relaxed and happy. Besides, it gives me free time to myself.

As much as I enjoy being doted on and constantly with my men, a moment alone can be very nice.

I'm not sure when things changed.

I used to look forward to Sunday's Margaritas, Movies, and Mayhem and the relaxed Mondays with Master that followed. More and more often he is working on Mondays, leaving me alone, which makes me long for Tuesday, my day to play with Lord Fyre, which usually leaves me wrung out for days. We've never discussed why things are different or how we feel about how things are turning out.

And now this baby. *Holy fuck.* It isn't Garrett's. I didn't know that he was infertile when I didn't tell him about the baby right away. I was under the assumption it could be either man's equally. I wasn't really concerned or even interested in knowing which. That wasn't why I didn't want to talk to Garrett about it. I was afraid of the repercussion. I was afraid of losing the unconventional, kinky life I live.

I like being Master's *Kitten*. I really like being Lord Fyre's *Sophia*.

I like being the CEO of *The Darkness*, an alternative lifestyle daily tabloid, and a full partner at Lewd Larry's.

I don't know if I am going to like being *Mommy*.

I fear that I am not very maternal. The thought of nursing makes me ill. I cannot even imagine what else goes with motherhood. At my father's parish, I used to feel sorry for the women being pulled in a dozen different directions by their small children, leaving them no time for self-care. They would drop into the pew like lead weights, obviously relieved they were being given an hour's reprieve, their children in someone else's capable hands. I wasn't that someone, though I tried once, putting in my time at the nursery. Crying, screaming, snot-nosed, poop-covered babies were not my forte.

"Oh God, I can't do this." I look away, avoiding Master's gaze, wondering if I spoke out loud. If I did, he doesn't acknowledge my words. I close my eyes, fear wrapping around me. *I cannot have this baby.* I would be a terrible mother.

Our gazes meet in the glass. Mine and Thomas's. He is worried, his face tight with it. As I watch his reflection, I see the slightest easing of tension around his lips, not quite a smile, but enough of a change that I begin to feel that *we* are going to be all right.

I still won't meet Master's gaze, not even in the reflecting surface of the window. Avoidance? Maybe. Fear? Probably. My arm is freshly scarred from the brand uniting us as a ménage. I won't give it up.

Thomas squeezes my hand. "Relax."

"How can I?"

"It's only a baby, not the end of the world."

"It feels like the end of *my* world."

I realize immediately my mistake and that it was the wrong thing to say when Master stands and walks to the window we've all been watching each other in. Thomas and I both watch Garrett. He is standing with his back to us, stiff as a board. It is hard to believe we will ever be able to fix any of this.

I finally manage to look Thomas in the eyes. "I'm sorry."

He kisses me. "Whatever for?"

I gesture chaotically with my hands between us and Garrett. "Isn't it obvious?"

He pulls me closer, maneuvering me into his lap. "This is growing pains. Every relationship has them."

I whisper, "You aren't worried?"

"We'll be fine."

I know we, Thomas and I, will be fine, but will the ménage survive this? I don't ask. He kisses my eyelids closed just as he does when a scene is about to begin. "Relax."

His command is magic, like a drug, medicating me into a peaceful place. I keep my eyes closed, remembering our first encounter, letting it play out in my mind. He'd kissed my eyelids closed, then covered them with a leather blindfold. I was terrified, my back against a wall and I'd had nowhere to go.

No, that isn't how it had happened at all. He'd produced the blindfold and lifted the leather to my lips. Just before I'd kissed it the thought went through my head: *shouldn't we discuss this? Limits and safe words and scene parameters?* But then I'd kissed the leather, giving him permission to start the scene. My mind had snapped, I'd felt it give, just a little, not like I was going to be insane or enlightened from the event, but snapped enough to know I was free to experience whatever came. It was a slow brain orgasm, a profound epiphany, as every ounce of resistance slid away. Then he'd kissed my eyelids closed and whispered close to my ear as the blindfold covered my eyes. "You know I won't hurt you. You trust me to keep you safe. Don't you, Celia?"

He'd waited for an affirmative response, but I hadn't been able to manage it because I hadn't known it to be the truth. He'd wrapped his hand around the back of my neck, raising gooseflesh, raising expectations of pain, but yielded only a gentle massage.

"I can't go any further if I don't have your complete trust, Celia."

I'd snapped, "I'm here, aren't I?"

Looking back, I wonder what I was thinking? I'd never been so disrespectful to *anyone*. Had I somehow been begging him to refuse me? Or had I been trying to bring out his worst? His response had been to laugh, a deep rumbling, fully amused laugh. "That you are. I had forgotten how full of spunk you are."

I'd thought, spunk? The notion was laughable. I was the opposite of spunky, whatever that was. I was the one who pleased everyone—I'd always been the good girl. Still, I'd mouthed off, "Look, this is just a test for me. I'm not here to have fun. I'm here to prove something—got it? So skip all the beginner Master-slave relationship bullshit and just tie me up or something!"

I was so naïve that day, so fucking stupid. I wonder now if I was testing him…or myself. The question never was could he really Master me? Could he help me find my darkness? The real question was did I want him to? Did I really want to face that part of myself and could I live with myself once I did?

In response to my disrespect, he'd hit me. Square in the middle of my chest. Even after the pain ripped through my sternum, making me feel like several vertebrae had collapsed and I couldn't breathe, I still couldn't believe he'd hit me. My knees had buckled, not from the pain but from the full mental impact of what I'd done. I hadn't just sought out Satan, I'd challenged him to a match of wills. It was *our* beginning.

Just remembering I feel all warm and fuzzy inside.

I still challenge him. Take me to the edge. *Take me. Take me. Take me.* Life. Death. Walk the fine line between with me. Lord Fyre understands the depth of my need. Pain. In all its glorious manifestations: mental, physical, emotional, or spiritual. Opening my eyes, I see Thomas still looking at me with concern, a fear I don't understand evident in his eyes.

Will having a baby change the way Lord Fyre treats me?

No, I don't think it will and that gives me hope.

I hug his face in my hands and pray he sees in my eyes that I trust him still. Mouthing, 'I love you,' I kiss him. I angle my head toward Garrett. "Can we have a minute?"

"That sounds like a very good idea."

Giving him a hopeful but not entirely optimistic look, I leave him to join Garrett at the window. "Master?"

He looks at me and lets out a long sigh. He's exhausted. We all are. It's been a long few weeks and an entirely too emotional day to boot. I can't remember the last time any of us had any real sleep. He asks softly, "Yes?"

I have no idea. When I was on the couch, sitting with Thomas, I knew I had to be the one to make things right, but how am I to do that? I walk into him, wrapping him in my arms, even if he is unwilling to be held. Thankfully he doesn't resist. He hugs me back.

I don't say things I don't mean. There are words frozen on my tongue, sentiments that might make everything better immediately. *I'm sorry.* Except I'm not, not for any of it. *I want this baby.* Except I'm still not one hundred percent positive I do. I finally settle on the one thing I can say with my whole heart and all of my soul, whispering, "I love you," against his neck. When he pulls me tighter against him, I am encouraged to add, "I can't imagine life without you in it. Please tell me how to make things right."

"I wish I knew, *Kitten.*"

Kitten. We're okay then, right? Because if we weren't okay he would call me Celia. "God, I'm exhausted."

He kisses the top of my forehead. "Me too. Do you want to go to bed?"

I look up into his face, wanting to ask but not asking, *the three of us?* Because it should be the three of us, shouldn't it? Even after everything...Eva...the unexpected pregnancy...my deception...it is still the three of us.

It's in his eyes he doesn't feel the same way. He wants to be alone with me. I've ended up saying the wrong thing after all. There's no out except to decline going to bed, and that will make everything so much worse.

Buzz. Buzz.

I am saved by the door. God, what time is it? Late? Early? We rarely have unexpected visitors, meaning it can only be one person. She loves Garrett, she loves drama, and last night's fight at the club had to have piqued her curiosity. I'm only surprised she waited as long as she did. Knowing Enrique the houseboy will answer the door, I look in anticipation, expecting Jackie to sail in.

Garrett's arms tighten around me, making me look into his face. Words don't have to be said to know what he is thinking. *This isn't over.* There's so much to talk about. *I can't imagine life without you in it either.* I wish he'd say it out loud because right now I really need to hear the words.

Enrique peeks around the edge of the door. "Sorry to disturb. A man at de door said dat I mus' give ju dis message immediately."

"Who is it?" Garrett demands irritably.

"Not you." Enrique looks at Thomas. "He did not give his name. He said to tell ju de words Alexiares and Aniketos."

Thomas jumps up and races into the foyer. Loud voices follow— his and a man I don't recognize. They speak in a foreign language. Thomas's native Greek, I believe. I look at Garrett. Shrugging, he takes my hand and leads me to the leather couch as the voices get louder. He leaves me to join Thomas in the foyer. Out of sight. God, what is happening? My heart is pounding. Something is wrong. Horribly wrong.

Looking white as a sheet, Enrique sits down on the section of sofa vacated by Thomas but doesn't say a word. He is so loyal like that, to Garrett. Unless Master wants me to know what is happening on the other side of the wall, I will not know.

What I do know is that our ménage's drama has been displaced by something even more intense.

"It came like magic in a pint bottle; it was not ecstasy but it was comfort."

Charles Dickens, *Little Dorrit*

CHAPTER 2

NIKOS

Shanghai, China

January 19

Smoke softens the edges of all the hard surfaces. The air reeks. Name your poison. It is here. Heroine? Opium? Ice? Hashish? I host big parties, I pay big bribes. You are nobody in China unless you are paying off somebody. I can say I'm the king here, because I pay everyone to forget they ever saw me.

Tonight, every night, there is a party in full swing.

Mr. Children fills the air, a lyrical love song. No, love-gone song.

The song makes my head ache as I try to not focus on the words, my brain translating even though I don't want it to.

"Too many things demanded. Only if it's possible, I want to be by your side. In between these times my breath is ceasing."

I do not long for a lost lover. I've never been in love. My melancholy is because I saw my twin brother yesterday for the first time in a decade. He looked the way I used to: tall, strong, proud. I cannot be proud of who I have become even though I have become the man I am at the orders of the country I serve. I say serve because none of the united European allies operating the WODC were the place of my birth. I am Greek. I have to remind myself of that. There is a pride to being Greek, and even when there isn't a single other thing on this world left for me to feel pride in, I will have my nationality. I am Greek. I am Demetres Aristotle Velouchiotis's brother.

Two things to be proud of.

I only hope Ari can still say he is proud to be the twin of Socrates Nikos Velouchiotis though neither of us has heard our birth names in a very long time.

It seems our lives have been predestined to carry us both on the paths we walk, all of our family...grandfather, father, uncle...having walked the same road. Ari and I were given knives and guns when boys the same age were still playing with toy trucks and trains. We were taught to climb and rappel in the mountains while our friends were still figuring out how to make a kite lift on the breeze. By the time we were teenagers, we were both masterful at all the skills required for our predetermined vocations: soldier, spy, assassin. Like a superhero, we would fight the evil-doers.

I watch the flow of traffic below. The wall-size window of my penthouse, high in the sky, shows me all of Shanghai. Bright red and white lights flicker, ebbing and flowing. I am reminded of glowing embers, a campfire, or the pit of hell. I am reminded, benignly that when my time is past there will be no heaven for me.

I was a good man. I can almost remember that time.

I turn my back to the window and survey my realm. I can see from one end of the loft to the other without obstruction, though the portion I stand in is raised by several feet. My "office." Open and accessible. The "pit" is a sea of couches, chairs and low tables, an area designed for the gathering of my loyal subjects, trusted men, beautiful women. Giggling girls flutter around the room, wearing brightly colored silk dresses. They will all be nude…soon.

"Alone late at night the loneliness explodes. The bittersweet candy was still in the pocket of my chest…please, eat it."

"Someone change the fucking song!"

The music stops, replaced with something more techno, less maudlin.

I control with fear. Bow down before me and if I like you, I may let you live. Pity if I don't like you, or if you cross me…death will be the blessing you beg for.

This is my empire, my kingdom, the one I built while no one was looking. While all had their eyes on my predecessor, King Cobra, I forged a new realm. I was his right hand man. For almost a decade I knew his every thought, his every deed, his malevolence, and his compassion.

I find it superbly funny that while I was an undercover agent planted by the WODC, he was posing as an agent as well. All along, while they looked for him, he was right under their noses. No one knew. Well, he obviously did. I discovered *his* truth and by some stroke of luck or genius he didn't discover *mine*. Somehow, I managed to keep him from killing me long enough to convince him what a great team we could make. However, to do so I had to be even more manipulative, more evil, than he'd ever considered being.

I could say he was an evil mother-fucker. A sadist in every sense of the word. Maniacal. Sociopathic. Terrorist. But I refuse to consider what I have become in order to complete the assignment. The first order of business, earning his trust and discovering every aspect of his organization, took years.

I'm not the same man I was when I took this job.

He is dead now, though not by my hand. That was the plan all along. At some point I would become his replacement, the Special Operations unit of the WODC's idea of how to control the outcome, the alpha dog able to keep all the other dogs in line. Left to a turf war of global proportions, bedlam would ensue. I minimize the chaos.

"Sir?"

I look down into the face of one of the women here for the party. *Young.* All of the women here are young, some too young, and she definitely falls in the category of the latter. She is a child, dressed up and made up, too much makeup for my taste, taught to walk and talk and breathe sensuality. I can't say she is particularly pretty; not considering the room is filled with perfection. My biggest problem isn't with her age, or that she isn't as beautiful as the others, but that I don't recognize her. That makes me nervous. Hundreds of women have rotated through my life and this one I have never seen before. "Who are you?"

She moves closer, touching the sleeve of my Tessori Uomo jacket. "I please you tonight?"

Her hand roves higher and I notice she is trembling slightly as she glides her fingertips from my elbow to my shoulder. She smiles, trying for seductive and failing. Fear fills her eyes.

I react, leaving a bullet-size hole in the center of her forehead, not even remembering pulling the small caliber handgun from my side holster. Shrill screams erupt around the room. Women hide behind furniture, knowing better than to run because if they flee, they too die. Anyone who has been with me more than a few hours knows this.

My men are at my elbow, surrounding me with a shield of bodies before I can take my next breath. Two men start to pick up the dead woman when I demand, "Gloves."

They pull latex gloves from their pockets.

"I want to know who she is, who she knows. Have her skin processed."

"Poison?" One of my men asks.

I don't bother giving him an answer. This is my life. Every day—sometimes many times a day—death comes looking for me. You would think I would lose track of the sheer number of enemies I have, but to become lax is to die. I know them by name, by face, by country of origin, by dialect, and by the timbre of their voices.

I fish three pills from my pocket, the flavor of the day.

I am called a fool by my enemies, an addict, but the truth is, I have the edge. I am alert when I need to be alert, I sleep when I feel safe enough to relax, and when the day or week demands that I do not sleep...I don't.

The threat has been eliminated today. Tonight, I sleep.

"You." I point at one of the exquisite whores. She stands immediately and walks to me. Her eyes are downcast. She is petite, thin, her waist-length raven-black hair hanging past her hips almost to her knees. The silk dress she is wearing leaves little to the imagination, clinging to her nakedness like a wet t-shirt.

Taking her hand, I lead her to my bedroom.

"What is your name?"

"Wen-Qi."

Sitting on the edge of my bed, I reach for a bottle of apricot oil on the nightstand. I hand it to her. "I tell you what, Wen-Qi. I'm tired. I want to sleep. Take care of me tonight."

She nods and kneels in front of me. She sits the bottle on the floor beside her before unbuttoning my shirt. Pushing the fabric off my shoulders, her fingertips linger over a section of my *horimono.*

"You like my tat, do you?"

She licks her lips. "It is terrifying."

I have to laugh. *Terrifying.* I suppose the dragons and demons covering my body might be just that. She helps me out of my shoes and the rest of my clothes before standing to remove her own. It isn't really necessary for her to be naked. Though she is perfection, I couldn't care less.

"Jerk me off, Wen-Qi. With your hands and the oil, not your mouth."

Hurrying to do my bidding, she picks up the bottle of oil and pours a good amount in her cupped hand. She starts to touch me, but I stop her. "No. Drizzle the oil over my cock and balls. I like the way it feels for the oil to drip over my flesh before you touch me."

She picks the bottle up and drizzles. I close my eyes, the cool liquid lapping over my prick like a bodiless tongue. She waits a sufficient amount of time before closing her warm fingers around my stiff penis. She squeezes me hard enough to remind me that I have metal bars piercing my frenulum. Four. They form a ladder of sorts up my shaft.

Keeping her palm wrapped around my length, she slides her hand up and down. I like the way the fine grit of ground apricot pits mixed in the oil adds to the sensation.

"Pull the lorum ring, babe."

She obeys, pulling on the piercing between shaft and balls with the opposite hand from the one she is pumping me with. She doesn't miss a beat.

"Rougher. Be rougher."

She tries, but I think she is afraid that if she hurts me I will blow her brains out.

"Please." I open my eyes, meeting her gaze. "If you do not cause me some serious agony in the next five seconds I will do to you something a hundred times worse than your imagination can come up with."

She pulls the metal loop at the base of my cock and twists. At the same time it feels like she is ripping the entire ladder of bars through the flesh holding them in place. I scream loud enough to cause four of my bodyguards to burst in.

"Get out!"

Her hand stills and I again meet her gaze, hoping she understands that I don't want to kill her tonight. I don't want to kill anyone else today. "Please, please, please. Don't stop again, Wen-Qi. Until I come or pass out, don't stop."

* * * *

Pop. Pop, pop, pop. Pop, pop. I dream of fireworks, but then the pain hits me.

Without even checking my vitals, my assailant flees and I am left moaning in the dark. Alone. Where in the fuck are my men? As I stumble from my room, I find bodies. Some dead. Some alive but dying. "God damn, amateur."

To have gotten so close but done the job so poorly…

"Fuck!" I wrap my arms around myself, trying to hold in all my spilling blood.

Wen-Qi stumbles from the bedroom and I see that she too is bleeding, a shoulder wound, nothing life threatening. As the room starts to fall into shades of gray I know *I* am in trouble. I reach under the bar for a first aid kit and start packing my wounds with quick-clot. Seeing a bright yellow dress lying across the back of a chair, I grab it and start ripping it into strips to wrap around my body. Two of my men, obviously late to the party, arrive and seeing the scene hurry forward to assist me. Only one do I trust. Sean Paul. We have been on–again, off-again lovers for more years than I can count. "Thank God you're here. Get me to the US."

Our gazes clash. He knows what I'm asking. I want Ari. If I am going to die, I want someone who actually gives a damn about my soul to be with me when I go.

As we flee the building, I don't have to tell him to trigger the self-destruct. *He knows.* Behind us the entire penthouse level explodes in a fireball that can be seen for miles. I know it seems cruel, knowing many will die in my endeavor to escape, but it is my attempt at compassion. I will not have the ones once loyal to me tortured in my enemies' efforts to find me. The explosion is also a nice distraction. With the tallest building in Shanghai burning, no one will pay attention to our leaving.

"I have heard there are troubles of more than one kind. Some come from ahead and some come from behind. But I've bought a big bat. I'm all ready you see. Now my troubles are going to have troubles with me!"

Dr. Seuss

CHAPTER 3

KITTEN

San Francisco, CA

January 21

A naked man lies restrained in the middle of our dining room table, not such an unusual circumstance for any particular night but an odd fact given Master is operating on him. Removing bullets to be exact. The man on the table I only just discovered is my lover Thomas's twin. Almost two years I've known him and never once did he believe the information was relevant.

I'm peeved.

As much because there are now blood stains on the wood floors as because I feel I know nothing about the two men I call Master. Take Garrett, for instance. I knew he had attended a medical university in Ohio and worked for a while in a trauma center, but that was his life before we met and I rarely consider it. I only know him as Garrett

Lawrence, owner of Lewd Larry's Underground, a BDSM nightclub. I've certainly never thought of him as a surgeon. He looks calmly confident for a man who hasn't held a scalpel in God knows how long. And really? A scalpel? I didn't even know we had one in the house. *Several.* Garrett has a full on triage kit and after starting a saline drip and adding an antibiotic bag, both hung from a metal coat rack to give them height, he started operating.

There didn't seem to be a choice.

"Shouldn't we call nine-one-one?"

Did I ask that? Did Enrique? I don't even know if the words were said out loud.

There is a black man standing guard, and I fear for all our safety even though he isn't waving a gun or making any outward threat. *Fuck. Oh, fuck. Is he armed?*

Thomas stands near enough to the table to watch but not be in the way. I watch him more so than I do Garrett. Even after more than a year together, he is still a mystery. He shares nothing of his life outside of our ménage. He too is my Master, and it is just as complicated as it sounds having two Masters to please. We wear each other's brands on our forearms—the three of us a united ménage—but as I watch Thomas's face etch with worry and Garrett's hand remain steady despite the lack of cooperation of his very awake patient, I become even more angry realizing just how much I don't know about either man.

I watch from the edge of the sofa, my knees tucked tightly under my chin. Not being one to miss anything exciting in the house, Enrique, our houseboy, sits beside me, holding my hand. He makes a great show of comforting me but he is the one who is as pale as a ghost.

God. Oh God. Thomas's brother is bleeding from more holes in his body than I can count. *This isn't good. This really isn't good.*

Though if the strength of the man's curses is any indication, he's going to be just fine. But what about the rest of us? Has he led danger straight to our door?

I shouldn't even being having such thoughts, but I am, because I'm not naïve. I know that when Thomas leaves on business trips, he isn't doing a normal job. He's always armed but especially when he travels. I like to think he operates on the right side of the law, but wonder if our views would even be the same on that. One thing is for certain. I knew the moment I met him, Thomas was a dangerous man. I don't doubt for a minute his brother is any less so. A dozen weapons were removed from Thomas's brother, along with his clothes. The evidence of Thomas's secret life being so blatantly exposed makes me more afraid than I've ever been. I hate his brother for showing up here. I suppose it wouldn't be a very Christian thing to do to toss him to the curb with last night's garbage, but that is exactly what I want to do. I don't care that he is Thomas's brother. He shouldn't be here.

And this stranger…who is he? He's wearing a jacket but beneath it he is armed. I saw the handle of a gun when he lifted his arm, and I doubt it is his only weapon.

I've never been overly superstitious but in this moment, I wish I were. I want to sprinkle salt over the eaves, spill brandy on the thresholds, hang dried wormwood on every wall. I need a bright blue Nazar Boncugu. *I want him gone!*

A scream fills the air and Thomas pushes his brother's shoulders back down onto the table, even though a dozen straps restrain him. "Hang on, Nikos. He's almost finished."

Nikos. His brother has a name.

It is obvious the man is out of his mind. The question is whether it is from pain, drugs, or if he is really insane. He is like a rabid dog. Crazy. His eyes make me believe no one is home.

He was right-minded enough to track and find his brother. How did he find Thomas *here*? I'm not so certain I want to know. Surely Thomas didn't give him our address.

The doorbell rings and only after a nod from Thomas does Enrique hurry to answer it. He emits George Fitzpatrick, Garrett's Number One at Lewd Larry's. There he is known as Dr. Psycho, though he isn't crazy, far from it. In fact, he is a retired psychiatrist turned full-time professional Dominant. I wasn't surprised when Thomas called him and asked him to join us, stating only that it was an emergency and his services were required immediately.

"What in the hell?" Seeing the scene, George is obviously alarmed.

I've been here an hour and I'm still alarmed. *Seriously. What the hell?*

"George, my brother, Nikos," Thomas introduces.

"Fuck you!" Nikos raises off the table as far as the straps will allow, trying to sit up.

Thomas smacks the back of his head.

Garrett pulls a bullet from the man's thigh and it makes a disgusting, wet popping sound as the suction around the bullet breaks. He drops the bullet into a metal bowl, and it clangs louder than it seems it should. I hold my breath, hoping that was the last bullet. I've lost count of how many have been pulled from him.

"Should we be doing this here? It isn't exactly sterile," George comments.

"There isn't anywhere else to do this, George," Garrett tells him. "Thanks for coming on such short notice."

"Thomas said it was a matter of life and death, but I see no one in danger of expiring imminently."

"That's the point, I think. I can patch up his body, but his mind is all yours."

"I'd be more concerned about infection setting in. If he's dead, his mind won't matter."

A string of what I believe is obscenities in at least a dozen languages issues forth from Nikos's mouth. If I had to guess I'd say he is trying to convince Master he is sane and rational, but as his glassy eyes dart all over the place, not focusing, he loses that battle.

"I see." George looks over his wire rims at his patient and it is obvious something has switched. The psychiatrist is in the house. "What drug's influence is he under?"

Thomas kneels beside his brother and whispers into his ear. It isn't quite clear whether he is trying to calm him or question him until Nikos starts listing his drugs of choice. "Opium. Heroine. Meth."

"Jesus Christ," George curses, but it soon becomes obvious that Nikos is not done.

He keeps speaking. "Hashish. Cocaine."

George ignores the man. "I'm going to need a complete toxicology report. It's obvious he didn't understand the question."

Thomas assures him, "I asked him what drugs he has used in the last thirty days. Would you prefer to know the last twenty-four hours?"

George shakes his head. "I'll trust the lab results when I have them. If what he states is true, Garrett's wasted his time getting all that metal out of his body because the detox will likely kill him unless he's in an appropriate medical facility."

Garret drops another bullet into the metal bowl and it *tings* loudly. He looks up to catch George's gaze. "That's exactly why Thomas called you. I'd like you to take him home with you, see to his needs. Of course, discretion…and Thomas will cover any expense."

George waves his hand dismissively at the offer of cash. The look on his face tells the tale. He's already accepted the assignment.

Thomas interjects, "We'll need George's absence explained, an extended vacation, several weeks."

George snorts. "A month at least."

"Yes, yes," Garrett responds distractedly as he stitches closed a wound. He speaks softly to Thomas's brother. "You're a very lucky man. No vital organs were hit. Unbelievably lucky."

An hour later Thomas and George are gone, thankfully, carrying Nikos out between them with the tall, silent, black man leading. With Enrique scrubbing away all evidence they were ever here, it seems my intention for no evil being able to linger in my home has been met, no brandy or salt scattering required. From across the room, I watch as Master pours a full tumbler of Scotch.

I haven't moved from my spot on the couch. I guess I'm still waiting to wake up. This was all just a bad dream, wasn't it? I wish it were. Making myself stand, I walk to his side and reach for the chilled glass, my fingers bumping his. "I could use a sip or two."

He catches my gaze and looks at me hard before his eyes drop to my belly, his message obvious even before he says, "I don't think so."

I cross my arms over my expanding womb.

"Hiding it doesn't make it not so."

I look away, unable to face him. It was easy to forget during the night's interruption that in the moment before Nikos's untimely arrival, we had been discussing my pregnancy and why I'd thought it was a good idea to keep it a secret as long as I did. We hadn't really gotten around to the part where I explained I'd only confirmed the fact myself.

It's ridiculous to say so now. I wouldn't believe me either.

You meant to completely shut me out of any decision making from the moment you realized you were pregnant and didn't share the news with me.

The words still hang between us though they were said hours ago.

He takes a long sip of the Scotch, half the tumbler's contents disappearing. He looks exhausted. No. He looked exhausted when I arrived with Thomas. Since then he has spent several hours bent over Nikos, trying to make certain he would survive. What comes after exhausted? I wish I knew.

"There is nothing more deceptive than an obvious fact."

Sir Arthur Conan Doyle, *The Boscombe Valley Mystery*

CHAPTER 4

THOMAS

In the privacy of the deserted parking garage, I face Sean Paul, a man who has been loyal to my brother and I since we all met at Oxford almost two decades ago. The last time I saw him was in France. He has been my informant, my brother's lover for almost as long. Our gazes collide. "Thank you for getting him to me."

He nods, grimly. "We part ways here. I'll be in touch."

After brushing his lips against my brother's feverish face, he disappears into the dark shadows. It is best for me to not know if he will remain here or go back across the ocean. He will lurk, eyes and ears collecting information, and will only appear again when he knows it is safe for all of us.

My brother is weak and delirious. I should be thankful he is alive. Pushing him into the backseat of George's Saab, I slap his face. "How dare you come here!"

"I'm sorry." His head falls backward onto the headrest.

"This is the home of the only two people on the planet I truly care about other than my children."

I climb into the backseat with him and buckle us both up. He rolls his eyes to look at me. "That isn't true. You love me. I'm your brother. I'm *your blood*."

His accent is as thick as I've ever heard it. His voice is full and deep. I am reminded of the man who raised us. Grandfather. He taught us everything that is important about life and family and duty.

You will keep each other safe and that is why you will need a word between you...a word that is not used in everyday speech, so the meaning will not be misconstrued and never used as a joke. In an emergency, you will use the word and it will mean you need the other's help.

We were young boys when we'd agreed Alexiares and Aniketos would be our secret word. The twin sons of Herakles and Hebe. It seemed appropriate at the time, their names meaning respectively, "he who wards off war" and "the unconquerable," lending much debate in future years as to which of us was the peacemaker and which of us invincible.

He'd used the words tonight, announcing even before he'd entered my threshold that he was in danger. I chose to drag him inside. I offered my protection without asking for any explanation.

His eyes close.

"Let him rest while he can. He's going to need it." George catches my gaze in his rearview mirror. "Detox may kill him."

"He's strong," I insist, looking away, not willing to consider losing him. *This is all my fault.* A decade ago I was supposed to go on an undercover assignment. He showed up ahead of me, convincing the leader of a terrorist cell that he was me. We'd been identical then. There's no chance of anyone ever believing that now.

I think he purposely changed his appearance to keep me from trying to switch us back. Now, his head is shaved and the goatee he wore is now trimmed down to a soul patch. He's pierced his cheek dimples, filling the natural indentations with pointed silver studs. His ears too are pierced, four hoops of various caliber and design through each lobe.

From our past encounter, I know he wears a wide metal spider stud through his tongue and bars through his nipples. Until tonight I wasn't certain if he was pierced anywhere else on his body. Post surgery I know he has a four bar frenum ladder, a ring at the base of his shaft, and two rings decorating his glans.

Then there is his tattoo, a *horimono* design. My brother's body has become a canvas of color, wrist to ankle and all the parts between. There is a pale strip of flesh down the front of his chest so that when the top two buttons of a dress shirt are parted, the ink doesn't show. Likewise his face and neck are free of ink, but the rest swims with color. A panorama of samurai, geisha, demons, koi and dragons, rolling into and out of each other, both connected and separated by smoky gray clouds or crashing waves. The art covering my brother is both masterpiece and tragedy. That he would go to such lengths to ensure we are never confused one for the other...

I watch the passing scenery through the window. Night has come and gone, dawn too passed. Somehow we managed to miss rush hour and the drive to George's house has been easy. Still, I take a close look at every car we pass, every pedestrian, looking for trouble I hope doesn't come. A ridiculous dream on my part. If my brother's enemies discover he isn't dead, things could turn ugly quickly.

In his sleep, he moans. My gaze again meets George's in the mirror. Both friends and adversaries over the years, we're close enough that I don't care that he sees my eyes fill with tears. "I can't lose him."

"I know."

George turns into his gated community. Top of the line security. I feel no safer than I did at Garrett's. The security systems that protect the wealthy and famous in this suburb would be nothing to bypass for the kind of men who would come looking for Nikos. I won't take any chances and immediately start making a mental list of what I will need to fortify his manse as he drives the car into his driveway. He presses his automatic door opener and parks the car inside the garage.

I feel they will be safe enough here today, but I'll feel better once I go pick up a few things. The last thing I want to do is put George in danger.

Hell, I don't know how Nikos found me. Unless...

Henri.

I mull that thought over while George and I carry Nikos into his house through the garage's interior entrance. George starts to turn on the lights, but I stop him. "I assume you know your way to the basement of your house well enough that you don't need light."

He keeps walking without flipping the switch. I do my best to not bang my almost dead brother's head on anything. Some light is filtering through the shaded windows, but everything appears gray. Reaching the staircase to the basement, George pauses. "Can we risk light in the lower level?"

"Once we're at the bottom of the stairs."

"Fuck."

I take Nikos's full weight, allowing George to descend the staircase unimpeded. Still, he hits a switch as soon as he is at the foot of the stairs. "No windows. It won't be obvious from the outside that anyone is down here."

He leads me forward. As many years as I've known George I've never been in his home. Finding myself in his basement, I am left envious at very first glance. "You have a rubber room?"

He splits a grin, seeing the direction of my look.

"Authentic. From Agnews."

Leave it to the good doctor to import an entire padded cell from an abandoned asylum. I keep walking, traversing the length of a medieval dungeon complete with iron cages. I don't doubt that the implements of torture on display are the originals. It is a museum quality collection.

I am led to a state-of-the-art medical facility. He answers the question in my eyes. "Never know when you might be in need of an intensive care unit."

"Garrett knew about this? Because if so, it leads me to question why he operated on my brother on his dining room table." We lay Nikos down in the center of the bed. He doesn't respond.

"Garrett has seen my collection, but we were both under the general impression that if he didn't act immediately to stabilize your brother there would be no need for any service I could provide."

"His color isn't so good." Ash. No other way to describe it.

George is a step ahead of me, setting up a saline line. A second bag is added to the tree. Antibiotics. And a third.

"What's that one?"

"Anesthesia. I want him to sleep through the initial withdrawal." He acts quickly, attaching lines, monitors, and restraints. When he looks up at me, I know he has done all he can, at least for now. "He's going to need some blood. I'll start a line on you, if that's okay?"

I nod, feeling like he might have done this a time or two. It seems the doctor has his share of secrets too. A second later he has swabbed my arm, jabbed me with a needle and my blood is filling a bag. I breathe a sigh of relief, thankful for the friends I have. I stockpile artillery, they store medical supplies. It seems we're a better match than I'd have ever believed.

"Be thankful Garrett was home tonight. From what I saw, a hospital somewhere is missing out on some amazing talent. *And*, I'm fairly certain you wouldn't have called nine-one-one."

I don't comment as George leaves me alone with Nikos, but I am very grateful. If not for Garrett, my brother would have been better off dying on the dining room table than being turned over to the authorities. Bending, I kiss his forehead. "You're going to live to see another day, Nikos. Believe that."

"Oh, haggard mind, groping darkly through the past; incapable of detaching itself from the miserable present; dragging its heavy chain of care through imaginary feasts and revels, and scenes of awful pomp; seeking but a moment's rest among the long-forgotten haunts of childhood, and the resorts of yesterday; and dimly finding fear and horror everywhere!"

Charles Dickens, *Martin Chuzzlewit*

CHAPTER 5

NIKOS

Flames lick my flesh while eight shades of agony wrap spiny tendrils of ice through my head, my veins…my tissue. Screams rent the air but I'm afraid to look for the source, fearful of finding someone in a worse condition than mine. Evil lurks in the shadows. I feel it coming for me. Laughing taunts whisper. *Too late for redemption. Too late. Too late.* Darkness has swallowed me whole. Red, beady eyes stare at me. Whispers haunt me, "We call you to be judged, son of Aristotle Socrates Velouchiotis."

"Leave me be!"

I fear hell has finally claimed my soul.

"Satan! Be gone from here."

I am not alive, I am not dead. Since I'm familiar enough with the differences of each, I realize I'm neither even though I seem to have forgotten my name, my purpose, my plan.

A robed, dark figure hovers over a book, reading my sins. One by one he names the people I've killed. I want to scream at him, "Get on with it! Announce your verdict already!" but I am too afraid of what comes after death to not gratefully accept this limited reprieve.

"Vladislav Lokshina."

I recognize the name as a young reporter who had uncovered military corruption which he'd connected to the WODC, which actually involved their agent Liam Dubh working as King Cobra. Vladislav was my first assassination working as Cobra's Executioner. Plenty of time...

Hundreds of names later the shadows come for me. "No! No!"

I have to escape. I struggle against tight bonds without any real form as I am forced down a long, dark tunnel. Fire licks at my heels. I have been condemned.

"God! Please! Hear me!" I drop to my knees, refusing to go farther but am dragged to my final destination. Scratching and clawing, I know I only have one shot at escape. "Ari! Help me, brother! Ari!"

Cool hands on my flame heated shoulders are my answer.

"He's pulled the IV loose. Hold him while I redo the line and increase the dosage. Talk to him."

"Nikos. Relax. Let us help you."

"Ari? You came for me. You rescued me. Thank God. Thank God. I can't go back there. Please don't let them take me."

Cool hands cup my cheeks, and I know it is my brother even though I can't see his face. "I can't see you, Ari! I can't see."

"It's the anesthesia, Nikos. Stop fighting it and rest. Give your body time to heal."

"Don't leave me, Ari."

"I'm not going anywhere. Sleep. I'll be here when you wake up."

My brother's voice is a comfort even though a weight holds me down. I can't move it's so heavy, but the flames are gone. For now at least, I'm no longer in Hell.

"There is no happiness in love, except at the end of an English novel."

Anthony Trollope, *Barchester Towers*

CHAPTER 6

KITTEN

It's been a long night and a longer day. Except for Thomas's absence there is nothing to prove the events of yesterday even happened. I don't know where Thomas went...but then I never know where he goes when he disappears...I only suspect danger is involved. This time there is no suspicion, this time my fears are made fact, proven by his brother's blood soaked clothes. I'm so worried my guts ache. I've never felt so utterly helpless.

Garrett is just as worried. I can tell by the grimness of his expression. That and the fact we aren't going to the club tonight. I don't know how we could even if we had to. If Garrett is as exhausted as he looks, he should have stayed in bed, not that it would have mattered. Neither of us could sleep once we crawled under the covers. Too many unanswered questions, too many worries and fears, none of which have we discussed.

Scotch has been his answer.

Crossing the room, I take the full tumbler from his hand and put it on the bar top. I step into his arms, hugging him, glad when he pulls me into him. We are in the living room, not the bedroom. Except for yesterday's exemption, the house rules are very clear. I am not allowed to talk here...only in our bedroom...but I just can't stand the silence another minute. I try to pull Master toward the bedroom, but he doesn't budge.

"You know I love you, don't you, Kitten?"

"Meow-meow," I murmur against his warm chest. Two meows for yes, one meow for no. Our rules are a comfort. Routine is a comfort. Closing my eyes, I inhale his scent, always the same...also comforting. His cologne invokes a feeling of peace and tranquility. I push my nose against him, trying to soak in the notes of rain and citrus, trying to push out the vision of Garrett's blood covered gloves and Nikos strapped to our dining room table. *God, what more can go wrong?*

Not even rules and routine can create reassurance in the throes of apprehension I'm feeling. I try again to pull Garrett toward the bedroom. He knows what I want. So why isn't he cooperating? "Please, Master. We need to talk. I need to talk."

"There is nothing to talk about right now that is worth the punishment you've just earned breaking the rules."

It hardly matters now since I've already fucked myself. If I'm going to be punished I might as well make it good. I ask, "Where is Lord Fyre? What is going on with his brother? Have you heard anything at all?"

He picks up his glass of Scotch and drains it. "If I'd heard anything you would have been the first to know. Put Thomas out of your mind until he returns."

Well, isn't that an answer. I start to argue, but the look he gives me tells me I've pushed hard enough and it is times like these that make having two Masters impossible.

It is an arduous path I've chosen, especially of late. I remind myself there is a verse of scripture my father often quoted when times seemed too hard for one of his parishioners to cope with. A verse meant to instill peace. I can still recite it in my mind though I've been long from a church. First Corinthians, chapter ten, verse thirteen. If I focus I can see the open page, the highlighted text for ease of finding. It said, *There hath no temptation taken you but such as is common to man; but God is faithful who will not suffer you to be tempted above that ye are able; but will with the temptation also make a way to escape, that ye may be able to bear it.* But try as I might I cannot twist the word temptation into trial, tribulation, or suffering, no matter how many concordances I reference. And yet for the life of me I cannot think of a single other reference for comfort when the trials become too difficult to bear, and so my mind goes to this one that I was taught as a child. I wish I could find comfort in it, but it only makes me feel worse.

I have brought this pain upon myself by yielding to the temptation of Lord Fyre in the first place. If only I'd not succumbed. Would I change anything if I could go back in time? At what point would I choose?

Before the auction?

That would seem wisest. I'd never been a part of the BDSM fetish world before taking an undercover journalism assignment to discover what a slave auction was like. I never expected to be purchased by Garrett Lawrence, owner of the fetish fantasy nightclub *Lewd Larry's*. If I had just avoided the temptation of that assignment, I could still be perfectly content as a very vanilla, very lonely reporter.

No, not that moment, I adore being Kitten, the treasured, pampered pet of Garrett Lawrence too much.

My only wish could be to have never met Lord Fyre or to have had the strength to avoid the temptation he represented. Though it took no more than our eyes meeting that first time for me to know he offered something I could never find with Garrett.

I didn't know what *it* was but everything had changed in that moment. I knew I could never be complete without *it*. He'd awakened an all-consuming need inside me, ever since referred to as *my darkness*. If only Master could have met that need, if only I'd never asked Lord Fyre…if only I had avoided that temptation.

If I truly wanted the Bible to provide an answer, I would follow the advice in First Corinthians. I would flee this current trouble by breaking up the ménage. I would cling solely to Master. I look up into Garrett's face. "You asked me once to marry you."

"Yes."

"You wanted a child and suburbia. You wanted *normal* and the idea terrified me."

He steps away, turning his back to me. "And now your greatest fear is being realized. You're pregnant."

He starts down the hallway toward our bedroom and I follow him. A small voice in the back of my brain demands I leave him alone. I ignore it. "Yes, but I'm no longer quite so terrified of normal as I was before. I'm still not certain how kinky and mundane can exist under the same roof, but I'm willing to figure it out if you are."

He stops in the doorway to the bedroom without entering and faces me. "What are you saying?"

"Ask me again."

"The child you carry isn't mine. Shouldn't this conversation be with Thomas?"

I wrap my arms around his neck and this time he doesn't hug me back. "I don't want to be Thomas's wife. I love you, Garrett Lawrence,

I always have."

Garrett laughs and it is cold and harsh. "We're having this conversation because I'm the dependable one."

"What?"

"I won't disappear in the middle of the night, leaving you worried and alone, scared to death it might be the time I don't return."

Our gazes collide. *He's right.* "I won't deny the obvious, but I also love you."

"You love Thomas, too. You carry his child."

I reach up to stroke his cheek but he pulls away, leaving me whispering to his back, "Marry me."

I follow him through the master bedroom to the master bathroom where he strips and enters the shower. There is no command to join him or even an invite to stay in the room. I sit down on the covered commode and pout, burying my chin against my fists. I stare at my sock covered toes. The socks are red, another reminder of so much spilled blood last night. I pull them off and toss them into the wicker hamper.

We didn't discuss it, meaning I wasn't given permission because I didn't ask, but I am dressed and ready…just in case we have to leave the penthouse in a hurry…just in case Thomas needs us.

Over the spray of the shower I hear Garrett say, "I don't doubt you love me. That isn't why I'm not going to marry you."

My heart drops to the floor, feeling like a weight is holding it there. My stomach turns over and for the first time in two years I feel doubt. "Then why?"

"You don't trust me."

"How can you say that? I'm asking you to marry me."

"You don't trust me to bring your darkness."

I slump, defeated, all the air leaving my lungs at once. He's right. It's why I left him to be mastered by Lord Fyre over a year ago. I wanted to embrace the deviant need singing in my veins, and I knew Garrett couldn't take me to the brink of sanity and back. I knew he'd never walk the fine line of life and death with me. He wouldn't hold my mortality in his grasp. And ever since I went to Lord Fyre and returned to Garrett there has been no mention of his wanting to bring my darkness. I know that there are people who pay him ungodly amounts of money to take them to the edge and back, but me, his property, he treats with kid gloves. Since becoming the ménage, I rely on Thomas to be *that* Master to me. That part is no secret. Garrett knows I dance a fine line of sanity with Thomas. Our play is dark and dangerous. I know he knows I love it. But with Garrett there is only pleasure and pain, no adrenaline rush. I've started to believe he isn't capable of truly mastering me, although Thomas assures me he could as *Lord Ice* if he chose to.

One step at a time. Get through *this*…

My head is spinning, heart racing, palms sweating…and my inner darkness is absolutely screaming bloody murder inside my head. *I can't give up Lord Fyre!* "What does that have to do with me being your wife? How can that mean anything at all when I am talking about raising a child with you?"

He leaves the shower, a towel already wrapped around his waist. He is a commanding presence, tall, lithely muscular. Need strikes hot, low in my belly, and I realize how desperately I want him to make good on a long ago promise that I will someday meet his alter ego.

Still dripping, he strides into the bedroom leaving me alone in the bathroom. *So that's it? That's how he intends to leave this conversation? I don't think so.*

I follow him and find he is already under the covers. Not knowing what else to do, I sit on the edge of the bed and look at him. His eyes are open, but he isn't looking at me. "I'm sorry about yesterday. I'm sorry about everything."

"You should be."

His sharp retort takes me by surprise. *Shit. I have really screwed up.*

"I know you won't possibly understand, but when I discovered I was pregnant, I was terrified. I panicked."

He sits up, the covers pooling around his waist. He looks deep into my eyes. "*That* is a normal reaction to pregnancy. Keeping the fact from someone you love and who loves you back with every ounce of their being *is not*."

"I just needed to think things through. I needed to get it clear in my head what I wanted to do about it before I told you *or* Thomas."

"And yet still you went to him first because not knowing him as well as you think you do, you assumed he would be on your side if you chose an abortion. Whereas, you thought I would be selfish and demand you have a child you didn't want based on a conversation we had a year ago? I wouldn't do that to you. It's your life. Your body. Your right to choose. If you came to me and told me you were pregnant and wanted an abortion, I would have found you the best doctor." He strokes my cheek, and I wonder what he sees in my facial expression. Whatever it is, he softens his tone. "I would do anything for you."

"I'm sorry I went to Thomas first."

"Because he's forcing you to have a child you don't want?"

"No," I whisper, wondering, *Maybe.* I've had weeks to think about this. Plenty of time to worry over every single scenario. How our relationship will be forced to change if I keep the baby. How I am afraid we will all be changed if I abort the baby. The one thing I never considered was that I would be completely wrong about their reactions. Thomas's adamancy I not abort. Garrett's insistence he will support me in any decision. I'd assumed the opposite. How could I be so wrong about them both? And how could I ever think I might be able to give up Lord Fyre...even if Garrett married me.

Nothing makes sense in my head. Nothing.

Beside me, Garrett is already drifting into sleep. I can tell by his shifting breathing pattern. How can he sleep? My mind is racing, worry gripping my guts, and he sleeps. Unfuckingbelievable. Angry and desperate, I close my eyes, trying to find some peace, some comfort. *God? Please hear this prayer. Let Thomas be safe. Let him come home to us soon. Amen.* I don't know if God still hears my prayers, but I continue to pray. What else can I do? I know I should pray for his brother as well, but what would I pray? Heal him? Keep him alive? It seems cold but I can't bring myself to. I fear him too much. I fear the danger he might bring into our lives.

This is why I wish Master was awake. I want to talk about this.

He is curled into himself, snoring softly. The fact that he is sleeping, not pacing the floors, irritates me even more. Standing, I pace for both of us. I feel so helpless.

I end up standing in front of a bureau looking at two jewelry boxes, one embroidered silk, one a roughly carved wood. I open the wooden box and look at Lord Fyre's collar I wore before the branding. With a shuddered breath and shaking hand, I reach for it. Lifting it to my lips, I kiss it and find that I feel stronger just holding it.

I look at my reflection in the mirror over the bureau and with some difficulty attach the collar. *I am his.* No matter what. No matter the sacrifice or the danger. A sob jerks from my chest as I realize I would have never been able to go through with marrying Garrett even if he'd accepted the proposal.

It doesn't matter how smart walking away from Thomas would be. I can't do it.

Reaching for the embroidered box, I take out the golden circlet Garrett placed around my neck in the storeroom the night of the auction. The ruby glitters and winks at me. *I am Master's.* I close the metal around my neck, the jewel dangling between my collar bones.

With both collars securely around my neck, I feel better.

The baby chooses this instant to announce its presence. I feel it, tiny flutters low in my belly. The softest, most surreal tap I've ever felt. *Tap, tap. I'm here, Mommy. I'm here.*

"Oh God." The flutter happens again, and I press my hands over the place where I felt the movement. *Oh God. I'm so sorry! I can't believe I even considered abortion. Forgive me.*

"What's wrong?" Garrett sits up in the bed, concern tightening his face.

"The baby *moved.*"

"You aren't far enough along."

His doubt and quick dismissal strikes me hard because when I was four months pregnant, Lionell and my father insisted I abort the baby. I tried to change their minds. I tried to convince them I was feeling it move. My father argued it was gas; Lionell argued that it was my imagination. I wish I hadn't been so young, so weak. *God damn them both!* I close my eyes, hoping to feel the baby move again.

"Kitten, come to bed."

Tap, tap.

"I felt it!" I shriek, turning on him, angry he doesn't believe me. Angry at myself for loving two men so much that I would consider not having a baby. I'm seething, the emotion sudden and irrational. I want to hit him but leave the room to keep from doing so, shouting, "God damn it!" and "Fuck you!" over my shoulder.

I can leave if I want to. *I want to.*

Running barefoot, I get as far as the parking garage.

"Kitten!" Garrett stops me from across an acre of concrete, my hand poised to open the car door. Thomas's 911 Turbo. I could have chosen Garrett's Cabriolet but I haven't driven it since the night I used it to follow Thomas to a soccer field in suburbia…and that night was…disastrous. And wonderful.

"Kneel!" Garrett shouts, and it is a command broking no refusal.

I am still looking at my hand, I haven't moved, my actions frozen by his voice. I have a choice to make. I can feel it. I don't know what the choice is but there is definitely a decision to be made. Garrett is near enough to touch now, but I don't reach out to him and he doesn't reach out to me. Does he know the answer? No, he can't, because it isn't his answer to give—but does he know the question? I don't even know the question.

Choose.

"What? Choose what?" I ask the question out loud. I must have because the question rings in my head. *What? What? What?*

Garrett is waiting. He pulled on sweats, leaving his chest and feet bare to chase after me, his hair is still damp from the shower, but somehow, even stripped down, his presence is more commanding than it has been during the entire last year. At least with me. I've watched his control of others, and it is a beautiful thing to see. Refined. Elegant. The opposite of Lord Fyre's raw, potent sensuality.

I love them both, please don't let that be the choice.

Opening my eyes, I kneel. My jean covered knees press against cool, unyielding concrete and something inside of me breaks. Tears well up and fall as I bend forward to press my forehead to the tops of his bare feet. I kiss his toes. *I don't want to choose!* The voice inside my head is screaming but I stay silent, holding back sobs that threaten to rip me in two. *My men or my baby, is that the choice?*

"Where did you think to go, Kitten?"

I don't answer because I don't know where I planned to go to. I only know I was compelled to react.

God. Please. You wouldn't be so cruel. I chose two men before. My father. My lover. I murdered my baby for them. I. Will. Not. Do. That. Again.

"Why would you leave?"

I swallow hard, feeling the rub of Lord Fyre's choker collar. It is uncomfortable most of the time, whereas Master's gold circlet is a comfort, the metal warmed by my skin soothing, the teasing tickle of the charm reminding. Tears and snot drip onto his pale skin. "I was angry."

He squats and pets the back of my head. "You've been angry before."

He cups my chin and makes me look up, though I stay completely bent over.

"We're going to survive this. None of us are reacting very well."

I nod, knowing the truth of his words.

He stands, leaving me kneeling. "Strip."

His command gives me pause. It isn't so much that we are in a public place, I've been naked in much more open and populated places than an empty parking lot, but that he is choosing to master me *now*, right smack in the middle of my much deserved nervous break-down. I pull my shirt over my head and unclasp my bra, neither being made more difficult by being bowed in obeisance, but unbuttoning and unzipping my jeans and shimmying out? Almost impossible, but I do it. Ditto for my panties.

Bared, bent, exposed. I wait. I rarely think about my nakedness anymore because I am usually so. Except for the four hours, four days a week I spend in my office at *The Darkness*, I am not clothed. Naked has become my normal. I have to assume having a child in the house will change that. The small voice in my head throws a temper tantrum. *I don't want my life to change.*

Life will be different. *It doesn't matter. I've already decided to have this baby.*

Come what may? *Yes, yes. Come what may.*

Even suburbia? Even if it comes down to having only one man?

I sag against Master's feet, and it seems to be what he has been waiting for.

"Come," he commands and walks toward the elevator.

I follow after first picking up my clothes, carrying them balled under one arm, crawling with the other. I am certain my hand and knees stride isn't as sexy as my well-practiced sway-slide-slide but it gets me to the elevator.

We don't see anyone on the way back to the penthouse. No one to witness my public display of indecency. It's quite disappointing. Once inside, Enrique is a witness that we are back and that I am naked, but he is used to seeing me so. I am not used to seeing him on hands and knees scrubbing an overlooked blood stain off the floor. We share a look. We are both owned and today, for the first time in ages, I'm feeling how that feels again. I smile, he smiles, and then the moment is passed. I leave my clothing in the middle of the floor for Enrique to sort out and continue crawling after Master.

He doesn't lead me to the bedroom. I find him in the library. I lick my lips, anticipation shooting down my spine, making my pussy wet, my skin anxious and needy. I remember the times I've spent here, one blurring to the next, the floggings, the canings, the hours of torturous confinement trapped in rope or leather or chains. *God, yes. Oh God.* It's been too long.

"Stand."

I obey, noticing when I do that my knees are stinging. He drops a suspended hook and motions me forward to stand under it. I do, feeling almost giddy with excitement. He takes my wrists gently in his hands and wraps them in leather cuffs attached by a chain before drawing my arms up over my head to secure to the hook. With a press of a button on a palm sized remote, my arms are stretched out as the hook ascends, my body too stretched out, and then I am forced on tiptoe. Higher. He leaves me balanced precariously on the bare tips of my toes. I am not in pain, barely uncomfortable, but the potential is there…within minutes I will be feeling just how thwarting the ticking seconds will become. He pulls up a straight back chair and sits down, straddling it in reverse so that the back runs up his front. He crosses his elbows over the top and settles in. *Oh, hell.*

I watch him, watching me. My toes hurt and I haven't even been standing on them that long. Mere minutes. I keep waiting for him to say something but he doesn't. I'm sure as hell not saying anything. Everything I have to say is inappropriate. Just because I knelt, stripped, crawled doesn't make me less angry. I am seething on the inside, and I don't know why. I feel like a long-watched pot, refusing to boil, and now…if I open my mouth I will erupt toxic venom. I won't be able to stop. There is so much *unsaid* between us.

If I was facing a mirror, I'm sure my stubbornness would be reflected on my face but I'm not, I have only Master, and his countenance is set in stone. Waiting.

I wish he would talk to me. It seems we haven't talked in a year, not about anything of relevance. We've gone through the motions; we've been so busy. We've discussed the club, we've talked about my day at *The Darkness*.

My heart breaks in two, looking at him, seeing *him* for the first time in months. I love him. I do. I love him with every beat of my heart, but Thomas is so...overpowering, intoxicating...especially as Lord Fyre. I sometimes forget how wonderful and special Garrett is. How could I? *God. Look at him.* If Lord Fyre walked into this room right this second, would Master pale by comparison?

Tears drip over my cheeks.

He stands, seeming to want to answer that question himself, and as he strides toward me I cannot understand how I ever thought he was less. What is changed? Me? Have the blinders been removed from my eyes?

Master closes the distance between us quickly, grabbing my jaw roughly, pinching my skin hard between bone. It hurts. A. Lot. I try to not moan, but lose that battle.

"Tears?" he asks sarcastically. "What thoughts go through that pretty little head that cause you to cry?"

I shake my head, refusing to answer, and he slaps me for the refusal. Shocked, I stare at him, realizing the difference. Not me. *Him.* "Lord Ice?"

"No, Kitten, you aren't ready for Lord Ice. Someday, but not today."

"Yet birth, and lust, and illness, and death are changeless things, and when one of these harsh facts springs out upon a man at some sudden turn of the path of life, it dashes off for the moment his mask of civilization and gives a glimpse of the stranger and stronger face below."

Sir Arthur Conan Doyle, *The Curse of Eve*

CHAPTER 7

GARRETT

She trembles against me. Nervous? Fearful? I like it, quite a lot actually, knowing I can affect her so. After so many months of watching her slip away, to finally have her full attention...

I could blame Thomas, but I won't. I knew exactly what we were getting into when this ménage formed. He is mesmerizing, all-absorbing...no one is immune from the spell he casts. I'm certainly not, I couldn't expect her to be.

I've spent my fair share of time with him, and he's made me remember who I am. It's a shame really that now that I am ready to be all Kitten needs me to be, I can't because she is pregnant. I must be especially careful with her. I can see the question still in her eyes. She isn't certain motherhood is a path she wants to walk.

I meant what I said. I will not force her to have this child. It has to be her choice. It is most convenient that Thomas was called away to deal with his brother. He would never permit her to make the choice.

I kiss her shoulder. "Tell me what you fear."

She takes a deep breath. "Nothing."

I stroke her face, softly, forcing her with gentleness to look into my eyes. "Everyone fears something." I caress her lips. "I'll discover yours."

She shivers.

I run my hands over her body. It has changed so much just from yesterday to today, or maybe I am just more aware. "Your breasts are larger."

She gasps when I stroke them, telling me they are extremely sensitive, and when I pinch her nipples…her eyes flutter closed and she grits her teeth to keep from crying out. I take her nipple in my mouth, sucking hard, drawing at her core.

"Stop. Please stop."

Stop and please are not safewords. I bite down on her nipple, making her cry out, making her keen. I pull as much of her breast into my mouth as will fit and bite, leaving deep impressions of my teeth when I release her. I am careful, being mindful of her developing milkducts, but not so careful that she will not remember this night for many nights to come. I didn't break the skin, but the dents are dark red, tinged almost purple. She will be bruised for days. I switch breasts, giving her a taste of agony for her second breast.

"Master? Please!"

I release her flesh and look at my marks on her. I stroke her arms, then her ribs. Bending, I cup my hands around her slightly distended belly. I should have noticed *this*. I kiss her just below her belly button before straightening, tempering her pleasure by pinching her clit hard.

She is so focused on her pain, she doesn't notice that I lower the hook just enough for her to stand flat-footed on the hardwood floors.

I try to not be obvious as I examine her, measure her.

Tapping her thighs to separate her legs. I smack harder to force them wider, my goal distraction. "Don't move."

Going to the toy cabinet I select lengths of rope, lube, a vibrator, a butt plug, and ankle cuffs. As an afterthought I grab a ball gag.

Using the ankle cuffs and ropes, I spread her legs as wide open as I desire and am certain she won't move. She cooperates, without comment. Sometimes, she does. She's quite the sassy slave, always trying to up the ante a notch.

It seems odd that tonight she doesn't say a word.

Obviously unnecessary, I lift the ball gag and she opens her mouth without being instructed to do so. Our gazes lock and hold. I wait to see challenge in her eyes but see only resolve.

With her gagged and bound, I hide what I am doing behind the guise of lubing her up, vagina and anally. Fingering her, I am more certain and even more concerned. She isn't outwardly showing, but the top of her uterus is level with her belly button.

I don't know how pregnant she thinks she is but my gut and limited medical training tells me she is farther along than either of us imagined and that worries me. I want to get her to an obstetrician immediately.

That doesn't mean I intend to end the scene.

I slide a small butt plug in place and attach it to the ball gag straps. Each jerk of her head will remind her she is filled.

I face her, holding a ball-top vibrator. "Don't even think about coming."

I've given her an impossible command. Squatting in front of her, I intend to prove to her just how impossible. I lift the hood covering her clit and keep the bud exposed as I apply the vibrator. It is an immediate shock that has her dancing in her bonds. The sounds coming from behind the ball gag aren't happy ones. I ease the pressure, but barely enough for the sharp jags of sensation to become pleasurable. I know the instant she is lifted into a stream of bliss, the moment there is no turning back. "Do. Not. Come."

She crashes through her need, orgasm exploding despite my command or maybe because of it.

I don't ease off the wand now that I have her sweet-spot targeted perfectly. Her orgasm doesn't let up. Wave after wave of pleasure turns into wave after wave of overstimulation. Eventually, the overstimulation becomes pain. She is screaming and crying, snot and drool covered by the time I decide she has had enough.

When I turn off the wand and remove the gag, she sags with relief but I don't give her a second's reprieve. I strike her. Slaps on the tops of her thighs and the back of her legs.

"When did you first suspect you might be pregnant?" I expose the bud of her clit and begin again with the vibrator.

"December."

"December what?"

She starts to keen, responding much more quickly to the sensation this time around. "The twentieth, maybe the twenty-first." She is crying. "I regret not coming to you the minute I suspected."

"You regret it, but you aren't heartsick. You feel no grief, no remorse, even though you lied to me, kept secrets from me, and planned to go behind my back to have an abortion." I think her blood is boiling, she is perspiring, and before she can answer the question another orgasm is lifting her. "Don't you dare come."

"I'm sorry!" She shrieks and I am not certain whether she's sorry for the secrecy or the orgasm.

"Yes. Sorry. But what I want to know is what exactly went through your mind that you felt your responsibilities as my slave included keeping such a serious matter a secret?"

"I was scared."

"You didn't trust me," I accuse. I remove the butt plug and reposition her, tying her in an inversion, feet secured with full-support ankle cuffs. She is upside down. This time rope is wrapped across either side of her pussy, trapping her genitals, cutting into her. More rope is attached to nipple clamps. All of the rope is anchored in front of her several feet away, forcing both nipples and twat to feel a constant sensation. It isn't comfortable. Or pleasurable. I make certain she is experiencing pain before I hold the vibrator to her clit. I begin again with the questions. "What did I do that you stopped trusting me?"

She is mid-orgasm when she screams, "You didn't trust me first."

What?

I allow her to ride the wave out before demanding, "Explain."

"When you found out I was a reporter, you chose to believe that everything we'd shared was a lie. It wasn't a lie. You left me. I loved you and you left me."

She is upside down and sobbing. She chokes. I get tissue and command her to blow. I command she stop crying, but she doesn't, and so she is forced to blow again and again to keep from choking on the snot going down her throat.

I do not try to explain how betrayed I felt at the time, because she is right and I was in the wrong. I should have tried harder to see the truth. She was in an impossible situation, feeling emotions she'd never felt. I left her bottoming out with no one to turn to except Lord Fyre…and he was there…ready, willing.

Damn it.

"So, because I failed you once, you can never trust me again?" I do my best to keep my voice in monotone and my emotions in check. I dip my head to lick her clit, a gentler stroke than the vibrator can provide. I want her to come down a little. Not too much. But a little. Enough to make the next pleasure plateau her highest yet.

"Yes. No!"

I squat down, catching and holding her gaze. "Which is it?"

"I trust you."

"Yet you went to Thomas, hoping he would support your decision to abort the baby? And I'm here to tell you, I'm shocked. Because the woman I knew the day before yesterday—or at least the woman I thought I knew—abhorred abortion. Or were you lying to me before?"

She gasps, my meaning clear, but I don't leave it at that.

Standing, I expose the bud of her sex and hold the vibrator to it. "Tell me again how Lionell McCain and your father forced you into a car and drove you to an abortion clinic. Tell me again how you fought them and how you struggled for years to find absolution from murdering your child."

Her body jerks under the pressure of the vibrator. She screams, "Stop it!"

"You had me convinced." I repeat what she told me in the past, mimicking with cruel exaggerated sentiment, "I imagined that I'd felt her move the days before. I wanted her. I did. But I had no one, except Daddy, and I thought that giving up my daughter was the only way to keep my father."

"Shut up!" She screams, her body bucking defiantly.

I should stop. I don't. Interrogation is the one thing Lord Ice excels at and I wouldn't want her to not have the experience before she decides if she wants me or Thomas, if it comes down to a choice. I fill my voice with the emotion she expressed almost two years ago. "Oh God, I couldn't lose him too, not so soon after Mom. I wouldn't have had anyone."

"No. No. No!" Her orgasm crashes over her.

I lie down on the floor so that we are eye to eye. "Did you lie? Were you just playing a part?"

"No," she sobs.

"You wonder why I left? Why I couldn't stand the sight of you after learning you were a reporter."

"None of it was lies. I promise. None of it was." She fights her bonds, but there will be no freedom for Kitten, not anytime soon.

"I know, Kitten. That's why I'm here. If I thought for a minute you were false I wouldn't be."

She cries harder.

"Tell me, at what point did you decide abortion is an acceptable form of birth control?"

"Master, please!"

"Answer the question."

"I didn't want the ménage to change!"

"The ménage changed dynamics the moment you conspired with Thomas against me."

Her eyes widen. "No! That's not—"

I wipe the tears from her face. "It's how I see it."

"I'm sorry! I'm so sorry."

I kiss her even though we aren't through. She thinks we're through, but I'm just getting warmed up.

"What frightens you, Kitten?"

* * * *

When I do untie her, she collapses into my arms, completely sobbed out. She falls asleep as I carry her to our bedroom and tuck her into bed.

She is bruised, bitten...emotionally devastated...marked by me both mentally and physically. And pregnant. Only time will tell how this plays out. In the meantime, I have to make an appointment with a community-friendly obstetrician.

I crawl in bed beside her, completely jazzed on adrenaline though I should be exhausted. I feel good, better than I should following the events of the day. I hold Kitten, knowing that after the intense scene she just experienced she will need me when she wakes and even though her slumber is easy, I don't sleep.

Hours later, she awakens in my arms and her eyes immediately fill with tears. "Do you hate me?"

I kiss her. "I love you. I was trying to help you figure out how *you* feel."

"You would support me in the decision to have an abortion?"

It is almost impossible to say the words but I force myself to. "If that is what you want."

"I don't, I'm just..."

I wish I could read her mind. She is wearing the same expression she wore to her father's funeral, lost, broken, dread-filled. "Tell me what you're thinking."

"I'll be a terrible mother. I'm selfish, self-centered. I like having the party revolve around me."

I laugh though I don't mean to, explaining, "You just described Jackie."

"No, Jackie is maternal, compassionate, selfless."

"We are talking about the same Jackie, right?" I ask sarcastically and receive a well-deserved look of contempt.

"You know we are."

"Two completely different sides of the same woman?"

She smirks, my meaning clear. I hug her closer.

"What if God takes my baby anyway to punish me for the past?"

"God doesn't work that way."

"You're joking. You were exposed to the book of Genesis in the Catholic church you were raised in, right? Lot's wife was turned into a pillar of salt for daring to look upon deviants *like us* as they fled Sodom. What will He do to me if I try to raise a child under this roof?"

I kiss her. "God isn't going to smite you or your baby."

She sighs and cuddles closer. I close my eyes, hoping she won't notice how truly upset I really am. I do not want her to even consider abortion. I thought we had this worked out…I know she told Thomas we would have this baby.

There's no slowing my racing heart, but she doesn't seem to notice. I excuse myself to retrieve my cellphone and make a few phone calls. Within a few minutes I have an appointment scheduled—the soonest available being almost two weeks away—I don't know how I'll ever survive the wait.

"Dark, dark! The horror of darkness, like a shroud, wraps me and bears me on through mist and cloud."

Sophocles, *Oedipus Rex*

CHAPTER 8

NIKOS

The room is pitch black and I am hanging by chained manacles. My wounds flare, pain striking red hot through my body. Sweat-soaked, chattering, I don't know how long I've been here. Whether it is yesterday or whether today has become tomorrow. All I know is that Shanghai is far behind me, and I long for the lush green mountains of Pelion overlooking the perfect azure of the Aegean. I haven't been *home* in so, so long.

If I close my eyes I can smell the salt mingled with fir in the air, the musky sweetness of the olive trees surrounding the stone house I was raised in. If I listen closely, I can hear Grandfather's voice: *Take good care of your brother, Nikos, and Ari will take care of you. Protect him. All of your days. Don't forget.*

I took his place, protecting him, because Ari would have never survived King Cobra. That isn't to say that Ari isn't a dangerous motherfucker, it just means that he isn't a sociopath. He still cares. He loves. He has hopes and dreams and ideals I can't even fathom.

I not only survived King Cobra, I succeeded him.

What in the hell happened?

My tower was impenetrable. Whoever came after me didn't kill me.

At first, I thought whoever shot me, whoever shot my men, was a puissant amateur, but no, my men were left alive for a reason. *I* was left alive for a reason. Why?

I close my eyes but it is not Greece I am transported to.

"Daniel? What the fuck happened to you, man?" Sean Paul, my beautiful, dark, sometimes-lover caught me as I fell. I'd lived in Paris then, and in all of Paris, he was the only soul I trusted. *Cobra happened.* That isn't what I say. "Hold me for a while?"

He stripped us both and laid me down on his bed, but he didn't fuck me. He held me while I cried. Sobbed. Retched. I could still see their faces, a dozen women, barely old enough to even be called women. Girls. Their eyes so trusting. I'd killed them. All of them. *Oh. God.* I'd crossed a line. I could never go back to normal. And I'd done it for the sake of Ari. I thought about what would happen if Ari saw me in the condition I was in. If he ever learned what I'd had to do in order to convince King Cobra of my loyalty. I heard my grandfather's voice that day as I lay in Sean Paul's arms sobbing. *"Take good care of your brother, Aristotle, and Nikos will take care of you. All of your days. Don't forget."*

I couldn't let him.

We are twins, identical even to the pain we feel when the other is hurting. He would feel my pain, he would know that something was horribly wrong, and he would come for me. I'd prevented him from taking the assignment because I knew King Cobra would destroy him. I couldn't fail him now.

Sitting up in Sean Paul's bed, I made several rapid decisions. First, I'd have to deaden the pain. Emotional. Physical. With a storeroom of every narcotic known to man at my disposal, I decided that shouldn't be too hard. Second, no one would ever mistake me for Ari or Ari for me again.

Turning to Sean Paul, I said, "I need you to help me do something."

A hundred hours of tattooing later, I looked nothing like my brother.

Now, I pray to God that Ari remembers the words of our grandfather. "Take care of me for a while."

"You're safe, Nikos. Just rest."

I open my eyes to see Aristotle. He looks haggard. Pale. "You look like shit."

"You have no room to talk, brother."

I chuckle but pain slices through my middle. I suddenly realize I'm lying in a hospital bed. "The chains?"

Aristotle gives me a questioning look.

"You've got to get me out of here. I'm being held prisoner—" I realize I sound like a lunatic. I look at my hands and wrists. There is no evidence that I was manacled. I'm in a hospital bed, surrounded by blinking monitors. I must have been dreaming. "I hurt, give me something for the pain."

"Not a chance. Rest."

"How long have I been here?"

"Seven days."

"Jesus." I try to sit up but straps hold me to the bed. I struggle uselessly.

"You are restrained to keep you from hurting yourself. Once we are certain you are lucid, the restraints will be removed. We're weaning you off the anesthesia, but you need to sleep."

I relax, knowing that fighting the straps won't prove I'm coherent.

When I awake again it is hours later. Maybe days later for all I know. I'm confused but lucid, lucid because I recognize the fact that I'm in agony.

Restraints no longer hold me down, but I lie flat on my back. If I try to sit upright tight jabs of pain stab through my middle and ricochet off my spine. There is little I can do but focus on remembering to breathe as it all comes back to me—waking in Shanghai as bullets pierced my body and making it to the United States. I'm still alive, that surprises me. The brightly lit room makes me feel like I'm in a hospital but there is just enough not right that I realize immediately I am not.

I remember my brother grabbing me as I fell.

He would not turn me over to any other than one who would keep me safe.

After a moment of deep focused breathing, I manage to sit up, forcing my way through the agony, recognizing the pain now as tight stitches, holding closed my wounds. I'm weak, but my body is healing. *God, how long have I been out?* I pull at a piece of gauze to see the damage, hoping to know by looking if it has been hours or days.

"Ten days."

I jerk, having not realized a man was in the room with us. I don't recognize him but then I wouldn't, would I? One of my brother's confidants I can only hope.

"I kept you sedated because I didn't think you would survive both your wounds and detox, but you are alive and on the mend. My name is George Kirkpatrick, though your brother usually just calls me Doctor

Psycho."

"Where is—" Damn, I don't know what name he is using with this man. Should I assume Thomas? That is the name I used to find him, but… "—my brother?"

"Sleeping. Finally. He has gone too many days without rest. It seemed as good a time as any to bring you around. See how you're doing in the department upstairs."

"The department?" I am confused until he taps his own head. "I see. You want to know if I'm insane."

"There is no doubt in my mind you have an antisocial personality disorder. You would not have been able to do your job if you didn't."

He knows what I've done? He knows that I am an agent? "Who are you? What hospital am I being held in?"

"I am your brother's friend, and you aren't in a hospital. You're in my home."

My brother has some peculiar friends.

"Your brother has asked me to determine if you will be able to function in normal society within the constraints of urban civilization."

"Meaning can I control myself when someone cuts me off in traffic, or will I kill them?"

"That's what I intend to find out." He chuckles and my blood goes cold. Few men have the power to intimidate me. This man, my brother's friend, terrifies me. "Now, let's get you out of this bed, get you up and moving."

I push up, intending to launch myself out of the bed and almost pass out from the wave of dizziness.

He catches my elbow and steadies me. "Easy."

God, I'm weak as a foal.

He helps me swing my legs over the bed and stand. Pain shoots through my middle to race up my spine and down my legs, and I release a line of expletives a mile long.

"That make you feel better?"

"No!"

"All right then. Let's try walking."

"God damn." I take a step forward. "Holy mother of God." I take another step.

The doctor laughs. "Nothing like pain to set a man to praying."

I don't see the humor and endeavor to grit my teeth through the rest of it. As he leads me out of the small room equipped with enough medical equipment to make me believe I was in a state-of-the-art hospital, I see it isn't his only *specialty* room. We stroll past a door with a small window, a quick peek inside revealing a rubber room. We keep walking and we are transported back in time as we enter a stone walled dungeon from the Medieval Ages. There is a wooden rack, an iron maiden, a spiked metal and wood chair. There is a glass case I linger over, in part because I'm exhausted by the twenty-five paces it took to get me here and in part because I'm fascinated.

On display is a metal device only describable as a head crusher. I saw one once displayed in a Paris Museum, but have never known anyone to have one in a private collection. The doctor interrupts my thoughts. "Fascinating gadget, that one. With the chin placed over the bottom bar and the head under the upper cap, the torturer could slowly turn the screw pressing the bar toward the cap, resulting in the head being slowly compressed. First the teeth are shattered into the jaw. Of course there would be the obvious agonizing pain, and dependent on the executioner, he could reverse and forward the process as many times as he liked to prologue the agony before his victim died."

I nod, bending forward to inspect the piece. It is elaborate with metal cups in front. "This is different."

"To catch the eyeballs as they are squeezed out of the sockets."

"Ah, of course." I shift my focus to three perfectly preserved Pear of Anguish. "These are very nice. Originals?"

"Yes. French."

Pointing at each, I guess, "Vagina, anus, mouth?"

He smiles. "Very good. You're an aficionado of the ancient art of torture as well?"

"To understand the past is to have better control of the outcome in the present."

"Indeed." He smiles and helps me amble deeper into his demented space where he has all manner of modern torture devices. He quips, "And this part of the dungeon is for my own pleasure."

Delightful.

"Do you play?" he asks.

"Not really. Sadomasochism isn't really my thing."

We make a wide turn and he starts me walking back toward the medical room. I can't say I'm not relieved, partly because I'm exhausted, but partly because the man is terrifying. He sounds truly disappointed when he says, "More's the pity."

"Footfalls echo in the memory, down the passage which we did not take, towards the door we never opened…My words echo. Thus, in your mind."

T. S. Eliot, *Four Quartets*

CHAPTER 9

KITTEN

Life isn't back to normal, but we're following our routines, which is a small comfort. We went to the club last night and although it wasn't a jam-packed madhouse, it was a much needed distraction from the fact Thomas is still *away*. As we drive back to the penthouse, dawn is breaking, another morning's arrival without Thomas. I miss him.

He's been gone little more than a week but it seems like a lifetime since I've seen him. If he was with us, he would be driving. I would be in Garrett's lap. I might be half-asleep, lulled by the car's motor and the contentment filling my soul, but I would be touching Garrett. Stroking him. Kissing him. Holding his hand. Why is it that with Thomas not here we can barely look at each other?

Garrett's hands are almost white knuckled on the steering wheel and I wonder if I caused the tension? It could be anything but I'm betting it's me. I've been sulky all evening, I can't help it.

I reach out and touch the top of his leg, feeling him tense even more, but I don't pull my hand away. I tease and stroke his inner thigh, following the crease in his slacks that allows me to also tease the bulge of his trapped balls. He doesn't say anything, he doesn't react positively or negatively to the attention and that is encouragement enough, especially since he didn't come the last time we were together. I think he believes I didn't notice, but I did.

I dip my hand lower, cupping his ball sac and squeezing lightly. A moment later he is shifting in his seat and I can follow the length of his erection with my fingers. The silky weave of his pants adds to the sensation, feeling good against my fingertips, it has to feel as good on the receiving end. I break the silence. "I want you, Master."

"How do you want me?"

"Rough and dirty." Until I said the words I didn't even realize I was thinking it. Garrett and I don't have that kind of relationship. Thomas and I do. I close my eyes, regretful and embarrassed. Wasn't the failed attempt at a little rough kitty play enough to make me realize he just isn't into me anymore?

He does a U-turn in the middle of the road, startling me, gravity pushing me hard against the door. He doesn't apologize, and he doesn't explain. He just drives and I keep my mouth shut.

"Anxiety is love's greatest killer. It makes others feel as you might when a drowning man holds on to you. You want to save him, but you know he will strangle you with his panic."

Anais Nin

CHAPTER 10

GARRETT

There comes a time in every young, new Dominant's life when he realizes that the person he is isn't enough to take the game that one step farther and that in order to survive the slightly off-kilter world he has entered into, a new identity must be forged. I experienced that day with Lord Fyre. Thankfully, he was experienced enough to see the change in my eyes and christened me Lord Ice.

We are the same, he and I, though as Dominants, we have distinctly different mastering styles. I know the dark places he mentally and physically takes Kitten to, because I have traveled those paths with him, and thus far I have refused to push her as far as I know she can go. Partly, it is because I cherish her so much I could not bear to lose her should the depth of my inner depravity disgust her. But more, the loss of Tony has given me a greater reverence for life. Kitten is so fragile, mentally, physically, spiritually…

Especially now that I know she is pregnant. Or maybe that is merely the way I see her, and Thomas sees her quite differently.

I know she clings to him tighter every time they dance the wire between safe and sane and whatever lies on that other side, and until I am willing to challenge her in the same ways, he is winning. I know...I shouldn't see it that way. Our relationships are not a competition.

I want her to meet Lord Ice, the way I can be, the way I want to be with her but for some reason have held back. Now is not the time. Now is specifically the wrong time. She is pregnant after all, the proof of her expanding waistline more evident with each day. If anything happened to her baby because of me, I could never forgive myself...but that said. God. I want her.

She'd been naked in my lap most of the night, eating from my fingers, drinking from my mouth. Her changing body left me crazed, and my blood was already boiling nicely just from running my hands over new curves. Then as we readied to leave, she pulled on some clothes from the staff closet, a tight white oxford shirt and a short plaid skirt. She's never done *schoolgirl* for me and doesn't know how it affects me. I reach over and pop the top button of her shirt, my fingers lingering between cloth and skin a moment before undoing a second button. I like that her breath catches and she goes still, already anticipating. I take my hand away, glancing over to see the opened shirt reveals the slightest peek of bare breast. Her breath is shallow, and she is trembling. Her pleasure has started already with the smallest change in me. I imagine the anticipatory tingle speeding through her veins.

Rough and dirty. Her request would have sent Lewd Larry running, but Lord Ice stretched inside me and yawned...slightly bored, slightly intrigued...and as a result I race across town to the one place I know we can play awhile that might curb her desire for filth. I honestly don't know that I can be rough and I am not out of control, far from it. If anything I am in supreme control of my every thought, my every action, but I will take her to the edge...

Freddie is the mechanic downtown who services my cars. I've done business with him long enough that I know exactly when he arrives for the day. Six a.m. I also know he won't mind if I "rent" his space for an hour, asking him to disappear, maybe get a cup of coffee to afford me some privacy. I pull into a full-service auto repair garage and drive into one of the open bays. Before I even climb out of my seat, I see he is already elbow deep in an engine. He glances up to see who has entered and smiles when he sees me.

"Garrett Lawrence. It's been awhile."

I'm wearing my work clothes, a tux and silk shirt, but have no qualms about reaching out and shaking his grime covered hand. "Freddie Martinez. Still keeping crazy long hours and refusing to pay anyone to help you?"

He scratches the back of his neck, looking sheepish. "I'm a greedy S-O-B."

"If you worked a crew, you could have five times the business."

"And ten times the headaches." He laughs but then seeing Celia in the front seat of my car asks, "So what brings you to my borough?"

"Let me use one of your pits for about an hour?"

He looks behind him at the engine he was working on, sucking his teeth as he contemplates if getting behind schedule is worth my good will. When his gaze collides again with mine, the look is one of greed. *So, okay, this one is gonna cost me.*

"No blood."

I laugh at his only concession and pat him on the back. "Go have some breakfast. I'll take care of your place."

Without regard for whether Freddie lingered or hurried away, I walk back to the car, stripping out of my jacket and rolling up my sleeves as I go. As I near Kitten's door, she trembles visibly, and need speeds up my spine. *I've wanted this too.*

I jerk open the door and grab her by her hair, pulling her out, at least until the buckle locks, holding her bound to the seat. She hurries to unlatch it, and as soon as I feel the belt's tension release I pull harder, dragging her out by her auburn tresses. She stumbles but catches herself. I remember belatedly, she is wearing stilettos. "Lose the shoes before you break an ankle."

She manages to hop on one foot, pulling off her shoe as I force her forward, my hand still wrapped in her hair. She repeats the action, dropping the second shoe, and is left barefoot. My eyes travel up her bare legs to the edge of her purple and black mini-kilt. She has the longest legs, and I allow my gaze to linger. I push her to the metal ladder that leads into an open pit. "Go."

She does, I follow her down. The walls are lined aluminum cabinets and some mounted tools, the ground is grime and oil covered. The air is heavy with engine fumes.

Facing her across the pit, I watch her as she stands in the corner, wrapped in her own arms, looking none too impressed. I command, "Take off your clothes."

Her lips part in a soft gasp and the sound is like lightning speeding through my veins. *God, what she does to me.* She had to expect this, had to know this command was coming. She doesn't argue, she starts unbuttoning her shirt and I notice her fingers are trembling. I wonder if she trembles for Thomas. It is an odd thought, one I wouldn't normally have, but as I watch her slow moving fingers it is my only thought. He would cherish each prolonged motion, soaking in her nervousness and fear, reveling in it. I am a more anxious taskmaster and impatiently cross the small space to push her hands out of the way. Grabbing both sides of the shirt, I rip them apart, sending small white buttons flying. I jerk the shirt off and throw it onto the floor.

Made even more nervous, she covers her breasts with her arms and stands shaking.

"Take off your skirt."

She fumbles with her zipper but manages to get the skirt off, leaving her standing completely naked in front of me. I smile. I was a very negligent Master, not realizing she was both braless and panty-less on the drive home. I must endeavor to be more observant.

"Lie down."

She looks at the concrete floor with obvious revolt, but kneels, picking her spot carefully. It won't matter. She finally stretches out on the cleanest section of floor available to her.

"Roll."

I honestly don't think she expected the command and it confounds me why she wouldn't. Despite her doubts, she obeys, rolling onto her back.

"More. I want you to roll from one side of this pit to the other without stopping." I step back to make room, trampling her white shirt as I do so. It is immediately and irreparably soiled.

She rolls, filth clinging to her with every movement. Her skin goes from pale white to grease and grime coated. When she reaches the far side, she looks at me.

"Stand up."

Once I would have felt bad for leaving her so grime covered. Not other men or women, but her, for some reason putting her on a pedestal which didn't allow for dirt in our relationship, but then I discovered her covered in mud from playing with Lord Fyre. We weren't a ménage then. She'd gone behind my back and sought him out. The evidence was all over her body, inside her body. So much mud. A little grease seems minute in comparison.

I walk over to her and swipe my hand across her shoulder. My palm comes away soiled. "Dirty." I draw a finger down her arm, leaving a white streak through the grime. "Girl."

I step back and look at her, surveying the damage.

I leave her standing, shivering, though at this point I don't think it is fear or anxiety, I think she is quite literally cold. I dip my fingers into a large barrel half-filled with reclaimed oil and they come out dripping black. I gesture her toward me. She hurries forward and it is evident in her eyes she knows what is going to happen, or at least what she thinks is going to happen. I stripe her face with the oil. "Not dirty enough."

I pick her up, making her gasp with surprise, and lower her feet first into the barrel.

"Oh!"

I back away, leaving her standing in the glop. The sludge hits her in the middle of her thighs.

"How does that feel?"

"Disgusting. Master."

"Do you feel dirty yet?"

"Yes, Master."

"You aren't nearly dirty enough. Scoop handfuls of oil over yourself. I want you to take a bath in that black sludge."

She looks disturbed by the thought and makes a disgusted face as she dips her hands into the liquid, but she manages to cup enough grimy oil to splash onto herself.

My dick has been aching since we entered the pit. I regret taking off the schoolgirl uniform quite so early in the game, but I promised Freddie an hour. Watching her cover herself in black oil may be my undoing. She splashes the liquid onto her shoulder, then slides her hand down her arm, leaving black tracks. She covers her breasts, letting the oil roll down her flesh.

Her fingers linger over her stomach, and I think she is beginning to enjoy herself. She makes swirling patterns before cupping her breasts and squeezing them. She pushes the two orbs together and there are white lines between the black from where her fingers were a moment earlier.

"Your face."

She dips her hands and manages to cover most of her face with a quick swipe from hairline to chin.

"Turn around."

She shuffles in a tight circle, turning her back to me. I dip my own hand into the cool oil and splash up, covering her back and buttocks.

"Turn."

She does a little baby-step shuffle to face me again.

"Do you think you are dirty enough now?"

"Yes, Master."

I grab her hair and pull her face toward mine, kissing her, making her mouth open under the force of my kiss, making her take my tongue into her mouth. I taste oil as I kiss her, the smell of it fills my nostrils. I kiss her savagely, the need I am feeling makes it seem like I am fucking her mouth with my tongue. The metallic bite of blood mixes with the motor oil. I whisper into her mouth. "Dirty. Girl. Is this what you wanted?"

"Yes-s."

I pull her hair, lifting her on tiptoe, pulling harder so that she has no choice but to leave the oil and come into my arms. My shirt soaks through as her breasts collide with my chest and her leg catches high on my hip. She uses my body as a ladder, leaving a cascade of oil running down my pants leg. I pull her into me so that she is out of the vat and back in the center of the pit. I pull on an engine hoist chain, looping it around her wrist and hooking it in place. She still has a hand free, but my purpose wasn't necessarily to restrain her but to hold her in place.

I step back and look at her, adrenaline pouring through me. If she is in sub-space, I am as surely in a place of my own. Other Dominants know this state of mind where everything stops. Time stands still. The world becomes silent. It is as if I am wrapped with her in a bubble of our own creation with an electric storm swirling around us.

I reach out and pinch her cheeks together, my fingers sliding through the grease. "Enough dirt to satisfy you?"

She nods, tears sliding over her cheeks. I somehow don't think she's sad but rather believe the emotion is one of joy.

I release her cheeks to slap her, the sting running up my wrist. I slap her again on the other cheek. "Not yet. You aren't dirty enough yet." I rub my hand between her legs, finding her wet and ready. "Unzip me."

Her free hand fumbles between us and she undoes my fly with a quick pull. She pulls my underwear down in the front, enough for my erection to pop free and just the sudden freedom from the clothing's tight restraint is bliss. Grasping her hips, I lift her and impale her. Her legs wrap tightly around mine as I thrust. She moans deep in her throat and it is almost my undoing. Not wanting to gain my own satisfaction too swiftly, I drop her as quickly as I scooped her up. I pinch her face cruelly and whisper close to her face. "You *are* my dirty girl. You probably want me to hurt you now?"

She nods and I pinch harder, making her squeal.

"A naughty, dirty girl deserves to be punished."

Echo of Redemption | Roxy Harte

"Please, Master."

I kiss her, less viciously than before, but still forcefully. "I'd like nothing more than to do just that."

I release her, not saying that any pain play will have to wait until after the baby is born. Turning my back to her, I take enough time to adjust my clothes, zipping and buttoning. My oil soaked pants, a sorry state of affairs.

Turning around, I drop to my knees and wrap my hands around the backs of her thighs to pull her forward. My hands slide as my face dips to catch her clit in my mouth. The oil makes an adventure out of merely going down on her. I like it that the grip on her shifts as my hands lose traction and I have to start again, pulling her close, only to have her slip away. She moans with frustration, adding to my enjoyment. I wipe my hands clean on my shirt sleeves before sliding my finger inside her to anchor her. It is enough stability for her to ride my face, my teeth and lips and tongue teasing her to an overdue orgasm. I pump her with my fingers, eliciting course growls from her throat.

"You like that, dirty girl?" I pump her hander. Standing, I push my cum coated finger into her mouth. "I don't like being dirty. Lick me clean."

She sucks my fingers and licks them. I push them deeper, making her gag because I find the sound arousing. When I pull my fingers out of her mouth, she smiles. Our gazes lock and I realize then she's stayed because she's been waiting. She had faith all along that Ice would show up sooner or later.

I smile and kiss her gently. "We're not quite finished yet."

I leave her for a moment to rummage through Freddie's cabinets and come away with an acrylic rod. I have absolutely no idea what he might use it for but for my purposes, it's perfect. I bend over and pick up her ruined white blouse. "Is this any way to take care of your clothing?"

Her eyes widen, but because role-playing comes so easily for her she responds easily. "No, Sir. I'm sorry, Sir. I promise I'll take better care of my things in the future."

"Shut up. We both know you won't. You're a dirty, lazy girl. You could have folded this blouse and put it away neatly. It only takes a moment."

She fidgets. "I'm sor—"

I cover her mouth with my hand. "I said, shut up. No excuses. I'm going to punish you now."

I slice the acrylic rod through the air, appreciating the whistle produced. Conscious of her pregnancy, I avoid her stomach, back, or buttocks. The tops and backs of her thighs however are fair game. This is the part I enjoy most, feeling my own lift of endorphins as I allow the swing of my improvised cane to overtake me. I beat her soundly, stopping only when she is sobbing.

I stop, seeing her. God, she is beautiful. Spent and panting, she sags against me as I release the chain. I steady her, not expecting her to cup my face in her hands. "Thank you, Lord Ice."

"Let's get you home."

Less than twenty minutes later, we are hurrying through the parking garage. We are a sight, barely dressed, covered in filth. Running ahead, she is giggling, and I realize my soul feels lighter than it has in years. Catching her hand, I pull her close as we enter the elevator. "I love you."

She looks up at me from beneath lowered lashes. "I love you."

Covered in grime and wearing my mark, she is more beautiful than I've ever seen her. I want her. Again. *Now.* I press the emergency stop. No alarm sounds but the lights power down to a minimal glow. I push her against the back wall, sliding my hands over her face and down her neck. I pin her against the wall with my hand wrapped around her narrow throat. "Have I ever told you that school uniforms make me crazy?"

Eyes wide, she shakes her head.

"Yeah. Must be the parochial school thing. All I can think about is pushing up your skirt." As I tighten the hold I have on her throat, I slide my hand up her thigh and under her skirt. Her hip is covered with oil and sandy grit. "Dirty, dirty girl, I want to fuck you, right here, right now. Is that okay with you?"

She nods, but I don't release her throat. If anything, I tighten the pressure, effectively cutting off her air while she fumbles with my pants. They fall to my ankles and she has to work at the elastic waistband of my jockeys. I smile at her, my wicked intentions speeding need up and down my spine.

I release her neck and with a quick under arm lift, pin her against the wall with my body. Her legs wrap around my waist but that isn't what I want. Grabbing her calves, I lift her legs higher, forcing her ankles onto my shoulders. She is bent and trapped between me and the elevator wall. Neither of us giving an inch. I spit on my fingers, natural lube to spread over her asshole. She tenses. "Relax."

I push into her, making her squeal and squirm, but she is wedged so tightly all she can do is open for me. She moans as I force myself deep inside her. Muscles contract against my cock, trying to stop the invasion. I smack her ass and push deeper, making her cry out in pain and need. The sound is raw and guttural.

"Yes. That's right, open for me. Take all of me, dirty girl."

She gasps, opening and I fill her to the hilt.

Thrusting, I grab her wrists and pull them high over her head. She is trapped, she is mine. "I hope you aren't tired *little girl* 'cause I'm worked up enough to go all night."

She laughs and the sound is nice after so many weeks of not hearing it.

I look at her, really look at her, seeing a change I hadn't expected. Beneath the dirty streaks, she is glowing, and I don't believe for a minute it is because of the pregnancy. She looks like I feel...lighter and happier than I've been in a long time. I almost feel like Lord Ice is ready to come back.

"Each has his past shut in him like the leaves of a book known to him by heart and his friends can only read the title."

Virginia Woolf

CHAPTER 11

THOMAS

I've completely taken over George's dungeon, rearranging to make room for a computer station complete with six monitors and a server. For almost two weeks, I've done nothing but wait and watch. Overnight there was confirmation through the WODC's site that international business tycoon *Daniel Parker* was confirmed dead. My lips twitch wondering how Henri pulled off that feat without a body. The easy answer was that it served his purpose to put a quick end to the investigation. Regardless of his reasons, I can breathe much easier knowing that no one will be looking for Nikos now. My brother has a clean slate.

Assured of his safety, I seek out a real bed in George's guest room, instead of napping in the chair in front of the computer, and sleep well for the first time in ages. Since before I went to Paris.

When I awake there is no heavy weight of panic in my chest, no quick reach for my Glock. I linger, listening, hearing absolutely nothing beyond the walls of the bedroom. As I shift in the crisp sheets, the sound of fabric against skin sounds loud as it hits silence. I'm not so certain all of George's high-tech sound-proofing is comforting. World War III could be going on beyond the bedroom door and I would not know it. I close my eyes, forcing myself to relax. *Nothing is wrong.* Just to be certain I climb from the bed and crack open the door. No screams, no gunfire. Somewhere deep in the house I hear the sound of a knife clicking against a chopping block, deducing George is in the kitchen.

After a long, hot shower I almost feel human again.

Walking through George's house, I am surprised to find the sun shining through the upper half of his windows. The lower half covered in a sheer accordion blind which allows for both natural light to filter through and complete privacy. I hadn't noticed them before. The clink of dishware draws me into the kitchen where I find George making omelets. He is humming and seeing me, he smiles. I think it is the first time he's smiled since he showed up at Garrett's to rescue my brother.

"You're in a good mood."

"Your brother is much improved."

I'd thought so myself, but I'd been afraid to ask. Relieved, I sit at a bar stool in front of the center island workstation.

He looks at me over his shoulder. "I hope you're hungry."

I hadn't considered it before he mentioned it, but my stomach rumbles with definite interest. I know I've eaten the past few days but I don't remember doing so. Food suddenly sounds good. My head is nodding before I answer, "Definitely."

Our gazes meet and I am suddenly faced with the huge debt I owe him. "Thank you."

He barely nods in acknowledgement before turning back to his stovetop. It occurs to me that George Kirkpatrick is an odd man. I don't know nearly enough about him. I know he rules The Attic with an iron fist and he is completely loyal to Garrett. Other than that? We've almost always butted heads, our personalities a major clash, making me surprised that he's been so willing to help me or my brother.

He sits a plate in front of me, a mushroom, spinach and cheese omelet from the looks of it, served with fresh fruit and a toasted bagel. My stomach grumbles impatiently. "This looks fabulous."

"Eat. I don't need praise."

I shake my head, happily shoveling several forkfuls into my mouth. *He's definitely odd.*

Across from me, he eats as well, but I get the feeling he wants to talk. I watch him take a swig of orange juice and am surprised to find myself lingering over the bob of his Adam's apple. Disturbed to find the vision erotically charged. *Hell no, not George.* I look away, embarrassed.

"We need to discuss the next stage in your brother's recovery."

"Okay." I keep eating.

"Aside from the obvious injuries that brought him here, your brother is an addict."

"He's clean now, right? Completely detoxed."

"Detoxed but not rehabilitated."

He's stopped eating. Regretfully, I lay down my fork to give him my undivided attention. The tension in the room thickens, making me realize how silent the house is, no ticking clock, no air exchange through ducts, not a single sound from outside. There should be sound. In the window behind him I can see the movement of trees. Wind maybe, and if not wind, the chirp of birds. I hear a trickle of water and remember seeing an elaborate fountain in his foyer. My mind concludes that his entire house is soundproof.

"There are many treatment facilities—"

I interrupt him. "No."

George lets out a heavy sigh. "I was afraid you were going to say that. The only other answer is for me to treat him here. He's going to need counseling and support for at least four weeks, maybe six, and even at that, unless he changes his lifestyle once he leaves here, avoiding narcotics is going to be a tough feat for him."

"Whatever it takes. I'll make sure you're compensated for your time."

"I'm not worried about the money. My concern is what life your brother is going to return to after he's *fixed*."

"Not the same one he left, I assure you." I push my plate away, no intention of finishing my meal. "Is he up to a visitor this morning?"

"Go see him."

I can only imagine what the confinement is doing to Nikos. In his shoes I would feel like an impounded dog, waiting for the rabies test to come back negative or positive, determining if he is going to be put down or not. The thought is depressing.

I find him kicked back on the hospital bed, playing an online game on a borrowed laptop. He looks better than I could have guessed, the last twenty-four hours a huge improvement.

"How's it going?" I ask.

He gives me a lopsided smile which I guess I could interpret as a good sign before lifting his shirt to show me the puffy red scars of his wounds. "All healed up."

I sit on the edge of the bed. "So George tells me. We should talk about your drug rehabilitation."

He logs out and powers down before closing the laptop lid. He gives me a long look. "What's there to talk about? System flushed clean thanks to the doc."

"It was hard on your body."

He lets out a heavy sigh. "You're telling me that? I'm the one who *survived* it."

"Surviving," I correct. "You're still an addict, Nikos."

"Yes. I *was*."

I ignore the comment. "George is going to spend some time counseling you, now that you can hold your head up off the pillow. You're going to need to get your head screwed on straight."

He shakes his head, his expression all tough guy. "I'm good. One hundred percent, and I think if I spend one more day in this bed you are going to have to put a bullet through my brain. I'm ready to get back to work. Of course Henri is very likely to kill me for this disappearing act I've pulled. Tell me you've been in contact with him."

"Not at all."

His eyes fill with pure panic.

"The world thinks you're dead," I tell him. "I want you to stay here. With me. I'll set you up with a place to live, a job if you want it. New name. New identity."

He licks his lips, and I can see the hope in his eyes for something *more* even if he doesn't have a clue what that is. For the first time in three weeks I start to believe that saving his life hasn't been a supreme waste of time and energy.

"What's the catch?"

"No drugs. No alcohol. No killing."

"Basically give up all my vices at one throw."

"Something like that," I agree.

He pours himself a glass of water from a bedside carafe and takes a long swallow before saying, "George is concerned I've lived so far from *normal* for so long that I won't be able to reacclimatize to mundane life."

"What do you think?"

"Do you know anything about who I've been or what I've done over the last decade?" he asks.

I swallow hard, remembering the sight of the circular saw grinding into Eva's chest. I've tried to not consider what atrocities he's been forced to do.

He doesn't wait for my answer. "You don't want to, brother. Don't let your imagination wander there." He pauses. "My life has been a nightmare, but I don't regret it. Not a single second of it. Because you have been here. You have been alive. You have been happy."

At a big cost to you. I don't say it. We both know the truth of it. I owe Nikos my life, my sanity.

"If you could see your face. Just say thank you." He laughs and the sound is good to hear. It makes my guilt even greater.

"Why, Nikos? The job was *mine.*"

He gives me a long serious look, like he's contemplating how to deliver bad news, before saying, "You wouldn't have survived King Cobra."

"You did."

"We're different. You still have a conscience."

"You don't?"

"No."

His answer makes a cold chill go up my spine. I've met other agents who have lost all sense of humanity and they're scary things, not people anymore, just machines, very deadly machines. When I look at Nikos that isn't what I see, but maybe my judgment is clouded by wishful thinking. He is a mere shadow of the man he once was, but he is also much more. He is scarred, mentally, physically, morally, and I am bound to an oath to take care of him. I will, more than willingly, if he will let me. "Stay here, with me. Let me protect you while we figure the rest out."

"Each of us has to find out for himself what is permitted and what is forbidden—forbidden for him."

Hermann Hesse, *Demian*

CHAPTER 12

GARRETT

Kitten peeks around the corner into the kitchen but doesn't enter. Sitting at the table, drinking coffee, I see her immediately. "I smelled the java," she explains, sounding like she is apologizing.

The tension between us is growing. I could blame it on the pregnancy. I could blame it on Thomas's abrupt departure. And then there was her conspiracy with Thomas in an effort to keep the pregnancy secret, I can't forgive that. Or I can just face the fact recent events are playing a part in opening my eyes to the relationship we've had for months. I've tried to ignore the facts. The more Thomas is away working, the more she clings to him when he's near, and instead of trying to draw her closer I've allowed a rift to grow between us.

I gesture her closer with a pat to my knee. I cannot remember the last time I shared my coffee with her. When she is settled onto my lap, I take a sip, then offer her my lips. She sucks the caffeine nectar greedily. She is and always will be a caffeine addict, which will make my next request a hard one to follow. "Enjoy today, tomorrow begins your withdrawal."

"My what?"

"No more caffeine. It isn't good for the baby."

She pouts, looking angry, but doesn't comment one way or the other.

"Do you want another sip?"

She nods, making me lift my brow.

"Yes, Master."

I give her another sip from my mouth, holding her closer. I enjoy holding her naked in my lap. Soon, our intimacy will be changed by the patter of small feet and I can almost understand why she was so reluctant to have the interruption now. *Abortion.* I push the thought away as soon as it enters my mind. Dredging up old anger isn't going to help our present. I stroke her head. "This pregnancy is going to change things before the baby is even born."

She takes a bite of banana offered from my fingers.

"I'll tell security any punishment has to be cleared by me, but I'm asking you to behave. There isn't going to be any isolation sphere or whipping posts in your immediate future."

"What? I'm not even fat yet!"

I didn't think this conversation was going to go well. "The rules of the house have deteriorated to nonexistence. You speak what is on your mind even when you are not in the bedroom, but I will not stand for you arguing with me."

She opens her mouth but doesn't say anything. She rubs her face against mine, meowing softly. I pet her hair and continue feeding her. She eats, but the silence filling the room is tangible. Like *this* is better?

I push her onto the floor, leaving her wide-eyed. She is trained well enough that she doesn't stand or say a word. I notice the tightening of her jaw a moment before she lifts her chin haughtily and then she crawls away, using the long extended arms, exaggerated sway of her hips sensual stalk she invented while under Lord Fyre's tutelage. If she thinks to push my buttons—she is. She circles the room before crawling back toward me and as she does her gaze meets and holds mine. I couldn't look away if I wanted to. She is like a great cat of the African plains, angry. Her stealth is provocative and exotic. I've never seen a more sensual pet, and this kitten is mine. It makes me proud to know others see her like this.

Her breasts have swelled with her pregnancy, not much, a little. Not enough for them to sway with her movement but enough to add a very feminine curve. Add her swollen stomach and she is luscious, all woman, all animal. I still can't believe I didn't notice.

She reaches my legs and butts her head against my calves in a definite defiance.

She backs away, sitting, lifting her face to glare before turning to look at her hand. So very feline-typical, she pretends she didn't just issue a challenge by lifting her wrist to her mouth and licking. Her tongue follows the long line of her gracefully posed hand. I warn, "Kitten."

She lifts her face and hisses before bolting across the floor to slam her hand against the lip of her water bowl. The metal dish flies into the air, spreading water over the floor. She hits the food container next and the cocoa flavored dry cereal I keep in it scatters.

I lunge for her, very aware of her pregnant state, and not willing to hurt her in an effort to contain her. I am surprised when she doesn't dodge but rather launches herself at my chest. On the slippery floor, we both fall, I taking the brunt of the landing.

She paws at my face, and her nails are every bit as sharp as claws.

I taste blood on my lip and try to grab her hands but she is a fast tiger, pushing my t-shirt up to bare skin. She sinks her teeth into my pectoral muscle and I realize this isn't a play for dominance, this is a staged scene for attention. She's done it before, always at the club, and always when I've spent too much of my evening directing employees and dealing with business-related drama. Never at home. But then she's always had my undivided attention at home, she hasn't had to resort to instigation tactics.

Moaning with very real pain, I finally manage to capture her jaw, and although she doesn't release my flesh from her teeth she holds the pressure steady. She hasn't broken the skin, so I'm not bleeding, and I won't be unless I jerk away. I'll have a heck of a bruise in a few hours though.

Our gazes lock, and then she releases my flesh and squirms away. She is crawling as fast as she can across the wet floor, looking over her shoulder to see if I am pursuing. I pull my shirt over my head and fling it into the mess of water and scattered cereal. Standing, I unbutton and unzip my pants. Two can play this game, and I am still the king of beasts in this house. I strip and drop to my knees. Letting out a roar, I charge.

She bolts from the kitchen but I catch her halfway across the living room floor, clamping my hand around the back of her neck and pulling her back toward me to take the brunt of the force of our collision with her hip. Rolling her, I straddle her legs and the wrestling match is on.

Her hair is wet and has puffed cereal pieces caught in its tangled tresses. Her skin is flushed, her eyes bright. She's raw and beautiful. Glowing. Happy.

Laughing, I realize that I too am having fun. It's been too long since we've played. But then she's subdued, exhausted too quickly, and she melts against the floor, giving up. I immediately worry I've been too rough and start to roll off her, but she grabs me and holds me tight. I've never seen her eyes filled with such worry.

I don't kiss her.

I do push her legs apart and kneel between them. Grabbing her wrists, I pull her over me to straddle me and her arms go around my neck with the desperation of a drowning victim. I do not thrust into her as much as she impales herself on me. I try to rock her gently, but she is crazed and rides me hard. She sinks her teeth into my shoulder, asking for roughness in return, but I can't give it to her. Even though rationally I know this will not hurt the baby, my intelligence and pure emotional panic war with each other. Within moments, she is gasping with her orgasm, not even realizing my erection has lost its might. Rearranging, I hide the fact from her and go to the kitchen to get my clothing. She doesn't follow me and I dress privately.

Coming out of the kitchen, I find her sitting where I left her. "I need to go to the club."

"It's the middle of the day."

"I know. I have an Attic session scheduled."

She pouts, standing reluctantly. "I'll get dressed."

"No," I say too quickly, too sharply. "Have Blake bring you by later. There isn't any point in you being there day and night as well."

"Oh, what a tangled web we weave, when first we practice to deceive!"

Sir Walter Scott, *Marmion*

CHAPTER 13

KITTEN

Following a two day honeymoon-like renewal to our relationship, I realize nothing has changed. If I thought calling out to Lord Ice was going to fix things between us, I was sadly mistaken. I am covered with bruises on the tops and backs of my thighs, but I woke up this morning alone, no one beside me to worship the marks with gratitude. It was quite anti-climactic and to find him sullen over breakfast was more than I could take. I went back to bed, citing morning sickness. I think we both knew it was a lie. The truth is, Thomas isn't here and we just don't seem to work well as a couple without him.

I would still be in bed sobbing if Thomas hadn't text me, asking me to meet him. I didn't tell Garrett, and I'm not going to. *So much for being a good submissive.*

"I'm going into the office this morning." My announcement doesn't make Master happy. I've caught him staring through the large front window at the skyline. He could as easily be looking at a bare wall because I don't think he's seeing the view.

When he turns to look at me, his eyes widen and I think I might have tried too hard to be believable. I took time, styling my hair with the curling iron, carefully applying my makeup, even choosing sensible if not completely conventional pumps. They are leopard spotted. I just couldn't resist funking-up the conservative brown tweed skirt-suit a little. Ditto for beneath my jacket, two layers, a white oxford shirt with a brown t-shirt pulled over the top, which proclaims: *Got pussy?*

Garrett doesn't say whether I look good, or ridiculous, but does arch his brow.

"I know. Doctor's appointment at four. I'm not going to forget, but I've neglected the paper for weeks and you know it." I grab my briefcase which is stashed in the credenza.

"Sit." Garrett gestures to the sofa.

Oh God, I do not want to argue about this. My coat and car keys are already in hand as I'd hoped to race out and not get into a conversation about whether I should or shouldn't go to the office. The clock is ticking, though I left myself plenty of time, knowing this might happen. *Damn it.* I sit. My pulse is racing when he joins me on the edge of the sofa and takes my hand. I hope he doesn't notice my sweating palms.

"We need to talk about Thomas."

He knows. My heart stops beating, fearing somehow that he has guessed I am lying to him. "You've heard from him?"

"No, and I'm not so certain we're going to. His brother brought danger into our home by showing up here. He's obviously in trouble, on the run. Thomas took him away as quickly as he could—against my medical advice—because he was more worried about our safety than his brother's life. He was protecting us. He may have left the country for all we know."

This is why he's been moody all morning? I swallow, hard, my heart in my chest. He misses Thomas as much as I do. I should tell him about the text. *Oh God. The lies, the lies, piling one on top of the other.* I take a deep breath, considering carefully how I would respond if I didn't know that Thomas was in fact okay and still in the city. "You're thinking he might be gone for a long time. Months maybe?"

He takes my hand in his. Holding my gaze, he kisses my knuckles. "I'm trying to prepare you that he may never come back."

"Did he say that to you?" I try to sound affronted. *God, what am I doing?* Garrett and Thomas have both on separate occasions accused me of being such a good actress they hardly know what to believe. It isn't true. I just keep getting put in these situations...where the truth isn't always the best thing to say.

"I haven't heard from him." His eyes ask if I have, even though he doesn't ask, or maybe I am just feeling guilty.

I jerk my hand away and stand. I'm on the verge of hysterics, I can feel it. My chest weighs a hundred pounds, I can't breathe. I want to scream, but I know if I start I might not stop. *I have to get out of this house.* "He won't leave us, not completely. We'll hear from him soon."

I start toward the door. I'm being a horrible slave. All protocol has gone out the window of late and Master isn't enforcing the rules. It would be so easy to be good if he would just lock me in my cage. But no, he's letting me run amok.

"And if he does, if he asks you to join him wherever he is, will you leave me to go to him?"

What? I hadn't considered that. *Thank God and the angels of mercy Master didn't ask me that before giving me a glimpse of Lord Ice.* Is that why Thomas text me and wants to meet with me privately? No, I won't believe that. He's committed to the ménage as much as I am.

Circumstances have changed though. Garrett's right about his brother bringing trouble into our lives. What if the only way for us to be together is away from here? What if he does ask me to go away with him?

I would refuse him.

I would.

This has been long coming, the last six months driving the point home as more and more business trips lure him away and all that time desperation has made me cling to him and in many ways left a wedge lodged between me and Master. Master has been the anchor keeping me grounded. *That* I see clearly now. "I love you, Master, my place is at your side."

"You love him as much, if not more."

There is a hurt in Garrett's eyes I wish I could erase. I've caused this doubt with the chaos that is mine and Lord Fyre's relationship. I press my fingertips to his lips. "No. Not true."

"You can say that *now*? With him God knows where?"

"I can promise you that I am not going anywhere. Even if he asked that. Thomas may come and go from our lives as he pleases, but I will never go with him. I was yours first. I will be yours always." I look away, remembering how easily Thomas left us for Eva, the pain of his betrayal still fresh and unexplored. There hasn't been time to think of that. So much has happened in the last few months. "I'm going to the office."

* * * *

There is a deli around the corner and down the block from the penthouse. I know of it though I've never eaten there. His text said *DELI*, nothing more, nothing less. No day. No time. I do not know how he will know when I will be there; I only expect he will show up. It seems silly really that I have such blind faith.

The breakfast rush is in full swing, making the deli crowded and noisy. There are few tables, eight to be exact, and a bar that seats ten. Every seat is filled. I stand in the doorway, waiting for an empty seat. My heart skips a beat when I realize he is already here. I didn't notice him at first though he sits at a corner table in plain sight. There are two seats, he occupies one, a man with his back to me fills the other. Thomas meets my gaze and his magnetism pulls me forward. *God, don't ask me to leave with you. I already promised Garrett I wouldn't, and there's been too many lies already.* The other man stands and leaves before I get halfway across the long room. He doesn't go out the front, choosing to exit through a back door instead, and I never see his face completely. He could be any man for as much as he stands out.

The same cannot be said about Thomas.

He is the face you notice when you walk into a room, stunningly handsome. He is wearing his hair loose today and his long dark waves cascade over his shoulders. He is wearing a knit tam, the kind I've seen Jamaican musicians on the wharf wear, and round sunglasses. Torn and distressed jeans, a tie-dyed t-shirt, and a well-worn leather jacket complete his *look.* If this is his disguise, he needs to work on it. I would not mistake him for anyone other than Lord Fyre.

I take the seat opposite him and just stare at him a moment, wordless. I have so many questions, but none of them are important. He is okay, he is fine. That is what matters.

"Thank you for coming."

"How is your brother?"

His eyes give away the emotion he is feeling. "He is alive."

I nod, understanding. What else is there?

Condensation drizzles off the side of his untouched glass of water.

It is obvious he has been here awhile and has not ordered. For a place so busy, I am surprised the waitress isn't haranguing him. "How much did you bribe the waitress to leave you alone?"

His lips twitch. "No bribe. I tipped her when I sat."

"Must have been a damn good tip."

He laughs and the sound is good to hear.

His hands are hidden under the table, out of sight, reminding me of an old western and making me wonder if he has a gun trained on the front door. I reach across the Formica, hoping he will take the hint that I need to touch him. Leaving one hand hidden, he puts the other in mine and the solid warmth of his palm is a balm to my soul.

"I need you to run an errand for me."

"There are a dozen people in this town you could ask favors of."

"Not. This."

His gaze holds mine an extra long minute, his intensity a worry. Wishing I could lie to him, I say, "I would do anything for you."

Reaching inside his coat, he retrieves a checkbook, driver's license, and social security card. Taking the items from him, I see the name on all three reads Blaire Harrington but it is my face on the license. *No. No, no, no, no, no! Do not ask me to runaway with you. Please.* My hand trembles as I look the items over. In addition, he hands me a business card advertising a real estate agent. It has her photo on it.

"I need you to meet with this real estate agent and buy a property. The address is noted on the back of the card."

As if I don't believe him, I turn the card over. An Artist District address is written in his hand. It can't be more than a block or two from Lewd Larry's.

"It's a foreclosure. The asking price is nine hundred thousand."

I look at him stupidly.

"Pretend to negotiate. Offer seven-fifty." He assures me, "There's more than enough money in the account to cover the full price, but I don't want you to appear overly eager. The most important thing is to close the deal. All the paperwork can be taken care of in-house today. As soon as you have the keys, call me using this cell." He hands me a phone. "It's registered to Blaire, remember that. You are Blaire. The number I want you to use to contact me is programmed as *work*. Do you understand?"

"Tell me you don't have time to explain all the cloak and daggers to me, Thomas, so that I can walk out of here and not look back." Issuing what amounts to an ultimatum, my heart is pounding so hard I think it will explode. Is this his every day workday? Always pretending to be someone else?

"Nikos is going to need a safe place to live. No one looks at eccentric creative types too closely."

I snort. "Is that what you think? Because *you* stand out, even in this getup."

He smiles patiently. "Only *you* see *me*."

I tap the business card on the tabletop nervously. I know the address. He's right, eccentric about covers it.

"And…the sooner I have my brother established someplace safe, the sooner we can be together."

"Do you think your cover here has been blown?" We've never discussed what he does for a living, and right now no one could convince me otherwise of my suspicions. Undercover cop. Spy. Assassin. Mercenary. He is something and to deny that would be ludicrous.

"It hasn't."

"Do you honestly believe I won't be followed?"

"I wouldn't put you in harm's way. Right now, no one is looking for Nikos in the United States. I want to make certain I have him well hidden if anyone ever does."

I tuck all of the documents into my bag. "I can't keep this a secret from Garrett."

"You can. You must."

I shake my head, not liking that he has put this responsibility on my shoulders. Garrett could have done this for him. George. The man who was just sitting here. *Unless he is testing me.* Why would he? I knew about Eva long before I ever admitted to him I did. I saw him with the senator I was never supposed to see him meeting. I didn't mention it to anyone, surely to God he knows he can trust me. It suddenly dawns on me that he does, and right now he trusts me with his brother's life.

"Fine. I'll do it."

He squeezes my hand, but his eyes are sad. "Thank you."

I am suddenly worried there is danger he isn't admitting to. "Do not die, Thomas! I mean it."

The look he gives me tells me how very much he loves me. "You, Garrett, and the new life you carry in your womb give me every reason I need to come home. Give me time to make certain no danger follows me."

I am angry and upset. "I wish I could have gotten to Paris in time, maybe then, Eva would have never come here."

"This has nothing to do with her."

"You are changed. *We* are changed."

He shakes his head in denial. "I promise, soon, everything will be as it was before."

"How can you say that?" I demand, insisting, "Everything is different."

"Do you love me?"

I gasp. *He knows I do. Why ask?* "Yes."

"Then we will survive this. All of it." He lifts my hand to his lips and kisses my knuckles, lingering. "I. Love. You. I'll come *home* soon."

Neither of us have to say it. We need each other. Now. Physical intimacy to seal the promise. When I am near him, I feel like an addict, or a horny adolescent. I don't look over my shoulder when I stand and cross a small hallway to the ladies' room, having no doubt he'll follow. I don't lock the door behind me. I just lean against the wall, waiting…

"Nay, call me not cruel, and fear not to take me, I am yours for my life-time, to be what you make me. To wear my white veil for a sign, or a cover, as you shall be proven my lord, or my lover."

Alice Cary, *The Bridal Veil 1820-1871*

CHAPTER 14

THOMAS

Sophia is so utterly beguiling; I don't know how Garrett ever lets her out of his sight. The things I want to do to her would make grown men whimper, but when I whisper my interests in her ear she only blushes.

There is no time for such pleasures today, and so I push her back against the porcelain sink with its bare pipes, thinking...if only there was more time.

She surprises me, twisting her fingers into my hair and pulling my head down. She is rough and needy, making me crazed in response. Grabbing her hair, I keep her from kissing me, holding her so that our lips barely meet.

This is no kiss, this is torture...for us both.

Her breath fans over my face as she begs, "Please."

She is dressed for a day at the office, skirt suit and heels. I imagine she is bare under the skirt, and I'm not disappointed when I run my hand up her silk-hose covered thigh, pushing up her tight pencil skirt, to find her wearing a garter belt but no panties. Grabbing her ass, I jerk her into me, leaving no doubt that this will head exactly where we both want it to when she feels my hard length pressed between us. "Is this what you want, baby?"

She tries harder to kiss me, but I jerk her hair, maintaining the distance between our mouths.

"God, yes. Fuck me."

I kiss her then. Hard. It feels like my lips are bruising as I crush her mouth against mine. I need the pain, need the distraction, to slow things down, but it has the opposite effect and suddenly we are on each other like animals. Teeth colliding, tongues dueling.

I spin her around, so she is facing the sink and looking in the mirror. Her hair is mussed, her lips bright pink from the ferocity of our kiss.

I push her skirt higher, before unbuttoning and unzipping my pants.

Behind us the door knob jiggles, and she meets my gaze in the mirror with panicked eyes. She calls out, "Occupied," as I lift her ass, spread her, and thrust deep into her pussy, making her voice sound slightly higher pitched and desperate. She looks surprised that I didn't wait, and I chuckle against her neck before biting her shoulder.

I cup her mons, pressing her clit between the v of two fingers. She is bent over the sink, holding on to the porcelain lip. She is standing on her tiptoes even though she is wearing high heels. I ride her hard, making her gasp as her pelvis slams again and again into the sink. She is moaning already, and I cover her mouth with my hand. She bites my finger, saying, "God, oh God," around my flesh.

She lifts her ass and pushes back into me, meeting my thrust, and I know I won't last long but then we really don't have time for more. I don't slow my pace, meeting her again and again. Pounding her.

I know the second her orgasm hits, her pussy clamping down hard on my cock. I flush the toilet beside us to muffle my moan as I lose the thin hold I had on my own control.

A moment later she turns on the water to the sink.

We are breathing hard and laughing.

It wasn't our most intense encounter, but it was satisfying, and when I turn her in my arms, seeing her flushed and beaming. I know I won't be able to stay away.

As we adjust our clothes, she takes me off guard, announcing, "I asked Garrett to marry me."

She meets my gaze and I don't really know what to say.

"He refused."

I find my tongue, barely. "I'm sorry."

She smiles and stands on tiptoe to kiss the corner of my mouth. "Don't be. It's not what I wanted, not really. I want the ménage, for better or worse, the three of us. I'm just afraid of what a baby means to us. I'm so desperately afraid of normalcy…it was an attempt to meet my fear head on."

The water is still running and I reach behind her to turn it off. She hits the chrome button to the air dryer.

"I'm assuming Garrett guessed that."

She shrugs. "I don't know if he did or he didn't. He accused me of wanting safe because I can't count on you."

I nod, hurt, feeling like a knife has been thrust into my chest. "Is that the way you see it?"

She kisses me, gently, and I let her, savoring the sweetness of her mouth. "I wouldn't be here if I felt that way. I trust you with my life. Just don't be long. I need you. *We* need you."

I hold her close, ignoring the jiggling door handle behind us.

* * * *

I no more than return from my errands when George informs me, "Garrett called."

I am immediately filled with guilt, knowing she might be in hot water with Garrett when she returns home to him, but my culpability takes backseat to my greater fear that he called here and the conversation may have been overheard by anyone *listening*, which makes me very nervous.

Kicking off my shoes in the foyer and then placing them in a small cabinet for storage, I join George in the living room where he is seated with his feet propped on an ottoman and doing a crossword puzzle.

Seeming to read my thoughts, he assures me, "Don't worry. He didn't say anything that would lead anyone to believe that *you or your brother* are here. He actually inquired as to whether or not I might be willing to shorten *my vacation*, and I assumed it was his way of inquiring about the status of your brother."

Sitting in a chair opposite him, I ask, "What did you tell him?"

"That he needs to be prepared for me to be absent another few weeks." George sets the crossword puzzle down and readjusts, putting his feet on the floor and leaning forward. "While you were away I took the liberty of having your brother's first counseling session."

By his tone I can imagine how badly that went.

"He refuses to admit he has a drug problem. He insists that his drug usage was a choice." Dismissively, he adds, "We'll get there, it will take some time, but I've cracked tougher shells. To be honest, I'm more worried about you."

I meet his gaze and he covers one of my hands with his. *Oh, hell.*

"You're avoiding Garrett and Kitten. I believe there is more going on than your fear that trouble may have followed your brother to town. Want to talk about it?"

My hand jerks under the weight of his hand and his fingers close tighter, holding mine. I warn him, "Don't try to analyze me."

"That isn't my intent. I thought you might need a friend to talk to. You've been through a lot." Thankfully, he releases my hand and sits back in his chair.

Since when did George start seeing us as friends?

"Your wife and children have been out of contact for almost a year?"

Don't do this, George.

"You sought out an old flame that could have destroyed the ménage…has it?"

"No! Eva is past."

His lips twitch. "Is she? Or was your brother's arrival merely a convenient interruption?"

I let out a long slow breath, repeating, "She is in the past."

"I assume you know that Kitten is pregnant?"

I nod, unacceptable emotion filling my chest.

"How do you feel about that?"

Stop. I stand abruptly, having taken all the interrogation I intend to.

"Your children are all but lost to you, and now you have the opportunity to start over with a new baby."

Only supreme self-control keeps me from hitting him. "The baby she carries is not a replacement. My children are not replaceable!" I leave the room, cursing. I don't need this. No one asked George to analyze *me*.

"Is love a tender thing? It is too rough, too rude, too boist'rous; and it pricks like thorn."

William Shakespeare, *Romeo and Juliet*

CHAPTER 15

KITTEN

The loft Thomas sent me to is in one of the few timber buildings left in San Francisco. An old factory converted into live-in, work-in units for artists. Not that I have ever understood how a struggling artist could afford almost a million dollars.

The real estate agent smiles too widely as she shows me the amenities. She is short, chubby, a little too perky, and afraid of getting her hands dirty as evidenced by the look of disgust when she has to turn a corroded door handle to show the bathroom.

"Twenty-four hundred square feet. And the light here is amazing. You didn't say, do you paint?"

My palms and pits start sweating. *Don't ask me any questions, lady.* "I'm not much into small-talk. Will you accept a check today for seven hundred and fifty?"

She looks aghast. "Well, no. The bank is quite firm on the price."

"You're certain?"

She licks her lips, making me feel like she is lying. By taking less, her commission gets cut. I prop the checkbook on a countertop and write out *eight hundred thousand dollars*, hoping that she will not notice that my hand is shaking. I hand it to her. "Will this buy me the keys today?"

She doesn't even blink. She hands me the keys. "I'll draw up the papers. Will you be available to sign the deed in the morning?"

"I will." *God, please let me be available to sign the damn papers in the morning.*

She leaves me and I look at the property Thomas just purchased. The walls and floors are painted black. The bathroom is a health hazard, and the kitchen is smaller than what I had in my dorm room at college. Remembering his brother stretched out on my table, tattoo covered and bullet-riddled, I decide the place is perfect.

I call Thomas from the provided cellphone. "It's all yours. She wants me to sign the deed in the morning. Tell me how I'm supposed to escape Garrett's notice a second morning in a row?"

"I'll take care of Garrett."

I'll take care of Garrett. "Before or after he kills me?"

"Sophia, you worry too much."

Disgusted I ask, "What do you want me to do with the keys?"

"Toss them in a dumpster. I won't need them."

I blink, suddenly remembering my obstetrician appointment. "Oh, shit! What time is it?"

He doesn't answer fast enough, and I hang up on him in an attempt to read the time on the phone's screen. *Shit! I'm late.* Or will be by the time I cross town. No question about it. The cellphone immediately starts ringing and knowing it's him, I don't answer. I went two full weeks without a single word from him and there is nothing he can say to me now that I need to hear. The phone immediately starts ringing again, but I still don't answer. *Let him worry about me for a change.*

* * * *

My day couldn't be easy. Dr. Moran's office is downtown and midday traffic is a nightmare, the parking situation worse. By the time I reach the twelfth floor office, I'm frazzled. I peek around the corner between foyer and waiting room before entering. I'd hoped to arrive before Garrett but seeing him sitting across the room, I decide I will never have any luck at all as far as that man is concerned.

As nonchalantly as I can, I cross the room and sit down in one of the leather upholstered chairs. "I know. I'm late."

He doesn't say anything.

"Only a few minutes."

He doesn't respond, not a look or a blink, or even a tap of an impatient finger.

The doctor's waiting room is almost empty. Garrett, a woman who is so pregnant I don't know how her stomach has kept from splitting wide open, and me. The woman's name is called and she lumbers out of her chair. It is not an easy thing to do, standing, when you are trying to lift such a swollen stomach. Seeing me watching, she blushes. "Triplets."

Her voice seems to waken Garrett from a slumber and he hurriedly stands to give her a hand up. I think she is made even more discomfited by his assistance, but she doesn't refuse the help. It's hard not to stare as she waddles...yes, waddles...out of sight. Oh God. I do not want to be here. I want desperately to wake up and find this is all a bad dream.

Another woman enters the lobby. She is carrying an infant car-seat-a-ma-jig, pink blanket dangling over the edge. A squeal of delight comes from the general area of the receptionist's desk. Suddenly three women appear, bouncing up and down impatiently as the new mother unwraps layers to expose the baby. Although I never see so much as a head or a hand, I have to assume there is a baby by the amount of "oohing" and "ahhing".

"Come around! Come around."

The woman and bundle disappear through the entry door, after which much excited chatter ensues. Eavesdropping, I learn that she is an employee and that she is on maternity leave. Obviously, she waited until closing time to arrive.

One of the nurses comes to the door and calls my name. I stand, thinking Garrett will stand too, but he doesn't. "Will you come in with me?"

He finally looks at me, but I can't read his expression. I wonder if he reads guilt in mine. I'm trying, really, really trying not to betray Thomas, but I don't know how I'm going to get through tonight with Garrett acting this way without giving him some explanation. *I was at work. I was at work.* I reinforce the lie in my head. *I haven't done anything out of the ordinary today.*

"I'll come in with you if you want me to."

"I do, why wouldn't I?"

He stands and takes my hand, making me feel better instantly, but then he whispers, "You didn't go to work."

Reaching the nurse, I plaster a smile on my face. *I will not do this here.* I keep my back turned toward Garrett so I won't have to look into his eyes and see the accusations or the hurt I might find there.

We have to pass the woman who brought her baby to show off. I finally see the baby's face, a deep shade of red, made to seem very red by the soft pink knitted cap and frilly pink dress she is wearing. She seems unbearably small but when she yawns, obviously bored by the entire showing-off-thing, her mouth is a wide, deep cave.

How could such a small baby have such a wide mouth?

The women meeting the new baby for the first time are all overwhelmed by her cuteness and there are more "ahh's"...and I am not unaffected...not by any means. Her adorableness makes me sad. The woman shifts the baby's weight and her left hand flashes a large diamond and a simple band. Married. At a glance I decide she has a very normal life, a husband and house in suburbia. She doesn't have to worry about which man to please, which to lie to...or which to obey.

I think the nurse leading me to a scale is in a hurry to see me gone, because as I am weighed and my vitals taken a second nurse asks medical history questions. Led to a large, well-appointed examination room, I am told to take off my clothes from the waist down and handed a paper sheet to cover up with for privacy even though as soon as the doctor comes in he will lift the sheet.

I am left alone with Garrett and fidget nervously with the button at the waistband of my skirt.

Softly, he asks, "Where were you?"

He has a right to ask. We're in a relationship. He's my Master. But still I bristle. I never expected to want space or privacy, but today I need both because I don't want to lie to him again. My brain quickly spins lies, and I start thinking of metroparks I could have escaped to for meditation and reflection. I *am* facing a huge decision today.

I slide down my skirt and step out of it. Step out of my shoes too. I am left wearing the garter belt and stockings, suddenly a pain after being so convenient before. Without pressing the issue, Garrett kneels and unclasps the hooks. He rolls the stockings one by one down each leg. His caress on my bare skin draws goosebumps.

I step away, suddenly fearful he'll realize I had sex.

Shakily, I climb onto the examination table and the paper cover rattles and I am embarrassed it seems so loud. Probably because the room is deathly still, waiting along with Garrett for which lie I will decide on.

I drape my lower half with the paper sheet, hoping Garrett is right that this doctor is community-friendly. My thighs are criss-crossed with deep bruises.

"At least tell me *he* looked well."

My gaze collides with Garrett's at the same time there is a light rap at the door. The doctor and a nurse enter without waiting for my approval. Garrett steps nearer the table to make room for them both. I reach out my hand and am surprised when he actually takes it. "He is."

"Excuse me?" the doctor asks, sitting on a stool at the base of the table.

"Nothing," we both say together. Garrett squeezes my hand. I am nauseous and filled with dread. I don't want to face the questions I know he is going to fire at me as soon as we get home.

"Place your feet in the stirrups and scoot your bottom to the edge of the table for me." I scoot, he pushes up the drape. His eyes widen at the sight of my thighs, but he recovers swiftly. He is quick, cold hands, colder speculum. "Nurse?"

She hands him the tip to an ultrasound wand.

"What is that?" I ask nervously. *I didn't expect this.*

"An internal ultrasound wand. Just relax."

The cold plastic slides in and I squeeze Garrett's hand harder.

The nurse turns the lights off and a monitor screen on. Waves of light and dark create shapes and patterns on the screen. I don't have to be trained to know an arm and a hand when I see one. *Oh God.* The images squiggle out of focus as he moves the wand. *Go back, go back!* The image swirls back into focus.

"I'm really pregnant."

The doctor glances at me. "I wasn't aware there was any doubt."

I look at Garrett. He is transfixed by the screen. I look again as the doctor starts drawing on the screen. The nurse measures between the lines. He points to a flickering on the screen. He points again.

"Surprisingly, you are quite a bit farther along than I expected." He runs his hand over my stomach. "You're barely showing."

Usually I am quite sunken between my pelvic bones. Not anymore. It seems since the inverted bondage session my gut is permanently pooched out.

He withdraws the wand. "The other one, please."

The nurse wheels over a second machine.

Garrett asks, "Is there a problem?"

"Everything is fine."

He spreads gel over my stomach. The cold surface of the transducer slides easily over my skin. Shapes appear and define. Three dimensional shapes. I gasp when a face appears. "Fuck!"

Garrett squeezes my hand harder than I am squeezing his.

The shapes go in and out of focus. The doctor smiles and announces dramatically, "*Voila.*"

There is no doubt why he is excited. The monitor screen frames two babies, picture perfect images. Two faces, four arms. It looks as if one of the babies is rubbing its eyes and the other could very well be sucking its thumb. "Do you want to know their sex?"

"Isn't it too early for that?" I panic, my knees are shaking.

"Not at all. You're eighteen weeks." He waits for a response.

Garrett nudges me. "Do you want to know the sex, sweetheart?"

I look at the monitor and jerk my feet out of the stirrups to sit up. I start to hyperventilate.

"Could you give us a moment alone?" Garrett asks, and both the doctor and nurse leave the room.

"Oh God. Oh God. Oh—"

Garrett pulls my face into his chest. "It's okay."

"I was twenty weeks before. Now—" Hyperventilating has escalated into full-fledged hysteria. "I didn't know for certain but I felt like she was a girl. I killed her, and she had a face and fingers and toes."

Garrett kisses my cheek, smearing my tears. "You can't go back and change the past, Celia. You can only move forward. What do you want for your future?"

I am panting hard when I look into his face, but I am certain when I answer, "I want to be a mother. I might be a really, really sucky mother but I want the chance."

He pulls me into his arms and hugs me. The cynical thought goes through my mind that he arranged for me to have a three-dimensional ultrasound on purpose. He wanted me to see exactly what I would be giving up. I push the thought away. What if he did? Everything is going to change in his world too because one thing is definite, we can't go back to the way it was now.

A tap sounds at the door. "Everything all right?"

"Yes," Garrett answers loudly.

"I want to know," I whisper.

Garrett opens the door to face the doctor. "We're ready to know the sex now."

"All right." He comes into the room and sits down. He runs the transducer over my stomach again. Pointing out body parts as he finds them. Knees, toes. Penises.

"Boys," I whisper. *Thomas's sons.* I look at Garrett and his face is filled with an awe and wonderment that makes me start crying all over again. *Can they be Garrett's sons, too?*

The doctor wipes most of the gel off my stomach and scoots back. "You can sit up now. Why did you wait so long to see me?"

"I didn't know I was pregnant."

Both he and Garrett look skeptical.

"I rarely have periods on a normal schedule. How was I supposed to know?" I sit on the edge of the table, feeling exposed and accused. "Is the baby—" I correct myself "Are the babies okay?"

"You are going to have to add more calories to your diet. Your babies are substantially undersized for the amount of development I am seeing." His voice is concerned. "Have you experienced excessive morning sickness? I can prescribe something to settle the nausea so that your meals stay down."

"No morning sickness," I assure him. "I've just always been very, very thin, and when I'm stressed…I don't eat."

"Are you stressed?"

Am I? I try to not think about Thomas's brother's bloody body on my dining room table or the fact that I just wrote an almost million dollar check under an assumed identity. That hasn't been my excuse for the last four months. "Not especially."

"She works very long hours," Garrett explains. "She's the owner and CEO of *The Darkness.* Perhaps you've heard of it? When she isn't working there, she helps me at my club. I'm afraid neither of us have regimented meal times."

He pushes his plastic rim glasses higher on his nose. "Try fewer hours and regular meals. I suggest six to eight small meals a day. I'm going to prescribe a prenatal vitamin. I want to see you every two weeks."

"That seems excessive. Do you suspect a problem?" Garrett asks, seeming a little more abrupt than I would suspect. I wonder if he is speaking of time between visits or the sheer volume of meals, because there is no way I'll be able to eat that much food.

"Your partner and babies are undernourished. Until I see some improvement in their condition, I want to keep a close watch. I would also advise you to refrain from impact play for the duration of the pregnancy."

Garrett flushes scarlet, and I am not certain if it is anger or embarrassment.

"I understand that you are both quite renowned in the BDSM community."

"I do not starve or abuse my partner."

"I didn't mean to imply that you do, but as her doctor I am concerned about the bruises on her upper thighs and want to caution you on areas which could pose health risks to the developing fetuses. If I may?"

The tension level goes up ten-fold in the room.

The doctor tells Garrett, "I respect the work you've done as an educator in the community, and I would just like to use this opportunity to help get my message out as far as what is and isn't safe play when your partner is pregnant. By having this discussion with you now, in these early stages, you can lead by example."

"Yes, I can see where that would benefit the community," Garrett answers and just like that the tension deflates.

The doctor is very thorough in what we should and should not do and I am left believing that the missionary position might be our only option.

As we leave, the parking lot becomes a battlefield when Garrett accuses, "You saw him today. Have there been other times?"

I don't answer and by the time I reach the car, my hand is shaking so hard, I drop the keys.

Garrett picks them up and holds them ransom until we have the discussion he wants to have. "I have to be able to believe you when you go out the door!"

"Can we please talk about this tomorrow?"

"So you can have time to coordinate your lies with Thomas's?"

"No!" I wrap myself in my arms. I knew this fight was coming, I was just hoping we could have a ceasefire for a little longer. "I do not want to discuss this now."

He stares at me and I give him credit for not throttling me. If I were him I'd have shaken me senseless by now.

"I lied. I'm sorry."

"Thank you."

The sun is setting and the sky is absolutely beautiful. Shades of orange and pink and purple swirl into and out of each other. I drop my head back and just take it all in. Delaying the inevitable? You betcha. I let out a deep sigh and look bravely into his face again. He looks exhausted and worried.

"Beautiful," he says.

"The sunset is beautiful tonight." I'm surprised by the reprieve. "I wish we were sitting on the beach so we could really enjoy it."

He steps closer and takes me into his arms. "Not the sky. *You.* I don't always tell you how absolutely beautiful you are and I should."

I let him kiss me. Thankful for the moment. I could wish I hadn't met with Thomas, that I hadn't allowed myself to be put into the position of lying to Garrett yet again, but as long as I wear two collars I am accountable to both of them. That's a problem. I kiss Garrett back with everything I have. I want to forget for a second that I am torn between the two of them. I just want to have one man at a time in my head and heart.

"This isn't the kiss and make up part, if that's what you are thinking," he warns.

"It could be."

He lets out a shaky breath, and I realize it has been an equally emotional day for him. From his point of view, he didn't know where I was or who I was with. I might have been with Thomas or I might have come face to face with the man who shot up his brother.

I take his face in my hands. "I am so sorry I worried you. I do love you."

He nods and the lines of exhaustion around his eyes deepen. "Let's go home."

"I would love that."

He pulls me to his car. "I'll send someone for yours. I'll drive."

Once I'm buckled in, I take the ultrasound photo out of my purse and just look at it. "They seem so real."

"They are real."

"You know what I mean."

"Yes. Three dimensional ultrasound is extraordinary." He leans over and kisses me. "When did you decide to not abort?"

"When I felt them move the other day. I know you don't believe me, but I felt them. From that moment I was lying to you and myself if I thought I could go through with an abortion."

"Knowing how far along you are, I have no doubt you felt them. I'm sorry for doubting you. I know you're scared, but as long as you want me by your side I'm going to be right here with you."

I pull his hand from the gearshift and kiss his knuckles. "I know. We do have to figure out this Master thing though."

He tenses. "This. Master. Thing?"

"Yes. As in me having to obey two men. It isn't working. I can't keep choosing who to obey and who to disobey. It isn't fair."

I earn an angry glance but my hand stays holding his as he downshifts to stop at a red light. "I am your *Master*. Thomas is your—"

"Other Master," I interrupt. "Tell me you see it any other way."

The light turns green, but he doesn't drive. Even after the car behind him honks and goes around us, he just keeps looking at me. *Say something!*

"Master?"

He shakes his head and looks forward again without saying a word. Shifting gears, he drives.

Really? This is the way we're handling this? "Seriously? What is your problem? You are my Master, Thomas is my Master. Nothing at all has changed from yesterday to today." My voice sounds pinched and frustrated...and disrespectful. What has happened that suddenly I am standing up to him? Arguing with him?

"I know. Drop it."

"No. You're acting like this is suddenly a problem."

"I want to protect you. I want to help you raise these children. I want—"

"The white fucking picket fence," I interrupt, making him glare at me in response, not because I interrupted him, but because our opinions are so far apart on this topic. "Our ménage does not fit into your suburban fantasy. I swear I feel like you are two different men sometimes."

We arrive at Lewd Larry's and after parking he turns to me and demands, "Do you really think it's suitable to raise children in my bachelor pad in the sky?"

Is that a rhetorical question, because I don't have an answer for that. I'm still struggling with the thought that I am pregnant. I am going to have a baby. *Babies.*

There is no *suitable* in this situation. I am Kitten, Goddammit. Kitten. Not mommy material.

Defeated, I follow Master inside and discard clothing as I walk. I am shedding the layers that define me as Celia Brentwood. Jacket. Blouse. Skirt. Shoes. I leave a littered trail not caring which server has to pick up after me. By the time I drop to my knees, I am Kitten. Sex pet extraordinaire. Owned. Collared. And for a little while I do not have to think about anything.

"Do not seek the because—in love there is no because, no reason, no explanation, no solutions."

Anais Nin

CHAPTER 16

GARRETT

The day's special arrives, crab cakes with a succulent orange and brandy sauce, fried green tomatoes, and salade du jour. It is Kitten's favorite, and I am quite surprised when she shakes her head the moment it is delivered.

"Eat."

"I told you I'm not hungry."

Hearing her voice here in The Oasis is unexpected. A single meow, a double meow, but not words, not here. It is one thing for her to violate protocol at home and quite another... Something rips inside of me and I am going back on my promise of no punishment in her immediate future. With all that is available to me, I can think of only one safe-for-her-condition solution. A hand signal brings security tableside. "Isolation Sphere."

She gasps, meeting my gaze for the first time. It is too late to change the outcome. She can cool her heels until she is willing to obey me.

As she is led to the sphere she doesn't struggle like she normally would, no hissing or baring teeth, no feline antics at all, and that worries me. Eddie, one of my men, positions her in the center of the sphere, secures her ankles and wrists in cuffs, leaving her spread eagle, arms over her head. She looks defiant as a ball gag is shoved into place. Once she would have cried, but that time seems an eternity ago.

As the sphere rises through the levels of the building, interior sphere lights come on so that all Kitten sees is herself, naked, bound, gagged. As it descends, the interior lights go down so that she can see her audience. For a while she is the main event.

Some slaves abhor isolation, Kitten loves it. For a moment I think I screwed up, in essence rewarding her bad behavior, but then I remember it will only take time.

Four hours later, she hasn't cracked and I am beginning to question my choice.

"I was told an intervention is required."

I startle, hearing Thomas's voice behind me, and give him an evil look over my shoulder. "Great. *Now* you're here."

He watches the ascent of the sphere, his eyes widening when he sees her. The interior lights are on so that she can't see us, but we can see her. Using the remote, I pause the sphere at our level.

"God, she's thin."

"Yes," I agree.

Stretched out, metal cuffs binding her wrists above her head, her feet pulled wide, her ribs and pelvis bones are painfully visible. It is hard to believe the slight swelling below her belly button is a baby, *two babies*.

I catch Jackie's waggling fingers from the other side of the dining room. Astonished, I ask, "Jackie called you?"

He shrugs. "She called George and suggested he call an early end to *his vacation* if he wanted a job to return to. She made it sound like you couldn't hold the place together on your own. George sent me to investigate since he feels my presence bedside is less necessary than his."

Standing, I give Jackie a hateful glance, not letting on that George talked to Thomas. Better she think her call to George and Thomas's arrival are mere coincidence.

"What did Kitten do?"

"What hasn't she done?" I don't have to tell him that I know he forced her to lie to me, his guilt is written all over his face.

He exhales, sounding exhausted. "What can I do?"

I shake my head and walk away, leaving him staring at our shared woman. I don't go far, only as far as the bar, ordering a Scotch. Eventually, Thomas joins me and convinces me to go back to the table where we have front row seats to the sphere. As he sits, he apologizes. "I've screwed up so much."

"You might say that." If he expected me to argue, he's wrong, although I'm not certain if he's speaking of Eva, his brother, or the lack of commitment he's shown the ménage of late.

"I could explain it to you the way Doctor Psycho explained it to me."

Keeping my eyes on Kitten's bound form, I cross my arms. "This should be good."

"The dreams I had of Eva were caused by the loss I was feeling following Latisha's desertion. Because I was unable to chase after my wife and children, my mind caused me to follow another ghost from my past. He's encouraged me to seek counseling to find some closure for a past I left unexplored and the present, which I am not dealing with."

"He wants you to make peace with Eva? Isn't it enough that she's gone?"

The look Thomas gives me isn't a happy one. "He wants me to figure out a way to bring my children home because I am so wracked with guilt that I am no longer an influence in their lives."

I kick myself in the ass for assuming his thoughts were left dwelling on a woman. Of course he is miserable with his children so far away. "Is that even possible?"

"Not without starting a war."

We sigh heavily and simultaneously. I think he's speaking metaphorically but after operating on his brother, I realize he might be telling the truth.

"Do you want to speak with Kitten?" I ask.

"No," he answers sadly. He hasn't taken his eyes off her the entire time we've been talking. "There would be no point. She wants nothing more than for me to return home with you both and I can't."

"Your brother?"

"He survived the detox with George's help. His body is healing well, thanks to you. The good doctor is working on his mind now."

I nod, hoping without saying so, and not knowing all the details besides, that George will be successful.

"I hope to have a clear idea of his mental state in the next few days. If he is able, I have a safe location arranged. The feelers I have out assure me no one is looking for him in San Francisco."

"That surprises you."

He nods. "A miracle."

"I can't control her. She doesn't respect me."

"Isolation is what she needs most. The sphere. The cat cage.

Humiliate her. Control her. Take away all of her personal freedom."

"Does that include secret meetings you arrange?" I ask icily.

He ignores the question but meets my gaze.

I ask, "For how long?"

"For as long as it takes to make her *yours* again."

He gives me pause, leaving me feeling like he isn't planning to come back. I could have her all to myself again…we could dissolve the ménage. Beneath my long sleeve, my concealed brand flares, itching.

I press the *STOP* button on the sphere's remote, locking it in place on this level. The interior lights go out and the door swings open. I know the moment their gazes lock because it feels as if all the oxygen is sucked out of the room. I can't breathe. Or don't want to. I have never seen two people so connected. They are One and as much as I could believe Kitten and I are so, I cannot. She loves me, yes, and I love her, but it is not and never will be the bond shared between the two of them.

"You're a bastard, Garrett."

"We aren't a ménage without you. We aren't a couple either."

He pushes away from the table and goes to her. It's like looking at a horrific accident on the freeway where you know someone has died. I don't want to watch, but I can't look away. He steps into the sphere and closes the door behind him. He starts the globe's ascent, taking them out of view as he cups her face in his hands and kisses her. I guess I won't be watching after all. I take the earbud out of my ear that has allowed me to hear the softest sound the entire time she has been inside. This is a private moment and one I will honor.

Just out of sight, the sphere stops moving. They are on the same level as The Attic, home to private rooms for play. Maybe he will take her out, maybe they will stay inside. I don't know. I don't care. I only want things right for all of us again. I don't begrudge her Lord Fyre because I understand. I am, as she is, made whole with him in my life.

"Cozy, cozy, the two of them all snug in the sphere like that. Too bad we weren't allowed to watch the show."

I look up to see Jackie's smug face. She seats herself in the chair Thomas just vacated without asking to join me. Our gazes collide and I manage to say, "Please, join me." It almost sounds sincere.

She looks astonished. I think she was expecting anger. "I know it's none of my business what goes on under your roof, but that girl is pregnant now and something has to be done to make the three of you act like you have half a brain between you."

"I know."

"That's it?" she demands.

I look away. "I just don't feel like arguing, not with you, not with him, not with her. Whatever is going to happen is. There's nothing I can do to make things right, and there's nothing I can do to make things any worse than they are."

"You're placing blame at his feet?"

"Yes."

She pats my back. "Well, as I live and breathe. I thought I'd never see the day Mr. Perfect could fall from his pedestal."

I snort. Thomas is a lot of things but perfect isn't one of them.

"The path is smooth that leadeth on to danger."

William Shakespeare, *Venus and Adonis*

CHAPTER 17

THOMAS

Her eyes are closed and her head sagged so that her face rests heavily in my palms. The tears trailing down her cheeks break my heart. I kiss the top of her head. "I'm sorry I've caused you difficulty with Garrett."

She doesn't move.

"I don't know how to fix this. I need your loyalty, I need to know that I can count on you and trust you, but I don't want to ruin things between the two of you."

Still, no reaction.

"No one ever promised you it would be easy serving two Masters."

She opens her eyes and meets my gaze. "Tell me what to do."

"Be good to Garrett. Love him while you're waiting for me." I kiss her, filling her mouth with my tongue, claiming her. Her tears leave both our faces drenched. "I. Love. You. With. All. My. Heart. And. All. My. Soul."

"I love you, Lord Fyre. *Thomas*."

I wipe her tears with my thumbs, as I still cradle her face in my hands. "Ari. My real name is Demetres Aristotle Velouchiotis. In private I'd like you to call me Ari."

She repeats, "Ari," and smiles. "I love you, Ari."

"I love you, Sophia."

She sobs against my mouth as I catch her lips. "Please don't say goodbye."

"You carry my child and I have just professed the depth of my love to you, I will never tell you goodbye. You are my heart. I could not live if I didn't have your strength to hold me together."

"Sh-h, don't say that."

"It's true and *knowing that* I want you to obey Garrett in all things."

She shakes her head. "You may need me to do you a favor."

"I may but if he refuses to allow you to come to me I will not hold it against you."

She sniffles, *understanding*. "He won't forbid my aiding you."

I hold her gaze a moment longer. "I need to get back to Nikos."

"Do me a favor before you go?"

"If I can."

"In Garrett's office. My purse. There's an ultrasound photo from my doctor's appointment. I want you to have it…to remind you why it's so important for you to return to us."

"I don't need a photo, sweetheart—" Seeing the disappointment in her eyes, I promise, "But I will get it before I go and keep it with me until I see you again."

She smiles and I step away from her while I still can. I press the *OPEN* button so that I can exit on this floor before sending her back down to Garrett. I watch her descent and keep watching, leaning over the metal railing that allows me to see most of The Oasis dining room. Garrett looks up, seeming to know I am here, watching. He nods before standing to go to her himself. I trust him to care for her while I am forced to be away from them, I just pray I'm not overly long.

I step into the shadows as he leads her from the sphere. I know she will look up, and I don't want her to see me. It is hard enough watching her melt against him without me there to hold her as well. She is broken, sobbing, and when she clings to him it is enough to get me through the moment. *They will care for each other.* With a final look, I take the stairs to Garrett's office so that I can do the task asked of me. I don't want or need the distraction. I know better. Staying focused on the task at hand is what keeps me alive...but I've promised.

Twins. My knees buckle, seeing the photo. *Dear God.*

In the corner of the photo it says *eighteen weeks*, and my mind travels quickly back to the memories I have of Latisha's pregnancies. By twenty weeks she was showing with each of the babies. Granted, not as much with the first, but still *showing*. And not pregnant with twins.

Angry, I leave the office at a dead run and make my way to the dining room. My only plan to shake her within an inch of her life and then force feed her. Reaching the room, I pull myself up short, seeing Kitten nestled in Garrett's lap. He is feeding her bites of food with his fingers. I swallow hard, realizing she was probably in the sphere for her refusal to eat. He has to be as worried as I am. I close my eyes and stumble back against the wall, remembering when I first took her to train. She was so thin, undernourished. She'd explained to me then that when she is under high stress she finds it hard to eat.

She's been starving herself, probably since I first left to find Eva. This too is my doing. I have caused her undue stress. *Damn me. Damn me to hell and back again.*

I force myself to get my emotion under control. From the shadows, I watch them. I should be hurrying back to George's and my brother, but I can't bear to look away.

Sophia is carrying my twins. *Mine.*

The one thing my talks with George have done is make me see how desperately I've missed my children. It is a hopeless situation as long as they are with their mother in Africa. And even though I know they are being well cared for by Lattie, her father, and more than a dozen servants, I worry about their safety and wish there was something I could do to influence the situation other than outright kidnapping my own children.

My enemies keep me from doing so.

Now, I am blessed with two more children. I am so undeserving.

Watching Garrett coax her to take another bite, I have no doubt how much he cares for her and if I am unable to return, he would be a good father. I don't like thinking the thought, but to think otherwise would be lying to myself. I do not know when, if, I will be able to return home. And now especially, I will not return until I know for a fact that Garrett, Sophia, and *our* babies will be safe.

An hour later I am pacing George's kitchen, my mood ripe.

He left a dinner plate in the warmer for me. A note on the counter says so. It also says he is "in session," which means he is behind closed doors with my brother and does not want to be disturbed.

I take out the plate and stare at the food, leaving it untouched. I keep thinking about Garrett, holding Kitten, feeding her bites with his fingers, and wishing I was there.

I can do nothing *here.*

Pace? Eat? Wait? George is doing everything that needs done. I am immediately filled with guilt. He has completely stepped away from his life to care for my brother. He hasn't been to the club, he cancelled all of his social commitments…

I hear his steps on the staircase leading from the dungeon and quickly stab a fork into the baked chicken breast on the plate. I cut a bite and shove it in my mouth. I am still chewing when he enters the kitchen. Under any other circumstances, I am most certain my taste buds would be experiencing nirvana, as it is I feel like I am chewing a piece of cardboard.

"I didn't expect you back so early."

I'm sure he didn't mean it sarcastically but I take it that way. I feel bad enough spending so many hours away, but it's taken time to convert the loft into an armed fortress. "How soon will he be able to function in society?"

George looks at me like I just asked him the meaning of life. He shakes his head and answers my question with one of his own. "Are you or I fit for society? We're damaged. We deal the best way we can. Do I think your brother will ever be able to have a quote-unquote *normal* life? Normal job? Normal commitments? Normal relationships?" He shakes his head, his lips pursed thoughtfully. "Not a chance in hell. I think in time he will be able to create a new life for himself and whether or not that will fit into the confines of civilized society is yet to be determined."

"I bought him a place, one of the artist lofts on Mission. When can I expect to get him settled in there?"

"His body is healing. Physically, he could go there today. Mentally?" He shrugs. "Maybe tomorrow, maybe never. I don't think he is a threat to himself or others, but anything could trigger something deep inside his mind and he could experience a psychotic break."

"But that might not happen? He might be fine?"

"I would expect it." He goes to the refrigerator, retrieves two small bottles of juice and hands me one. "He doesn't need institutionalized. He can live in society. Just expect the worst."

"Then let's ramp up efforts to get him to the point where he can *exist in society*."

I can't believe I am rushing this. I should be hiding him deeper, not forcing him back into the world. My gut tells me to hide him in plain sight. I just hope my instincts are trying to protect him and not just focused on being near Sophia and *our* babies.

I hide my fears behind a swallow of juice. If George senses I am mentally or emotionally torn, he will be like a dog with a bone and I do not want chewed on.

"So, what was the emergency at the club?" he asks. He has turned his back to me and started rummaging in the refrigerator for a snack.

"What is always the emergency? Too many customers, not enough workers." It isn't the true reason behind Jackie's call but it isn't a lie. "*We* need to be there. I owe Garrett a huge debt."

Pulling out several types of cheese and fruit, he meets my gaze. "Or he could hire some people."

Glad he hasn't picked up on my distress, I nod, agreeing, "Or he could hire some people."

"If all the world hated you, and believed you wicked, while your own conscience approved you, and absolved you from guilt, you would not be without friends."

Charlotte Bronte

CHAPTER 18

NIKOS

Thomas finds me playing chess in the basement with Doctor Psycho. I like this crazed doctor; he's highly intelligent, geeky to the extreme, and not a bit insane. I call him Doc and that does trip his synapses a bit. He likes control and by being unable to manage me...that makes him a bit nuts. We're at an impasse. He could beat me to death, strip the skin from my body, cut off my fingers and toes one by one, and still I would spit in his face and call him Doc. I find great joy in my ability to leave him slightly unsettled.

He made tea just before my brother arrived and I lift a too dainty, antique china cup to my lips. Black tea. Cream. Two lumps of sugar. Did he think this would somehow intimidate me? Or is his *very* ritualized tea service a part of his every day? Who knows? Not me. Occasionally, I'll pick up on words he says with an English pronunciation, making me wonder if his mother or father grew up in the UK. It is this constant mental guessing game of him analyzing me, me analyzing him that has made my time here bearable. I still *ache*. I walk with a cane and crave meth. I'm bored out of my mind and for me boredom has always led to dangerous activities.

Chess was today's answer, but the good doctor must know that he will not be able to keep me here forever.

"Who's winning?" Thomas asks, pulling up a chair.

He is being polite, making small talk. It is fairly evident from the playing field we are at an impasse and it is merely a matter of calling a draw. Doc's stubborn. I equally so. We may be sitting, sipping tea, and staring at the board for a magical solution for hours yet. Neither of us answers.

Sitting, Thomas asks, "Whose move?"

I answer, "His."

Hearing so, he stands. "Good. You have time to walk with me."

Walk with him? My blood thins and freezes, though I honestly don't feel he intends to kill me here, now, after so much effort has been spent keeping me alive. I wonder if George told him about our last session when I admitted that I think about meth constantly. The other drugs were just drugs...cocaine, opium, heroine, hashish...I can't say I miss them. The methamphetamines are another story entirely, and I would have never confessed before that I needed them. That's what I admitted to the doctor, breaking down. He suggested *we* try adding some mood stabilizers, non-addictive medications to help alleviate my anxiety, depression, and inability to sleep.

What I need is for him to stop saying that "we" need to do things because he isn't experiencing the urge to start running and not stop. If I could run out of my flesh and bones, I would. So far, I'm playing it cool. I'll be a prisoner for my brother, because I know he is keeping me here for my own good.

I don't know how much longer I'll be able to do this though. The doctor seems to think my long-term recovery will take more than a year. I've got news for him...I'm not hanging out in this dungeon for a year.

I stand and follow my brother to one of the many rooms down here, the one he chooses being small, tight, more walk-in closet than room. He pulls a dangling cord from a bare bulb mounted in a low ceiling. *You've got to be kidding.* Everything is gray, walls, ceiling, floor, furniture. With the room illuminated, he closes the door. With only two metal chairs and one small metal table for décor my mind fills with images of other interrogation rooms and none of those memories are pleasant. "Short walk. Should I be worried?"

Ari rolls his eyes, taking the farthest chair. He sits, placing his empty hands on top of the table. "I only wanted privacy."

It's hard for me to do so, but I remind myself that this is my brother, he isn't going to hurt me, and I sit across from him. "Privacy is good. So what exactly is on your mind?"

"You've been here a month, and we've barely talked."

"What is there to say?" I ask.

"I've missed you," he answers. "I love you."

Emotion I've trained myself to not feel bubbles to the surface, but I push it away. I don't offer him assurances. He knows I love him. I wouldn't have done what I did if I didn't love him. "What's this about, Ari?"

He flushes, a sure sign he is angry. "I've missed an entire decade of your life."

I chuckle. "Trust me, I wish I could say the same."

Our gazes collide. He hides it well but he is seething. Sure he's mad at me, I took his assignment. He hates that I endured what I did to spare him, and he's thinking now that it would have been better to have suffered as I've suffered, done the deeds I've done, than be sitting on the other side of the table looking at me. Does he see a ruined man with no chance of rehabilitation? Does he see a rabid dog that needs put out of its misery?

I cover his hand with mine, finding his flesh ice cold, mine barely warmer. I can only assume my gesture is as uncomfortable for him, but I don't pull my hand away. "Say thank you, Ari, and forget it."

His jaw grinds tight. "How can I forget when the debt I owe you is so great?"

I tighten my fingers around his hand. "Would you have done everything I did to spare me the pain of doing the things I've done?"

He looks away, heartbroken. He doesn't have to say he couldn't have—not even if my life depended on it—because we both know it's true. We may look alike, but we don't think alike. It is a long moment before he turns back to face me. "Thank you."

"You're welcome." I smack his face, making an unshed tear fall. "Now, stop dwelling on what was."

He nods. What else is there for us to do in this moment? There is no going back. There is only a hope we can move beyond the last decade, and neither of us will be able to move on if we don't forget.

"Tell me about *your* life."

He smiles and pulls out his wallet. He spreads four small photos in front of me. "You're an uncle."

"Huh." I pick up the first picture, awed when I see a young boy with wild, curly black hair and wide brown eyes staring back at me. His skin is darker, but he could be Ari, or me, at the same age.

"Hektor," Ari says.

"Hektor," I repeat, a name shared by both our grandfather and our father. "It is good." I hate to release the first image, so I keep holding it in my hand even as I add the second photo to it.

"Olympia."

I smile. "She's an imp, my God, what mischief in that face."

"Yes," he agrees.

The third photograph is another boy child, a chubby baby, but also with a head covered by curls. My heart jolts when he tells me the boy's name. I repeat it softly, rubbing my thumb over his cheek. "Nikkos."

"It is good there is another Nikos in the world."

I shake my head, my hand trembling. "You should have named him Aristotle."

"That's your job. Someday you will give me a nephew."

Surely he knows that day will never come. Hurriedly, I pick up the fourth picture to join the stack. It is an infant, newly born, not a standard hospital issue, but blurred and poor quality.

"Athena-Sophia. I took that one with my phone. She's almost one by now."

I can tell by the longing in his voice something is wrong.

"Where are your children?"

"Egypt? Sudan?" He shrugs. "Somewhere on the continent of Africa. They are with their mother. It's complicated."

"That's a very clichéd saying."

"There is no other way to put it. They are there, I am here, and there is no way for us to be together."

I return the photos to him and after a moment he pulls another photo out of his wallet and hands it to me, saying, "This is their mother."

"God, she's beautiful."

He smirks. "Yes, she is, but she's no longer mine."

His hand lingers over his wallet like he is considering showing me another. He finally decides, withdrawing the photo of another woman. "This is Celia."

I trade him photos. She seems so average compared to the exotic ebony beauty before, but I can tell by the look on his face that this woman has become the center of his universe. "Tell me about her."

"She's my perfect match. Our darkness melds well together." As an afterthought he adds, "And our light."

I look at him curiously, realizing the man I once knew as my brother is different, changed. Softer than he ever was before. Gentler. Kinder. Paternal. He became who he is now because of the sacrifices I've made and suddenly I don't regret a single thing I've done to ensure his health and well-being.

"Thank you for showing me these." I hand the photo back to him, and he keeps his eyes trained on the woman. *Celia.* "I think I'd like to meet her."

"She's pregnant. Twins. My children."

I watch emotion wash over his face.

"Why do I sense this relationship is even more complicated than the one with the other woman?"

"Because it is." Snorting unhappily, he slides the photos into his wallet. "It shouldn't be, but it is. I share her with another man, my best friend."

I whistle, surprised. "You are a changed man. I've never known you to share anything you didn't want to."

Our gazes collide. "It is only for her benefit I am willing to now."

"You should be with her tonight, not me. I'll stay here and entertain the doctor."

Thomas smiles, his eyes lighting up, and I see how desperately he wants to be with her. He makes no move to leave.

"Go on, get out of here. I have a chess rematch waiting for me."

"Your wish for me is impossible tonight," he answers, and the look in his eyes is heart-wrenching. He quickly adds, "And do not worry, I have seen her." I wonder if the assurance is for my benefit or his. I can tell he's forcing a smile when he says, "I do have some work I could be doing though."

"Sure, sure. I'm sick of looking at your mug any way."

"Hey, this work is for you. I've found you a place to live, I'm getting ready to outfit it with some nifty security measures tonight."

Now *that* gets my hopes up. Excited, I say, "Let me come with you," betting there isn't a chance in hell he will. Neither he nor the doctor is convinced I won't self-destruct the moment I leave my confines. Knowing that, I don't take his refusal too hard. I'm happy believing my freedom is imminent.

"Anger and jealousy can no more bear to lose sight of their objects than love."

George Eliot, *The Mill on the Floss*

CHAPTER 19

GARRETT

Tonight I am at the club alone and not at all happy about that fact. Last night Celia slept in the guest room. This morning she was gone before I rose. A phone call to *The Darkness* confirmed she was at work. I spoke to the receptionist, not Celia. It appears we aren't speaking, and it's entirely my fault. I just don't know what to say to her at this point that will make a difference. She wants absolutely nothing about our relationships or living arrangements to change just because of the babies she is carrying, and I think it is absurd to expect anything to stay the same.

I don't want her to choose between me and Thomas, I think we can continue to be a ménage, but looking to the future there are going to have to be a lot of decisions, and I feel like the first assessment we need to make is where we are going to live. *Her and I.* Not excluding Thomas, but not pretending we can be three in a bed every night anymore either. I couldn't get her to see past her question, "Why not?" no matter which tactic I took.

When she arrives at the club, I am so relieved I exhale and realize I have been holding my breath all day. Waiting. But now she is here, safe. I suppose the next move is mine.

She exits the elevator and crawls directly to our table. I've been sitting alone all evening...brooding, unfit for company...but I pat my knee, hoping.

Without a word or a glance, she arranges herself on a pillow at my feet. *Damn stubborn feline.* I didn't comment to her, but it's obvious she has returned to wearing my collar and Lord Fyre's. Once meant to remind her of her constant servitude, I think their presence is now a visual marker to remind me.

"Mr. Lawrence?"

I glance up to see one of my night shift receptionists. She is young, pretty, and very shy. She stands looking at her feet and whispers her message, "You have an appointment waiting upstairs. I rang your cellphone but you didn't answer."

Oh, hell. I'd forgotten I added myself back onto The Attic's schedule.

With both Thomas and George absent for three weeks now, there just aren't enough experienced Doms to handle the scheduled number of private sessions, and since this is an important area of income I can't allow anything less than perfection in service.

I'd forgotten how time consuming The Attic is. Our clients expect elaborately staged scenes, and they are willing to pay for quality. I'm going to have to speak with Kitten about hiring someone to replace Lord Fyre. She won't be happy. She expects him to return to us every day, and when he doesn't, she is even more disappointed than the day before. Telling her this will definitely make things worse, but it can't be avoided any longer.

Looking at her, I can't tell if she is asleep or faking it. I decide against waking her just to tell her I'm going upstairs.

"The shadows of our own desires stand between us and our better angels, and thus their brightness is eclipsed."

Charles Dickens, *Barnaby Rudge*

CHAPTER 20

KITTEN

I awake alone, not really a surprise. Master is always darting here or there to deal with business. I wish I was home sleeping, although it seems for the last few days all I've wanted to do is sleep.

Today, I skipped working even though I was at *The Darkness* all day. I locked myself in the office and slept. After putting in eight hours on my office sofa, I would have happily bailed on coming to the club and went home to bed if Garrett would have allowed it. It is ridiculous I am here since he's obviously left me to entertain myself in The Oasis.

Normally, I would be incredibly pleased. Left alone? Kitten time? I could pose on a tabletop, give myself a tongue bath, and definitely become a nuisance for somebody. Yes. Yes. Yes! But today? No. Not feeling it.

I scan the room and my gaze lands on Jackie. She is sitting alone, sipping wine, no pet on the pillow at her feet. It seems she is alone more often than not of late, and I wonder about that. Curious, I crawl to her and curl up on her vacant pillow.

Predictably, she is in a mood and turns her gaze in the opposite direction. Any other day, I would be pissed off. I would show my displeasure by crawling into her lap and pushing my face into her hand or her neck, or if she was being a real bitch I would rub my face against hers. Today, I curl into a ball and close my eyes. Sleep, sleep, heavenly sleep. That is what I want.

A pointed toe nudges my shoulder. "So you do that sexy sashay crawl all the way across the room to get my attention and now you want to sleep?"

I open an eye. "That wasn't for you."

She holds up three fingers to make a *W* then tips it on its side to form an *E*.

I scowl at her *whatever*, opening both eyes to do so.

"Oh, get off your ass, girl, and show me that baby bump."

I smile, I can't help it. My baby bump *is* sticking out there, especially when I'm naked. I'm not sure if it makes me sad or happy, but one thing is for certain, there is no denying it. I make a face, half pout and half embarrassment as I stand. "I'm fat."

She molds her hands around my extended abdomen, her hands deep russet against my creamy white flesh. "Precious life growing in there. *Precious.*" Her eyes tear up. "I never thought I'd see Garrett become a father."

She pats the chair beside her, definitely against house rules. Call me intrigued *and* it's a chance to be naughty. Kitten is not allowed to sit on the furniture. I smile mischievously and crawl onto the upholstered seat beside her, tucking arms and legs to pose cat-like and regal. I lift my nose at the security already headed toward the table but Jackie gives them an evil eye, making them stop in their tracks. The two stand watchful and ready should I break out my bag of kitty-tricks,

I assume because I have a reputation for trouble. I'm not sure why her glare stops them. I am breaking the rules. Perhaps it is because Jackie gets special privileges since she is Garrett's oldest and dearest friend or maybe because she is a huge financial contributor to The Oasis. But then there is no overlooking that she is a six-and-a-half feet tall, probably closer to seven feet with her sharp edged stilettos, she-male with attitude.

I rub my cheek against hers—kitty hello—and she tousles my hair playfully. I give the security guys a big 'ole theatrical wink.

Jackie rolls her eyes. "You have to tease them, don't you?"

"I have to have some fun." I pout, reciting all the can't-do's because I'm pregnant. "No bondage, no whipping, no caning, no electricity, no breath-play."

"At least he's taking good care of you and isn't putting that baby in harm's way. I'll stop worrying now." She takes my hand in hers, then pats it with the other.

"Hmmph. These babies are in like a gallon of water, swimming around all warm and happy. They are not going to care one way or another if I'm getting whacked on the outside."

"You'd be surprised," she says, and then her eyes go wide. "You said babies?"

Garrett didn't tell her? And here I thought Garrett confided everything to her.

She doesn't release my hand. She squeezes it harder. "Well, damn. So now you expect Garrett to help raise two of Lord Fyre's brats."

"Excuse me?"

"Have you even considered how much this is hurting Garrett?"

I jerk my hand from hers, feeling hurt. *Attacked.* A feeling that isn't lessened when she hurries from the table. What had I expected? I know how she feels about Thomas. Hate doesn't even begin to explain it.

Seeing security start toward me again, I wiggle out of the chair and resettle on the floor cushion. Arching my back, I bare my teeth and hiss in their direction before curling up tight. They don't come closer.

I almost wish they had. Punishment of any kind would be a distraction from Jackie's response. I don't want to think about Garrett's feelings. Yes, I'm carrying Thomas's twins, but we're a ménage, there was a fifty-fifty chance. Still, Thomas has children already, Garrett hasn't. *Damn it, Jackie!* And of course she'd been there when Garrett had his Cincinnati-meltdown, suddenly proposing, pitching his idea for babies and suburbia, so she knows exactly how badly he wants children.

Why couldn't these babies have just been *his*?

Oh, that's right, he had a *vas*! I don't share my sarcasm with Jackie.

I am still irritated at Jackie for messing with my head when she returns. She squats in front of me, precarious on her platformed spikes. Although her makeup is perfect, her eyes are red and puffy. "I'm sorry. I'm not saying I overreacted, but you are my friend and I am here to support you, regardless of who the father is."

I tear up, no reason for it, but suddenly I am crying. "No more brat comments."

"Not one." She holds out her arms, and I let her hug me. After a few more tears, she pulls me into a chair and reaches into her oversized leather tote to withdraw colorful brochures. She spreads the leaflets out on the table and points at each in turn. "Lamaze. Primal Birth. Bradley Method. Hypnobirth."

"Where's the info on drugs? Lots of drugs. As in I do not want to know what is happening at all."

Jackie titters but as quickly realizes I am completely serious. She pats my hand. "You're just scared."

I nod rapidly and she laughs. Picking up one of the brochures she reads, "Women's bodies are designed to create life, and giving birth is a natural process. We guide a woman to embrace her instincts."

"My instinct is to use lots of drugs," I insist. *I am not joking.*

Ignoring me, she keeps reading. "The emotions a woman experiences throughout her pregnancy will affect her birthing experience. A woman must be allowed to express her feelings completely."

She meets my gaze over the top of the brochure and asks quite dramatically, "Tell me what you're feeling right now."

Really? "I don't know. I'm tired. All. The. Time."

She looks at me like she is hanging on my every word, and the attention makes me tear up unexpectedly...again. She reaches out her hand and I grab it, tears flowing freely.

"I've been exhausted ever since the ultrasound. I don't know why, except that this—" I cup my baby bump in my hands for emphasis. "—suddenly feels so real. So important."

I pause, hoping she will say something, anything, because I feel so stupid talking about this. It isn't like I am the first woman to ever give birth.

Brightening, she demands, "Tell me the thought going through your head this very second."

"The part where I feel stupid for crying? Or the part where I feel this pregnancy is sacred?"

"The sacred part," she encourages, making me snort.

"That's what's so ridiculous. It's not like I'm *the virgin*, but I just feel like these babies are meant to be. I mean, I went to the doctor, still trying to convince myself I wanted an abortion. I was on the pill for a reason, you know? But then I saw their little faces and heard their little heartbeats and I swear I felt like the first woman ever to experience this miracle. Is that the most insane thing you've ever heard?"

She doesn't answer me; she just looks at me drop-jawed.

The abortion thing. I just freaked her out. I really should learn to keep my mouth shut. I assure her, "I never seriously considered an abortion. I was just terrified."

"Good. Because I couldn't have supported you in that, even if I do hate these babies' father. Everything happens for a reason. Even this. And I believe you have been *chosen* to be a mother." She passes me the brochure. "Read this one."

Congratulations. You are embarking on the greatest challenge and most rewarding experience you will ever face as a woman. Do not shy away from a single moment of the profound life-changing experience you will soon face: BIRTH.

My heart starts racing. I feel as if this brochure was sent directly to me.

At Primal Birth, the birth of your child will be a mind, body, and spirit experience. We are here to lend guidance and support as you embrace the natural instinct already residing inside of you to birth your child naturally and effortlessly.

There is a photo of a pregnant woman, sitting cross-legged in the middle of a field of wildflowers, meditating. Another photo shows a pregnant woman jogging barefoot on the beach, water lapping at the trail of her footprints. They look peace-filled, happy.

"I want you to know, I'm here for you. Need a birth partner? You got one."

I wonder suddenly if Thomas will be able to attend the birth. Seeing my look of distress, she thinks I'm worried about hurting her feelings. "I know, I know, you already have two men, one for each hand, I'm just saying."

"You're a good friend, Jackie." I just wish I could confide in her my fears for Thomas's safety. I don't make a big deal of it, but I crawl onto the cushion at her feet, taking the brochure with me. I don't have to pretend I'm reading. It is a welcome distraction, one leaving me enthralled.

In the wild, a mammal releases adrenaline to delay labor if a predator is near, leaving the soon-to-be mother prepared for fight or flight. It is only natural that a human mammal will have the same reaction to a stress-filled or dangerous environment. Adrenaline is the enemy of labor, making the use of drugs during the process so prevalent. No doctor wants to wait around for a mother to feel safe. At Primal Birth you will learn to prepare your birthing nest for a drug-free and stress-free natural birth.

I glance up from the brochure to see Master. Finally.

Garrett sees me and lifts his chin in a barely perceptible greeting before turning his back to me. He is watching a scene play out on the punishment dais. Morgana topping a man. She is small, petite, and also thin as a reed. All of her weight rests solidly in her double-D cups. Her bright auburn hair is pulled into a tight ponytail, exaggerating her naturally high cheekbones, and her cupid lips are painted a startling shade of red. She is layered in belts, one over her breasts, barely covering her nipples. Several are criss-crossed around her waist. Upper arms. Thighs. It seems like a medieval fashion statement until my eyes land on the big black strap-on jutting from her crotch.

She is beautiful and powerful in a way I will never be. Knee-high, lace-up black commando boots complete her look. It is her boots that have her slave's undivided attention as he licks them clean.

"Not good enough." She strikes his ass with a riding crop, leaving a bright red line on his pale buttocks cheek. I have to close my eyes against the beauty of it. *I want bound and whipped.* I can't imagine waiting six months to experience the sting again and decide that for the rest of the evening Master and I really need to focus on *us*.

He gives Morgana a long look of approval before turning away from the scene. Our gazes meet as he strides toward me, and I lick my lips in anticipation. I wish he could read my mind. If he could he would see a replay of the scene we played out in his library.

I want flogged. I really want caned. I lick my lips again, almost drooling with the need of my desire. I smile at Master, hoping he takes it for the naughty invitation it's intended to be. Wait. He's not looking at me, he's looking at a man who has matched his stride. They are close enough for me to hear Master tell him, "The receptionist is in charge of scheduling all Attic appointments. I'm sorry I can't help you with that, but I will be happy to have someone escort you upstairs so that you can make the appointment while you're here."

"Sir, no disrespect but I've been trying to get an appointment at The Attic for two months."

Master turns only slightly, the man steps between us, blocking his progress. I meet Garrett's gaze, catching the flair of annoyance before he gives his full attention to the rude man. Lust crosses his face. *What?* Their words cease to have meaning as my head spins around the thought Master is obviously attracted to the man. I take a closer look. He's mid-thirties, tan, buff, blond. I'm not blind, the man has the total package going on. Nice bod. Pretty face.

"You're so keen to do a scene with one of my Dominants, sub for me. Now."

My head swivels to face Master, hoping he'll notice my glare, but he doesn't meet my gaze and within seconds he is leading the man toward the elevator. My heart crashes as I watch them ascend. Through the glass walls of the elevator, I see that Master is already topping him. The man's face is lowered to look at the ground. "Well, la-de-fucking-da."

* * * *

I awake when Joel Winston, Garrett's security lead, lifts me and starts carrying me through the dining room. For a moment I am disoriented, wondering what I did to be in trouble this time, but he passes the cages and stocks, the whipping posts, and isolation sphere without even slowing down. Suddenly, I'm scared, considering the recent violence and Thomas's fear for mine and Garrett's safety. "Where's Garrett?"

"Working. You've been here long enough."

One of the other security guards opens the door that leads to the alley, and bright sun blinds me momentarily. "What time is it?" Shielding my eyes with my arm allows me to see the limo waiting. *Our* driver holding the door open. Unless there is a huge conspiracy I don't know about, I am safe. It just isn't like Garrett to leave me unattended so long and he has never sent me home alone before.

I am deposited into the backseat as naked as I was inside the club. "Hey. Clothes?"

Joel, never a man for many words—unless he's arguing with Garrett—points to a small bag I hadn't noticed on the floorboard. It is the one I normally keep stashed in the office. Since most often I leave the house in fetish-wear, or naked, and return in the same condition, I realized fairly early in mine and Garrett's relationship—the second time around—I needed clothing available for a vanilla emergency.

Frowning, I look from the bag back to Joel. "Did Master instruct you to send me home?"

"Miss Jackie asked me to see to your welfare before she left."

"Thank you, Joel." *He forgot about me.* I start rummaging through my bag as soon as the door closes and instruct Blake to take me to the office. I slept all night. I am certainly not going home to stare at an empty space. I know myself well enough to know *that* would lead to me getting into much trouble...

What I really want is to turn around and go back to the club. Now that I am awake I want to know what Garrett's doing. I imagine him in The Attic, still torturing the hotty he took upstairs—clamping his nipples, zapping him with a prod. God, I get wet just thinking about it. *I want zapped.*

"Damn it!"

I can't go straight home in this mood. I'd only end up hunting down Lord Fyre. Now that I know he's still in town, it isn't a far leap to know that he's holed up with his brother somewhere. I know where he lives and if not there I know where George lives...and if he was neither place...I'd just keep looking.

Better to find a *safe* activity.

"Hey, Blake, can you take me to the nearest bookstore?"

"It will be hours before one is open, Miss."

"Do you have something better to do?" I ask irritably, immediately regretting my sharp tongue. It isn't like my foul mood is any fault of his.

"No, ma'am."

"Well, neither do I, and go through a fast food drive-thru. I'm starving."

"Mystery and disappointment are not absolutely indispensable to the growth of love, but they are, very often, its powerful auxiliaries."

Charles Dickens, *Nicholas Nickleby*

CHAPTER 21

GARRETT

My favorite room in The Attic is one I designed with George for mind play. It's one thing to go into the nice sterile medical room. You can be fairly certain what is going to happen there. Or the room that looks like a Victorian boudoir, no big surprises, but room number eight is a mystery. The floor is wooden and overlaid with a maze of pipe that you have to step over again and again to navigate the room. Pipe on the wall, pipe hanging from the ceiling.

I have the man who introduced himself as Dean make his way to the center of the room. There, I have him strip. Completely. If I was in lust with him before seeing him naked, I am flipped now.

I lick my lips and try to not stare. Wouldn't want him to know I'm impressed, now would I?

I've kept on my clothes, dress shirt, pants. I work my tie loose and roll up the sleeves of my shirt. "What brings you to The Attic, Dean?"

He swallows hard and tries to look away. Is this more than he bargained for? The intimacy of questions...

Some people can handle it, some can't. Some don't want you to know anything about them at all. That's how I peg Dean. He didn't supply a last name. If I wanted I could use my PDA to pull up all of the secure personal information he provided before being allowed on the floor. I'm fine with Dean. *For now.*

"Curiosity." He finally answers my question. "Everyone talks about The Attic like it is such a big deal, like you can't get the same type of experience anywhere else in the world."

"Well." I scratch my chin. "Your expectations must be high then. Perhaps when we're through you can tell me if you were impressed or disappointed."

"Be glad to, *Sir.*" He's challenging my authority already with his sarcasm-laced answers. He probably dominates in all of his relationships, but in The Attic all clients are subs, he wasn't given a choice in the role he is playing.

"Think you can balance on that pipe there, Dean?"

Barefoot, he steps onto the pipe and smiles.

"Good boy."

He frowns at the praise. I don't think he liked being called boy, or maybe it was all of it together, "good boy," like a loyal hound. Or maybe, just maybe, he sensed my sarcasm and is beginning to realize the scene has begun, and it's all downhill from here. I push a button on my remote control, and the pipe suspended above him drops. I have him grip the bar, like he would if I wanted him to do pull-ups. He holds on. From a rack I grab some lengths of pipe, some galvanized elbows, and join him on the balance pipe. I make quick work of boxing his hands between pipe. He tries to pull his hands free, the design deceptively simple, seeming not effective, but he is trapped as surely as if I'd bound him in rope or leather or cuffs.

I hop down, pressing the button on the remote that lifts his hands above his head. "Comfy, Dean?"

"Yes, Sir." He's lying. The soles of his feet are burning already from balancing on the narrow metal pipe. He shifts his weight again and again.

"So, why don't you tell me the real reason you're here, Dean?" I withdraw a handful of clips from my pocket. They are shiny black and have a nice bite to them. I bring one into his line of vision just to watch his eyes widen a bit before I attach it to his scrotum.

He says, "Fuck," under his breath before answering, "I told you the real reason, Sir."

I don't expect a reaction so early in the game. *This is going to be entertaining.* I smile, relaxing for the first time in what feels like months but has only been days. I can feel the dom-space settling nicely through my cortex. It doesn't usually happen at work. Work is work. And to gain the slightly euphoric feeling so early on? This is an unexpected surprise. The room around me fades as I focus on distributing the clips in a pleasing pattern over his scrotum. He dances on the pipe, and to ease his suffering just a little I stroke the back of his thigh. It's a very small distraction. "Relax. So, you aren't here for the pain?"

"No, Sir."

His jutting erection labels him a liar, but I don't mention the obvious. I join him on the pipe and dangle a pair of nipple clamps attached by a chain in front of his face. "Tell me you want me to attach these to your nipples, Dean."

"I'd be lying, Sir."

I laugh at him and twist his nipple. "You'll have to try harder than that to convince me, Dean."

He writhes forward, gasping, "Please."

"Please is neither your safe word nor the response I was looking for." I twist his other nipple.

"Sir. Please attach the nipple clamps."

I don't leave him wanting. His breath sucks in and he makes a high pitched keen in the back of his throat. From experience I know the bite of the clamps I just attached. They are wicked. I won't be able to leave them on him long, but just the initial pain ripped through his chest and zigged down his spine to pucker his asshole. "Say, Thank you."

"Thank you, Sir."

I stroke his face, and he closes his eyes at the tenderness. "We're going to have a good time, Dean."

I attach the other clamp and this instance I don't have to ask him to say the words. He volunteers, "Thank you, Sir."

My cock is as hard as a rock and the session is just beginning. I smack his ass as I jump off the pipe and leave him standing. I cross the room in front of him, taking my time. I posture a little as I remove my tie. Seduction. It's what Lewd Larry has always been best at and now, consciously bringing Lord Ice more and more to the forefront of my psych, I decide this part of Lewd Larry I keep.

I take my time selecting the perfect flogger and though I'm not looking at the man bound behind me, I know he is watching me because a wave of his need ebbs through the room. I chuckle. *We are going to have a very good time.*

"Night, the mother of fear and mystery, was coming upon me."

H.G. Wells, *The War of the Worlds*

CHAPTER 22

THOMAS

I am filled with trepidation as I enter the hotel's lobby. At Glorianna's request I am meeting her in the bar after hours. I am surprised to find her sitting at the bar, instead of a small table tucked into a corner. We're alone except for a man playing soft jazz on piano...and of course, her armed bodyguards. Most senators aren't afforded such luxury as secret service at their beck and call, but Glorianna is an exception. She's swirling her drink like a woman with something heavy on her mind when she says, "Tell me you were surprised to hear from me."

I kiss each of her cheeks before sitting down on a bar stool beside her. She gives me a long, sensual look. Glorianna has always been a very beautiful woman, time and experience giving her an edge that adds to rather than detracts from her raw sensuality, especially now with at least one cocktail down, maybe two. She is toying with me, making me wonder why I am here. Am I to be bed sport? Or am I to be reprimanded for not bringing her my brother? She has most certainly heard news of his *death*.

"You do not look like a man in mourning, Thomas, and I've been so very concerned about you. That's assuming you heard about the blast in Shanghai?" She strokes the top of my hand. "Real tragedy there, fire out of control, no small loss of life. The question is did Henri eliminate your brother? After so many years getting him into place, I doubt that very much. Which leaves the questions, which of your brother's many enemies went after him, and what retribution do you have planned?"

I swallow hard. I hadn't considered what my reaction would be if my brother was really dead. There would have been a reaction. I've been blowing it without realizing I was and if she has been watching me, no doubt Henri has been watching, leaving the heads of two international organizations watching me. So not good. I like it when they forget I exist.

I take her glass of mostly melted ice and swill the remainder of her drink, although I rarely consume alcohol. "Sweetheart, I know you've heard that revenge is best served cold."

She lifts her finger for two fresh drinks. "I knew there must be a reason. So, you know who is responsible?"

"Not yet. I'm still working on it. Perhaps you can make my job easy and tell me who had him killed."

The bartender sets two glasses in front of us and she answers, "Ah, but if I knew."

Licking her lips, she runs her fingers down the front of my lapel. I am very aware of two things simultaneously, her perfume and her two bodyguards leaving the corners to step nearer.

Seeing my discomfort, she rubs her cheek against mine, whispering, "Relax. Don't you think that if I wanted you dead, you would be so already?"

I smile and laugh.

She too laughs. Still leaning intimately near, she asks with hope filling her voice, "Come to my room?"

By the question, it might be assumed I actually have a choice. I lean nearer, wrapping one arm around her back to pull her against me. Inappropriate for so public a place, for such a well-known political figure…because even after hours someone somewhere is watching…even if it is merely the piano man. Discretion is always called for, but tonight caution feels overrated. She and her men are watching me closely. Every facial reaction, every body movement. Reading body language is such an exact science and tonight I must convince them I am mourning.

I whisper, "I may not be up to my usual expertise. Events have left me emotionally and physically drained."

"Perhaps tonight, I can comfort you? No props, no play, no games…just two people using each other to relieve the stress and heartbreak of the day."

I allow myself to slump a little, like I have been holding myself rigid and have found comfort in her words. Meeting her gaze I tell her, "*That* would be nice."

I allow her to lead me to the elevator. Of course we don't enter alone. Three bodyguards, two in front of us and one behind. When we arrive at her floor, the two lead men exit first, looking left and right. I almost get the feeling there has been some breach to her security. Something is different. For a woman always so careful, so well guarded, it seems her men are especially on edge and I don't believe the difference is me.

She has a large suite of rooms and after a quick walk-through her men leave us alone in the master bedroom. Pulling her against me, I ask, "What's going on, sweetheart?"

She rubs her neck nervously and gives me a tight smile. "Nothing."

I lean my forehead against hers. "Liar."

She looks away but then quickly looks back at me, holding my gaze as she admits, "There was a threat. It's nothing."

"A death threat?"

She shrugs. "There are those who do not like one particular path I'm pursuing, and they want to make my success an impossibility. I don't want to talk about that. I want you to kiss me."

I kiss her gently, and she trembles in my arms. I push her hair away from her face so that I can look deeply into her eyes. She is a woman troubled by something greater than a death threat, but I don't press for answers. She called me because I am the one man she allows herself to be open and vulnerable with. For others she wears a constant mask of power and control. I surprise her, scooping her into my arms and carrying her to the bed. When I lay her down gently, she keeps her arms around my neck, holding tight, like she is afraid to let me go. She says urgently, "I need to know I can trust you."

"I won't hurt you."

"But I'm afraid you already have. I understand there must be certain secrets between us, but I cannot abide by an outright lie, Thomas."

She is a woman who has risen to a place of power solely on her own worth, most of her peers either loath her or fear her, and tonight despite her doubts in me, it is me she called. I sit on the bed beside her, allowing her to keep her arms roped around my neck as I gaze down on her. I ignore the insinuation that I've already lied to her and slowly start unbuttoning her blouse. Pushing apart the cloth, I reveal a delicately embroidered flesh-toned bra. I trace its scalloped lace edge with my thumb, liking the way her breasts rise and fall beneath the fabric with each breath.

She is not a luminous beauty, perhaps she never was, but nevertheless she is capable of captivating me, of making me desire her. She attempts to kiss me but I resist, knowing that the moment our lips connect we will get lost in the physicality of each other. We have to resolve her concerns. I will not be ordered dead a week from now because she felt I lied to her tonight. I tell her, "You can trust me in all things concerning your person, your security, and the safety of this nation."

"That was carefully worded, lover."

"I can give you no other assurances."

"Because you play for more than one team?"

"Since you have granted me asylum, I have worked only for you but you know that."

She nods. "Answer me this, has Henri forbidden you from telling me if your brother was recovered alive."

I answer her honestly. "Henri did not find a body, but then you know the physical amount of destruction in Shanghai would have made it impossible to identify any human remains."

She trembles and I know that it is anger, brimming just under the surface. She wants to slap me and ask me plain questions to which I respond with answers not twisted in wording that make them more true than false; but she also knows to do so would get her nowhere. She sobs against my mouth, "I want to trust you, Thomas. Please don't disappoint me," and I finally allow her to kiss me.

Reaching behind her, I unfasten her bra so that I can pull the fabric cups below her breasts. "You have beautiful breasts."

I run my tongue over the tops of each mound and nip at her flesh lightly. When I again look at her face, I find her head tipped back and her eyes closed. I take one of her tightened nipples into my mouth, biting gently until she moans. I suck softly, easing the pain before biting again. Arching her back, she cries out and I am compelled to treat her breasts even more roughly, sucking, nipping, squeezing them.

"God, Thomas! I cannot wait. You must fuck me."

I slide my hand between her thighs, pushing against the tight fit of her skirt. "Pantyhose? You've got to be kidding."

She looks at me with a smirk on her face. "They're practical, and I never said you wouldn't have to work for it. Besides, garters and stockings are the trademark of ladder-climbers and whores."

Roughly, I jerk her shirt halfway down her arms and roll her onto her stomach. She can't struggle and can barely resist as I force her skirt up to her waist and pull her pantyhose down. Forcing her onto her knees, I command, "Stay in that position."

Her face is pressed into the pillow, making it impossible for her to watch as I stand and pull my shirt off. I unhook my belt, unbutton and unzip, but otherwise do not remove my clothes.

"Please, take off your clothes," she commands in a muffled voice.

"Not *this* time." I climb onto the bed and straddle her legs. Probing her with my fingers, I find her wet, ready. "Urgent need is best vented quickly."

Reaching into my pants pocket, I withdraw a condom and quickly unwrap it. I slide it over my stiff erection and realize she is touching herself, rubbing her clit in earnest.

I thrust, filling her in one deep stroke with such suddenness she grunts. I push deeper, making her moan. "Too much?"

"God, no! Fuck me. Make me forget the doubts I have in you."

I thrust again before setting up a rhythm. Reaching around her, I cover her massaging fingers with my own, feeling her touch herself. "Yes, yes."

With a sudden sweetness our rhythm matches and I can tell she is close to orgasm. I thrust a little deeper and am not surprised when her orgasm overwhelms her.

A while later she is sleeping. It is the way our relationship works. Although normally I give her an intense scene before the sex, but after the sex she always sleeps. She told me once she never sleeps so well as when I am in bed beside her.

I don't sleep and even though it was after three when I met her, dawn seems a long time coming. It is a relief to escape alive but no comfort when, as I am leaving, she says, "I know you will do the right thing and should your brother actually be alive, know my offer still stands. I will give him protection, just as I've harbored you."

I wish I knew what benefit she hoped to gain by having his loyalty. If I did I might not fear turning him over to her as much as I do.

"We make our own lives wherever we are."

L.M. Montgomery, *Anne of Avonlea*

CHAPTER 23

GARRETT

I enjoyed being in The Attic tonight. It was a nice distraction, and Lord knows I need it. Work has always been my answer to stress. Long days and longer nights mean less time to think. Exhaustion is a good thing.

I've added myself as a Dominant on The Attic's private session schedule. With both Thomas and George away, it only makes sense. The hard part will be explaining to Kitten I intend to spend even more time away from her. It can't be helped. I just hope she sees it that way. Somehow, I don't think she will.

Returning to the penthouse after noon, I find Kitten stretched out on our bed. She is reading a book, and I am surprised when she doesn't stand and run to me. "That must be a damn good book."

She keeps reading, not understanding I am expecting her show of obeisance at my feet.

"Listen to this. Primal Beginnings believes there is a link between the primal period of our life and who we become as adults."

I'm too exhausted to make issue. I join her on the bed, lying down, resting my head against the pillow, closing my eyes. *Bed good.* "Primal period?"

"The time between conception and one year of age is extremely important. It says there is a correlation between what we experience in the womb and many physical and mental health issues."

"Um-hmm," I answer, feeling the pull of sleep.

"I want to take their childbirth classes."

"Sure, sure, childbirth classes. Good idea. Lamaze. Your doctor can arrange it."

"No. You aren't listening. I want a Primal Birth, doula assisted."

I am suddenly awake and sitting up. "Are you out of your mind?"

She looks hurt.

"You are having this baby in a nice, safe hospital with lots of medical staff around to help in the event of an emergency."

"No. I'm. Not."

She climbs out of bed and throws on a robe, storming out of the bedroom before I can get another word in. *What the hell? Where did this come from? Primal Birth? Doula?* I follow her. Finding her sitting on one of the sofas in the living room, the book she's been reading in hand. "What are you doing? Come to bed."

"I slept last night. I'm not tired. If you want we can talk after you wake up, before going to the club."

I tower over her. "Or you can put this ridiculous idea out of your head right now and throw that damn book of quackery away."

"Just because it's my idea and not yours doesn't make it any less important. I've studied all of the different approaches to childbirth, and this one resonates with me."

"Resonates with you? What are you talking about?"

"Pregnancy, childbirth, motherhood. They're all sacred journeys. I have to pursue the path which feels right for me. I do not want to feel like a victim of the medical establishment. People go to hospitals when they are ill, when they are injured, or when they are preparing to die. I am bringing new life into the world. I do not need medical intervention. I need a support team."

"You are not having this baby without a doctor present."

She smiles sweetly. Too sweetly. "That's why I have you."

"I am not a doctor."

She arches her eyebrow. "Oh, really? Because I thought our dining room table doubled as an operating table a few weeks ago."

"This is not open for discussion."

She stands up and confronts me nose to nose and eye to eye. "My body, my decision. Those are your words. If you don't want to be part of this, Jackie has already volunteered to stand in as my birthing partner."

Jackie. That explains so much.

I am her Master. I could force the issue if I wanted, but I'd rather her see the logic herself. "In a hospital, if you decide you need a medicinal intervention during the process you will have options."

"I won't need it."

"If you do."

She holds up the book she's reading and points to a line of highlighted text, reading, "Hospitals are unnatural environments where all control of the experience is taken away from the parents, leading to anxiety, especially for the male whose instinct is to protect the female. A hostile environment is forged when doctors interfere with instinct."

"My instinct is to protect you, and by having a hospital birth, we will be in the safest environment possible."

"Read the book. Please?"

"It won't change my mind, Kitten. I am resolute."

She crosses her arms. "Do you know what oxytocin is?"

"It's a hormone."

"Correct. It's released *naturally* by a mother unless a doctor intervenes using its synthetic version, Pitocin, to induce labor because he's in a hurry to get to a golf game."

I sigh, wishing Joel would have never sent her home alone. *Where in the hell did she get that book?* "Physician's do not misuse medication for personal gain. It's been proven that the use of Pitocin reduces the amount of time in labor for the benefit of the mother and the child, not the doctor."

Kitten rolls her eyes. "It blocks the natural release of oxytocin!"

She flips pages, finding more highlighted text. "My maternal instinct may be delayed or completely blocked. It's been scientifically proven that the lack of oxytocin crossing the placenta at the appropriate time can cause severe social problems. Our babies could have life-long issues with anxiety, trust, love…bonding."

"I'd like to read that study." I kiss her forehead before turning away to go back to the bedroom. I need sleep, not arguments. "Like it or not, this conversation is over. I have six hours to sleep and then I'm doing another double shift in The Attic."

She follows me back to the bedroom and stands looking at me with huge, disappointed eyes and a pouty lip while I strip and crawl into bed. I don't ask her to join me. "Are you coming to the club tonight or staying home?"

"Does it matter?" she asks sarcastically, a needling reminder that I have been a horrible, neglectful Master of late.

I scrub my face with my hands. I'm exhausted, no good will come from more conversation. "You matter, Kitten. Please come to bed, or go to the other room. I need sleep."

"Will you promise to read the book?"

I close my eyes to her pouting, knowing I would agree to anything to make her happy. "We have a doctor's appointment next week. Let's make certain everything is going well before you even entertain further ideas of natural childbirth. I know you haven't considered it, but there is a higher instance of Caesarian section delivery associated with twins."

"Go to one Primal Birth meeting?"

It seems ridiculous to my tired brain that we are even having this conversation since I won't allow her to have anything but a hospital birth. "I'm not going to change my mind, but I will listen to what they have to say at *one* meeting."

"Thank you, Master." She throws herself onto the bed, onto me, wrapping her arms around my neck and covering my face with kisses.

I regret agreeing, knowing how disappointed she'll be when I won't support her plans but at least with her stretched out beside me, I can finally sleep.

"The woodland's silent smile where flowers raise their heads and Venus bids you welcome. Loose your girdle, come to bed. Indulge yourself. Give in to love."

Tiberianus, *Vigil Of Venus*

CHAPTER 24

KITTEN

The Oasis is crowded, more members on one night than I can remember seeing in a very long time. Every table is filled, the curtained bed spaces as well. It doesn't dawn on me why until I see the holiday decorations. No doubt Valentine's day is the culprit, confirmed when Cupid shows up. Painted silver and wearing only a leather and brass codpiece, he totes a bow and arrows and tosses shiny confetti on anything and every person he passes. *Oh, joy. Love is in the air.* Or at least lust. Spontaneous play erupts in his wake, spankings, floggings, sex...

Even Jackie, alone so many evenings of late, has a new pet at her feet. It bothers me she never told me what happened between her and Bernard, or never mentioned this new guy. I thought we were best friends. *Damn it, I miss Bernard.* He was short and slightly pudgy. I've cuddled against him more evenings than I can remember while Garrett and Jackie shared a meal. We never spoke. I knew nothing about him, but I felt we were friends even if only as silent pillow mates reclining at our Masters' feet.

I look over her new pet with disgust. He is an Adonis. Tall, almost as tall as her, or so I guess by the sheer length of him. I haven't seen him stand and walk. I've only seen him crawl, led by a leash, milking the attention he earns with every sashay of his perfectly chiseled, ivory glutes. Do I sound jealous? *I am not jealous.* From the cushion at Jackie's feet, he sits up straight, surveying the room, looking regal and proud. Her hand rests lightly on the top of his head. I have to admit they are a striking pair, her so very dark, he so very light.

She has her hair styled as she did the first time I saw her, a platinum blond wig wrapped in an elaborate French twist, which captures her classic elegance perfectly and makes her long, graceful neck seem even more dramatic. Her beauty never ceases to overwhelm me, the she that was once a he, so much more feminine than I shall ever be. She is dark skinned, a pure, deep russet. She has almond-shaped brown eyes, made even larger and more dramatic by her false eyelashes. Her full, sensual lips are artistically lined and filled with a slick, glossy lipstick.

She is wearing white leather.

I smile knowing Garrett detests the sight of a Domme or Dominant wearing white. I wonder what he would say about Jackie. He couldn't say she is any less than stunning.

I realize that she is different tonight because she is exactly the same as the day I met her so long ago. She is utterly charismatic. There has been something missing of late, more than just her pet, Bernard, a sparkle in her eyes that is suddenly back.

I take a closer look at the new pet, still not certain if he is canine or feline, but I'm guessing cat. He's too fucking posed for a mutt. I narrow my gaze. I'm the one who perfected the feline persona around here.

His hair is cropped short, a military cut, and jet black. He is pale, pale white, or maybe it is only the contrast of being so close to her. I think his eyes are blue, too light to be any other color, but I refuse to crawl closer to get a better look. Nude, he is perfectly toned, pure muscle. I could imagine him on a stage, oiled and posing.

He doesn't seem like Jackie's type, maybe because he is so perfect, but seeing them together, I can't look away. Their beauty as a couple is breathtaking.

I crawl under the table, waiting for my Master to claim me, knowing he won't.

God, I hate Valentine's Day.

I've never been one to put too much stock in the holiday. Before Master there were no hot dates or roses or boxes of chocolate. Now, I have two Masters and neither are here for me to lavish attention upon. I try to not remember last year, which seemed so perfect. We didn't make it to the club at all, though we'd had every intention…

It had started with a meal. Master will use any excuse he can to whip up culinary delights and our ménage was so brand new, it demanded extravagance. Raw oysters followed by prime rib followed by decadent chocolate-dipped strawberries.

Lord Fyre had drawn me a bubble bath and bathed me.

Both of my men had pampered me so thoroughly, I'd felt like a queen…and this year, I sit alone. I wonder if either of them even realize what day it is?

Suddenly, I see Master, riding in the glass elevator with a blond man. My mind flashes back to a week before. *Déjà vu?* Or did that really happen? It must have. I remember the man so clearly…think, *think*…the day Master missed the doctor's appointment. Yes, because I remember the lust on Master's face vividly.

Screw this.

I follow them, but they are already sequestered in a private room. It isn't one of the suites usually reserved by guests because of its elaborate nature. It's expensive. Lord Fyre always called it the Room of Devices. Iron head cages and manacles, mostly mechanical props, the only time I was ever in the room I knew it was too extreme for my taste. I can't even imagine as I pace outside the door, wondering how long a normal session is.

My chest is heaving with emotion, my breath heavy as I try to calm down. *This is nothing new.* Master is with clients every day. The difference is that now he isn't playing with me every day...and I've never considered he might be *enjoying* himself. The lust I saw in his eyes chokes me as I press my back against the corridor's wall, staring at the closed door. I slide down the wall, sitting, waiting, not believing I am sitting alone in a dark hallway on Valentine's Day?

* * * *

Dreaming is the best part of the day, especially when Lord Fyre joins me. Except my tailbone hurts too much for this to be a pleasant dream. I shift my weight, realizing I am still sitting in the hallway outside of Attic Room number eight, Garrett is still inside with his client and Thomas really is striding toward me. He is smiling widely.

He's back! My heart leaps but I'm afraid to hope.

I try to stand, but my legs are asleep. Seeing my grimace, Thomas hurries to my side.

"Wait, I'll help you." He holds out his hand, lending support as I stand. Seeing my itty-bitty baby bump he whistles and cups its contour. "*Now* you're starting to look pregnant."

I make a face and he lifts my chin gently.

His smile is gone as he traces the tracks of dried tears on my cheeks. "What's this?"

"I'm fat, it's Valentine's Day." I cross my arms. "And I'm all alone."

He kisses my temple. "You aren't alone *now*. The night is yours, sweet valentine."

My arms go around his neck. "Hurt me." The words are out of my mouth before I even realize I've said them. He pulls away from me to gaze deeply into my eyes and I tell him, "Watching everyone else play is the worst torture."

He hugs me close, but before he does I see the dark shadow fall across his face that tells me he is angry. Not at me, or he wouldn't be hugging me.

"God, I've missed you."

"I have missed you," he assures me, his voice full of emotion. He hugs me tighter. "I want to be alone with you."

I think he might lead me to one of the play rooms but he doesn't. We go down to Garrett's office, where he closes and locks the door. It is a large room. Garrett's desk, file cabinets, and general business-related clutter taking a large chunk of the corner, a few tall, lush plants in front of the window and on the far wall a leather sofa. Thomas leads me to the sofa but neither of us sits. He caresses me. Face. Shoulders. Arms. Breasts. Belly. He pays extra attention to the baby bump, circling it with his fingertips. "Have you felt them move?"

"Yes. Garrett doesn't believe me, but I feel them all of the time now."

Squatting in front of me, he kisses my belly lightly. "I believe you."

He continues stroking my stomach and watching his expression fills a void I didn't understand was there until this moment. I want...I *need*...someone to share this pregnancy with and Garrett has been a real disappointment.

God, did I just think that?

Yes, yes I did. For a man who was all about the baby—marriage, family, and living in suburbia—he has shown a distinct disinterest. Watching Thomas stroke my belly, I wish I knew what he was thinking.

"Do you want me to hurt you now?"

I'm startled by his question as our gazes meet, so much so my heart skips a beat and my pussy clenches. "Yes. Please, Lord Fyre."

His hands slide over my waist then up, finding the sweet spot between my ribs. His fingers dig in between the bone and it is instant agony. I dance on tiptoe, instinctively trying to escape the pain, though honestly that's the last thing I want. "Oh. Oh!" I am trying to not scream. "Fuck."

He slowly releases me and within seconds it is as if the pain was never there because it does not linger. He strokes my face and kisses me. A second later, pain arcs down my spine and I realize he has attached a nipple clamp. He must have had them in his pants pocket. Don't all good Dominants stay so prepared? Maybe just my Lord Fyre.

He kisses me again, lingering over my lips teasingly, and although I know the second jolt of pain is coming and think I am prepared, the shock almost takes me to my knees. I moan against his mouth.

"Your nipples are very sensitive now that you are pregnant."

Holy mother of God.

"Kneel."

I drop to my knees and bow forward as much as my new shape allows. Stepping back, he looks at me. I close my eyes, soaking in the moment, soaking in his appreciation of my obeisance. "You are so beautiful, Sophia. Are you comfortable?"

I nod but he instructs me to change position. "Fold over the couch."

I do as I'm told, crawling to the couch and then laying only my upper body over the seat, arms folded above my head as I press my face to the cushions. The position lifts my bottom, exposing my genitals to him and I am very conscious of that fact when he commands, "Arch your back."

Arching makes raw need speed through my center.

He bends to slide his fingers through my wetness. "It seems pain isn't the only thing you need, Sophia."

I don't answer, believing it was a rhetorical question.

A sharp stab of pain through my labia makes me gasp as he attaches several clips. "I know you are probably craving more extreme play, but hopefully this will take the edge off."

Kneeling behind me, he leans over me. He is still completely clothed, and I enjoy the sensation of his shirt and pants rubbing against my skin. He caresses me as when we were standing, sliding his hands over my shoulders, my arms, my back. He massages my ass and thighs. The gentleness is such direct contrast to the pain inflicted on my nipples and genitals; it is quite a mind fuck. I know he will pull the clamps off and as much as I am enjoying the massage, I stay tense, waiting for the jolt I know comes.

He kisses my shoulder, leaning some of his weight over my back as he opens his pants enough to withdraw his erection. His stiff penis bumps against my thigh. *Yes, fuck me.* My hips rise, wanting so badly.

"Patience." He chuckles, then allows his stiff member to slide between my legs, not penetrating, just teasing.

Oh God.

He flicks off one of the nipple clamps and pain overtakes all thought. "Ahhh!"

He rubs my breast, cupping it, squeezing it, before massaging my other breast in much the same way, though he leaves the clamp attached. Waiting for me to relax so that the pain will be another shock. *Just do it. Do it. Do it. Do it.*

He slides inside of me and I close my eyes the sensation is so sweet. I've missed Lord Fyre. I've missed having his cock in my pussy. I push back into him, enjoying the sensation, the clamps still attached to my nipple and labia only a small distraction.

He moves in me, building my need to a plateau...and pops off the nipple clamp.

"Ahhh!"

He keeps riding me, kneading both breasts. *Oh God, oh God.*

He knows the exact moment I start to orgasm and I try so hard to not let him know. I expect he will start tugging at the labia clamps, but he doesn't. Not during the rise of pleasure. Not as I fall. I am panting, he thrusting hard, harder. It is as his need spirals up that he starts pulling off the clamps and my yelps of pain shoots him over the edge.

"Recollections of the past and visions of the present come to bear me company; the meanest man to whom I have ever given alms appears, to add his mite of peace and comfort to my stock; and whenever the fire within me shall grow cold, to light my path upon this earth no more, I pray that it may be at such an hour as this, and when I love the world as well as I do now."

Charles Dickens, *Master Humphrey's Clock*

CHAPTER 25

GARRETT

Hillary is waiting impatiently outside of Room Eight when I come out. She holds a clipboard and is tapping her pen on its hard edge. Not knowing the exact time, but guessing, she should have finished her shift hours ago. A good employee, she remains silent as I walk Dean to check-out and discover we just spent three hours together. He doesn't even blink when he's presented the bill. While his credit card is being processed, I help him schedule another session. I shouldn't. I'm enjoying our sessions together entirely more than is appropriate. I'm looking forward to our next session. Giving him a final pat on the shoulder, I escort him to the elevator. As soon as the doors close I ask Hillary, "Is there a problem?"

"No problem, Sir. I was asked by Lord Fyre to wait for you to come out and ask you to join him in your office."

Thomas is here. Now? "And Kitten? Is she still in The Oasis?"

"I believe she is with Lord Fyre. Waiting."

"I see." I wave her away. "Go home, Hillary."

"But, I—"

"Go."

I close my eyes, trying to regain my sanity. I shouldn't be feeling guilty for keeping a client overlong. Or for enjoying my job. But I do. There is no doubt Thomas is going to feel I have been neglecting Kitten. I can't even argue I haven't been because I'm feeling guilty about that too. *Damn it.*

Dreading the inevitable, I don't go straight to my office. Instead, I shower and change. Only then do I face them, finding Thomas reclined on the leather sofa, Kitten curled against his side sound asleep.

Closing the door, I cross the room quickly. "How's your brother?"

Thomas is reading the Primal Birth book. He looks up at me, amusement in his eyes. He holds up the book. "This is very insightful."

I sit in the chair across from them. He hands me the book. "I'm betting you haven't read it."

I'm not going to lie. "I haven't."

He nods. "In answer to your question, he is alive. He is healing."

"So, did you just pop in for a visit? Or are you back?" My question came out sounding more bitter than I intended, but now that it is said there is no taking back the emotion attached to it.

"I am here to spend Valentine's Day with the two I love," he answers, making me feel even worse.

I don't validate the accusation I hear in his voice. Standing, I cross the room and sit behind my desk. My territory. A safe zone. I know it's purely mental posturing but here I am king. A hiding monarch, but still the ruler of this corner. I do not want to fight and by shuffling papers I think maybe I can delay the inevitable.

"I have promised her I will visit the Primal Birth Center with her."

Hitting the keys on my keyboard harder than necessary, I pull up my email, gall rising. "Kitten has a very good obstetrician, the best in the city. She sees him again in a few days, you might be better served meeting him." I'm bluffing. I don't know when her next appointment is. I know I missed an appointment. I know the doctor wanted to see her every two weeks. But honestly, I'm clueless.

"The best in the city?" he repeats, voice rising enough to stir Kitten. "By best do you mean he has the highest rate of Caesarian Section in the state?"

"He's a high risk obstetrician. Of course his stats will be higher than a physician who does not manage high risk clients."

"And what exactly led you to believe Sophia is high risk?"

I bite my tongue, silently counting to ten. *I'm not having this argument.*

Kitten rises while I am counting to ten a second time. Thomas helps her rearrange and they kiss. She looks at him like he is a God. That pisses me off too. He asks, "Good nap?"

She smiles. "Yes, Lord Fyre."

He winks. "Ready to play?"

"No." I stand, taking a resolute position on this one. "If you haven't noticed, she's pregnant, and the obstetrician said absolutely no play."

Thomas helps her stand before turning to face me. "Join us or no, but we're playing, and if you think I would do anything to ever hurt these three—" He slides his hands tenderly down Kitten's arms to end wrapped protectively around her protruding stomach. "—you really have lost your mind while I've been away."

"The dream was always running ahead of me. To catch up, to live for a moment in unison with it, that was the miracle."

Anais Nin

CHAPTER 26

KITTEN

In the elevator Thomas presses the button for the fourth floor. Garrett shakes his head. "You're not taking her to The Attic."

Thomas gives him a hard glance. "Would you rather I take her to the cove?"

A dark expression crosses over Garrett's face, and the men share a look. I wonder what happened at the cove. Whatever it was must have been far worse than anything Thomas can do to me in The Attic.

The elevator doors open, and Lord Fyre leads us to Room Eight. He addresses Garrett. "This is your favorite room, yes?"

Master swallows, nervous. He doesn't have to worry, I already know it's his favorite room. Of course, I've never been inside but I've heard the rumors. Not knowing the truth of what Master does in there is both blessing and curse. I wonder but I can't drive myself insane knowing the intimate details. He looks at me and though I try to hide my excitement, I know I'm doing a fairly horrible job. Ever since Thomas pressed the button in the elevator, I knew he was bringing me up here for a scene and I started bouncing on the inside. My excitement of finally playing again is so great I might just explode from the euphoria of the anticipation.

Garrett reaches up and strokes my face. "I don't want anything to go wrong, Kitten."

He means he doesn't want me to lose the babies, and I don't honestly think Thomas would be so irresponsible. He had a kinky wife, they had three children together, and all three children were fine. I smile, I can't help it. I'm hoping for pain with a capital "P" but I'm trying to convince Garrett to not worry. "He wouldn't do anything to hurt me or the babies."

"I'll be near. Right next door in an observation room."

Thomas opens the door to Room Eight and slaps Garrett on the back. "Oh, you'll be closer than that."

He pushes Garrett into the room and holds out his hand to me. "Be careful. Watch your step here."

The room is pitch black but suddenly starts to glow with red lights recessed in the floor. The dim lighting tracks reveal a labyrinth of pipe attached to the floor. Some low, only a few inches off the surface, some a foot high, and a few several feet high. I'm perplexed. Looking up, I see that a similar structure hangs from the ceiling.

I see that Thomas is holding a remote control. He presses another button, and the sound of hissing steam precedes the mist's burst from pipe running vertically up the walls. I lick my lips, ready, impatient. I didn't think I'd be nervous, this is after all a very controlled, safe setting, so unlike the places Lord Fyre normally takes me, but I can feel the sizzle of adrenaline racing through my veins and can't deny being both nervous and excited.

Thomas leads me deeper into the room. Garrett has taken up a post near the wall, looking none too happy. "I don't know what you think you're doing. The doctor said no bondage and no impact play."

Thomas chuckles and smiles at me before calling across the room. "You didn't ask the right questions. Come. Be my assistant."

For a moment I don't think Garrett will come closer, but he does. I meet his gaze, realizing he is flushed. I think that just being in the room does it for Garrett on some core emotional level. If I touched him, I'm certain I would find he's hiding a tight erection beneath his slacks, but I don't have time to wonder why. Thomas directs me to sit on two parallel pipes which are affixed to the ground close enough together to form a bench. "Lie back."

I'm not certain how he expects me to maintain my balance but I obey him and am surprised when he holds my hand in an assist. Before I am even halfway reclined my shoulders collide with another parallel pipe. He leads my hand to the pipe and I grasp.

"Hold on with both hands."

I stretch my other arm out as instructed and grasp. A vision of Jesus stretched out on a cross flashes through my mind, but I kick the thought out of my brain. I recently concluded that *this*, my need to be restrained and hurt, would be one of the lesser things that would likely send me to hell.

"Comfortable?"

My head swivels. Lord Fyre has never asked me if I was comfortable during the course of one of our play sessions. Must being pregnant change everything? Like sitting on two pipes and reclining against a third is any less comfortable than lounging in a lawn chair. "I'm fine."

He looks at Garrett. "Satisfactory?"

He sighs heavily, still disgruntled despite his arousal. "So far."

Thomas kneels before me and gestures Garrett closer.

"You, my friend, need to start asking the right questions. No doctor in his right mind would give approval for any type of bondage or pain play. Even a community-friendly physician is going to fear a lawsuit if something goes horribly wrong." Thomas cups the mound of my pregnancy. "The womb is an amazing shock absorber, almost nothing that takes place on the outside of a woman's body will hurt the fetus."

Garrett objects but Thomas lifts his hand, effectively silencing him. "That doesn't mean I have any intention of spanking her, caning her, or whipping her."

I narrow my eyes, disappointed that Thomas, who I thought was on my side, is suddenly being overcautious. At least in *my* mind. How could a simple thuddy flogging hurt the babies? I press my lips tightly together to keep from screaming. Thomas catches my gaze and I see him smirking. My heart swells with hope that he hasn't turned completely.

Thomas separates my knees, spreading me wide. He strokes the inside of my thighs. "The veins here—"

Garrett names them, "Iliac, femoral, saphenous," while waiting for Thomas to make a point.

"—can be prone to blood clots during pregnancy, so even though you would think that a light spanking here might not hurt the baby, it could be deadly to both mother and child."

Garrett looks at me smugly. "And that is why bondage is also a very bad idea after the second trimester."

"Correct," Thomas agrees.

Turncoat. I don't break protocol though I'd love to interrupt. Since I am here, I have to assume that sooner or later Lord Fyre will arrive to save the day.

"The pipe can control without compressing."

Garrett nods, meeting Thomas's gaze. Something passes between them. Unsaid. I feel the ripple of energy as something changes. Have they found a common ground? Is the argument over? Are you going to do *something* with me now?

The men leave me sitting and go together to a wood workbench where they sort through bins silently. I sigh, impatient, wanting someone to tell me just what in the hell was decided. I don't have to wait long, but the interim seems to take forever. They return bearing flashlights, tools and parts. Without a word to me they go into motion, working in tandem to trap my wrists and ankles between pipe. Both men hold the flashlights trapped between chin and chest, making me wonder if perhaps it would have been easier to turn on the lights, but knowing them as well as I do, it is all about the ambience.

They are so synchronized it is unnerving. I know they've worked together for years, played together, played with me as a threesome, and every time we play I am left awed. It is like they have one brain between them, anticipating each other's moves.

I shiver, hating the noise the hand ratchet makes as they tighten down bolts to secure the assembly of pipe and metal elbows. *This* I wasn't expecting. They step away and look at their work. I don't feel bound. I'm disappointed in the effect for all the noise they made. "It's too loose. I don't feel anything."

"Can you get free?" Garrett asks, and I pull my hand. I'm stuck. I don't have to wiggle my ankles to know I'm not going anywhere.

Thomas closes the distance between us and slaps me. Hard. *Fuck!* Not Thomas. Lord Fyre. He is angry. Cheek flaming, adrenaline speeds through my veins. I want to run but understand too late, I'm not going anywhere. He slaps me again. And again.

I guess my face is fair game. I hate to be slapped. That is why with Lord Fyre I try really hard to behave. I'd forgotten. In only a few short weeks, with Garrett's irregular enforcement of the rules, I've become a very bad slave. He grabs my cheeks and squeezes. "Do we have an understanding?"

"Yes, Lord Fyre," I say through pinched lips. It must have been a satisfactory answer because he walks away to join Garrett at the workbench. Leaving me to sit and wait.

It's a funny thing how bondage which could have been perfectly comfortable a moment before can suddenly turn not so. Arms stretched to the sides, my back only supported by the single pipe, I am starting to feel the burn. I shift but it doesn't help. Closing my eyes, I try to relax. Harsh whispers are a distraction. No chance in hell of finding my zone with them arguing in the corner.

Garrett glances over his shoulder at me, looking resigned, but it is still several minutes before they rejoin me. Each man carries a tray set up with alcohol, swabs, gauze, and an array of needles. *Yes! This I can get excited about.* I've watched both of my men do piercing sets onstage, separately, with partners other than me, and though I've considered asking to do a set with either or both of them, I haven't and now that I am faced with the prospect of actually experiencing it, I don't know why I haven't. Well, actually, that's a lie, normally, with Lord Fyre at least, this type of scene would be absolutely tame, and I enjoy our edge play too much to spend our time with something so mundane compared to what he can normally dream up for us to do together. And Master? Eh. I'm happy to let him tie me up and torture me. He chooses to not use needles, and I've never requested them.

Garrett swabs me from shoulder to groin with a liquid surgical prep, which seems like overkill to me but I'm not arguing. *I get to play!* My heart is racing.

Lord Fyre asks, "Is this acceptable?"

"Yes, Lord Fyre." *Yes, yes, yes, a hundred times yes.* I wonder what part of my body they intend to pierce. I consider begging, 'not my nipples', because they've grown so sensitive, but I don't. Right now, I'll take anything they choose to give me.

He takes a surgical pen off of his tray and draws a spiral on my baby bump. He hands the pen to Master who draw three lines just above my breasts.

In concert, Master and Lord Fyre pick up alcohol swabs and needles. They wipe the top line of the design Master drew. The liquid cools my flesh, and a cold chill goes up my spine. They each pinch the skin over one of the lines and align their needles. Both needles pierce my flesh, the needle moving smoothly under my skin like a snake. *Oh!* Expected but an unanticipated higher intensity pain knives through me. I break out in a cold sweat and feel slightly dizzy. Is this *normal?*

"Are you okay?" Master asks.

I realize my hands are trembling. "Yes, Master."

Between my answer and their action, there is no delay. They pinch and pierce the second line. *Oh God.* I close my eyes as pain spreads between the two needles, a small dance of fire under my skin. I feel a third pinch and prick of pain. I open my eyes to watch as the metal slides between my skin layers, raising my flesh. Though I can only focus on one of the needles at a time and they are both piercing together, the needle I do watch seems to move in slow motion. I see the tip nearing the surface just before it pokes through the skin. *Pop!* I gasp, though the discomfort seems more tingling verging on numbness as I float above the soft comfort of pain. *This.* This is what I've missed.

"Continue?" Lord Fyre asks.

I am not certain whether he is asking Garrett or me. It seems unusual that he would ask, I have a safe word after all, but just in case Master would refuse, I answer, "Please, Lord Fyre. Don't. Stop."

Our gazes collide and I see such pride reflected back at me, my heart swells. Lord Fyre starts at the center of the spiral drawn on my stomach and works the design from a tight inner circle, widening outward. Master stands, arms crossed, not participating but witnessing.

The pain of the piercings ebb and flow and I float on the current, enjoying the rush. I float, forever suspended between the two men I love.

How much time passes? Minutes? Hours? I do not know as needle after needle slides under my skin to create the spiral. I know I am crying when a mirror is carried forward to show me the result. "It's beautiful."

I am immediately frustrated because I want to hug them both but I cannot move. *Hug me. Hug me. Hug me!* They don't, they walk away, leaving me bound, pierced, and alone with my thoughts.

"Love is like a beautiful flower which I may not touch, but whose fragrance makes the garden a place of delight just the same."

Helen Keller

CHAPTER 27

THOMAS

We leave Kitten under the close supervision of a room monitor, who will watch her via camera until we return. In an emergency he is seconds away. It is Lewd Larry's policy to have each room in The Attic under constant surveillance by both a team member and with an audio-visual recording.

As we leave the room, I don't mention it to Garrett, but I plan to check up on him by watching the last month's worth of his logged sessions. There are definitely some perks to being head of security, and I'm worried about him. He isn't playing with Kitten, he isn't playing with me, so it makes me wonder if he has lost his edge...or if there is something else going on. *Someone.* I don't want to consider that but I know Garrett, he's a monogamous kind of guy, except on the rare occasion he completely loses it. High stress affects people in different ways. I get that. But if he's being a slut, I want to know before Kitten. I'm not sure she would understand that particular personality glitch.

It may be more mundane than that and I may be concerned

needlessly. He's often distracted by the sheer amount of work that goes into keeping Lewd Larry's a well-oiled machine, and he's on occasion forgotten Kitten, regrettable but also the flipside of his personality. The man is a workaholic. From what I know about his father the same could be said about him. I don't know if it's genetic or learned, but it's definitely a family trait.

He's not happy that I'm dragging him back to his office for a chat, and his irritation bristles off him. "If you trust me to take care of her while you're away, the least you could do is support the decisions I've made in your absence instead of overriding my authority."

I don't offer comment even after we are behind closed doors.

"The doctor was fairly adamant that she not participate in any form of bondage." His back to me, he runs his hand through his hair. When he turns to face me I can tell he is spoiling for a fight. "And please, do not encourage this damn natural birth quackery. Jackie is a bad enough influence."

I sit down in one of two wing chairs, waiting for him to finish venting.

"You need to be home. She's carrying *your* sons. Do you have anything to say?"

"Nothing." I spread my hands out in front of me.

"I can assume you haven't returned? Your brother still needs you? So tonight whisk in and give Kitten all the answers she wants to hear and when you leave, I'm again the bad guy. What comes next? Another trip out of the country?"

He is so enraged there is nothing I can say that will calm him nor can I promise him I won't be called away. Anything I say at this point would only inflame him more. Silence seems the best answer.

He paces. "I can't believe you aren't going to say anything."

Standing, I block his path and step into him, bumping our chests together. The kiss begins gently but then becomes rougher as I take what I want from his mouth and he takes what he wants from mine. Both of us struggle for dominance.

It is a long moment before he relaxes against me completely. He says, "Stay."

"I can't," I say, though I know the safest thing for me to do would be to return to my regular routine. If Glorianna is having me watched, which I haven't been able to determine, she would immediately notice I am not following a normal routine. I have to try to hide my brother in plain sight. Only as a very last resort will I turn him over, and then only because I do trust her word.

Taking my frustration out on Garrett, I kiss him again, rougher still, ripping apart the closure of his silk shirt. Buttons fall to the floor and the *click, click* of their bounce mocks the ruination of his Stefano Ricci handmade original. He shrugs out of the designer weave and lets it fall to the floor while he lifts my plain black t-shirt over my head.

Garrett jerks my belt off and slings it over the back of his neck so that the ends dangle over his shoulders. He unbuttons and unzips my pants, sinking to his knees and sucking my cock into his mouth before he even has my pants pulled over my hips. *God.* He bites my glans, the sharp jolt of pain pure pleasure.

"Easy, tiger." I knee him in the chest, pushing him back and follow the motion, pinning him. I slap his face repeatedly. "You want it rough. Is that right?"

"Yes," he grits out between clinched teeth.

"You want to hurt me?"

"Yes."

"Well, maybe I'll let you...after I take what I want from your hide." I grab the ends of the belt, twisting then together before jerking his neck forward. I kiss him hard, tightening the leather to the point he can't breathe. He doesn't struggle, he pushes into the kiss. When I push him away, he is left gasping for air. His face is deep red. I smack his cheek. "You like that too much."

"Yes," he grunts.

I slide the belt off his neck and double it in my palm, using the folded leather to smack his chest, his arms, and his abdomen. He yelps but the force I'm using is nowhere close to what I know he can take.

"Have you gotten soft on me?"

"No, Sir."

I strike him repeatedly with the belt, making his chest glow a rosy shade of pink before straddling his face. "Suck me off. Fast."

He doesn't disappoint me. His face darkens as I force my cock deeper. He gags when I push as deep as I can go. I like the sound of him gagging around my penis. I withdraw and thrust deep just to hear the sound.

I feel his arms moving and guess he is undoing his pants. I pull out of his mouth. "Did I say you could do that?"

He grins guiltily.

"You want to touch your own dick?"

Catching his gaze, holding it, I watch his face, liking the lust I see as he grabs my hips and pulls me back into position over his face. I fill his mouth and slap the leather belt down over his bared side as he does so. He moans in pain, then laughs. I push deeper and he gags.

"God damn I've missed you, Garrett."

I pump his mouth, while I'm lashing him with the belt. He is going to be welted and bruised when we're finished.

I pull out, wanting to see my jism arc and spurt over his face.

While I am put slightly off balance by my ejaculation, Garrett takes the advantage by pushing me back. I'm gasping for breath when he pins me with his body. I could fight him, roll him off, and reestablish control, but I don't want to. He wipes my cum off his cheek and laughs. He moves to straddle my face, asking me, "Turnabout is fair play, eh?"

I smile and open my mouth, but he doesn't thrust in fast and deep as I'd expect.

He rubs his glans over my lips. "Lick it."

I lick the tip of his cock, rimming his piss hole. I hold his gaze, taking my tongue in a slow slide down around his cut head. With the tip of his dick wet with my saliva, he holds his shaft in his hand and circles my mouth, spreading my spit around my lips like he is applying lipstick.

He leans back his head and sighs.

I give a fast flickering lick on the ridge that runs along the backside and am rewarded with a moan, but soft lick and tease tickles isn't what he needs and we both know it.

Using the folded length of belt, I slap his hard shaft. Hard, harder, until I get the "Holy fuck," response I'm after. He coughs, grunts, laughs, and then begs, "Again."

I slap him hard enough to make him yelp, then swallow his shaft, taking him deep.

Holding him tight and deep, not gagging, I don't release him. I keep him tightly sucked where I want him, not giving him any wriggle room, and start wailing on his backside with the belt.

With his dick trapped in a cage of teeth and tongue and muscle, he is helpless against the belting I give his ass and thighs.

"Oh! Ahh. Oh, fuck."

I slap him harder.

"Holy fuck."

He moans and his fingers twine into my hair, pulling tight. I bite, a teasing bite, and his grip tightens. I run my hands down the leather warmed flesh of his ass and thighs. I flick his balls, making him jerk and cry out.

"Fyre." He growls my name softly.

Grabbing his thighs, I pull him deeper into my mouth and throat. Setting up a rhythm, I loosen my mouth enough to take him in and out smoothly, quickly. I feel the tension building in his thighs, he's close to coming when I pull away and his moan is one of disappointment. It is my turn to laugh. "You didn't think I'd let you come that easily."

I force him back and we wrestle for dominance. This is it. One of us has to yield and he's in just enough of a mood to not want to. I'm ornery enough to want to make him really fight for the prize, counting on one hand how many times I've allowed him to ass fuck me.

I don't expect the solid punch to my jaw.

He rolls me over, looping the belt around my neck and jerking my head back with it. He growls, then grunts with the exertion it takes to hold me. I never said I was going to make it an easy win. "Don't make this harder than it has to be. Lift your ass."

He pulls the belt tighter. I could get free, but I don't want to, not this time. I'm not sure what's going on in Garrett's head, but tonight he needs to be top dog and I'm man enough to let him. I lift my ass, taking the full thrust of him. He jerks on me like a jackrabbit in rut. He tries to slow the pace, to force down his own need, his own desires, but I don't let him, knowing he's close, very close. I push back against him, squeezing his dick with my anal muscles.

"Holy fucking God, Fyre. Holy fuck."

I collapse onto my chest, him falling against my back. We both lay there breathing hard, and I am surprised when he rolls off to lay beside me. I wrap around him, holding him with both arms and legs. Continuing our interrupted conversation, I whisper against his ear, "I wish I could stay tonight. And by the way, they will be *our sons*."

Still out of breath, he chuckles and I feel like we are going to be all right.

"I think we will disagree much on the raising of boys, Thomas. I won't allow them to participate in organized sports."

I hold him tight. "Oh, there will be sports. Football, baseball, soccer, basketball, archery, ninjutsu—"

"Only if you agree to ballet and music lessons, piano and violin."

I cuff his head. "Admit it's going to be interesting."

I loosen my hold so that I can roll up on an elbow and look down on him. It's been a long time since I've just looked at him. I run my hand over the flat plane of his stomach and note just how pale his skin is to mine. When our gazes touch, he looks concerned. He says, "You might as well say what's on your mind. I promise I'm calmer now."

"Why are you neglecting her?"

The defensive shield he throws between us is a thick, touchable tension. Perhaps I should have sugarcoated it.

"Have you thought I'm doing the work of three men here?"

"You always do the work of three men," I argue.

"Well, now I'm doing even more, covering your shifts and George's."

I sit up, suddenly angry that he is really going to blame work. "Hire more people."

He doesn't sit up. He rolls onto his side, putting his back to me. "I don't want to hurt the babies."

"What?"

"We're not playing, we're not having sex. She may have mentioned that."

I would not betray her if she had confided such to me. "It is fairly obvious your relationship is strained."

"If she would miscarry on my watch, the ménage would be destroyed. Neither of you could trust me again because both of you would look at me like I'd done it on purpose."

His admission leaves me stunned. "Do you want her to miscarry?"

He stands and starts pulling on clothes. "Of course not! I just want to play—*hard*, harder than I've ever wanted to play—and I can't do that with her, not now, and it leaves me wondering why I'm so filled with this need if not because I secretly long for the worst to happen."

Standing, I catch him mid-pace, holding his shoulders, and make him meet my gaze. I am met with a guilty look and feel he is more distressed that she carries my children in her womb than he would ever let on. "I know you don't want any harm to come to her or the babies. So what is this really about?"

He shakes his head. "I don't control her anymore. She's willful, disobedient."

I smirk. "Kitten has always required a strong hand."

"Moreso now."

I grasp the back of his neck and pull him into me, almost surprised when he doesn't resist. For a moment I just hold his face to my shoulder. "I told my brother that I share Celia because it is in her best interest to do so, and although that statement is truth, it is also a lie. She equally shares me with you and you with me because she knows we love each other even though the two of us rarely say so. Do you understand how much I've wished I could have you in my life as it was those first few weeks?"

I feel his sob against my shoulder. "It hurts too much. I don't ever want to feel as broken as I felt following Tony's death."

"And so you would cheat both Celia and I the full measure of your love?"

"No," he whispers, and we both hear the lie.

"I want all you have to offer, but Celia deserves it."

"I know."

"I'm not a greedy man, Gar. The babies will be as much yours as mine."

"And what if I turn out like my father?"

Therein lies the crux of the matter. "You will not ignore your sons."

He rears away, glaring. "Won't I? How can you say that knowing I give every ounce of energy I have to Lewd Larry's? After saying I neglect Kitten. I neglect you."

"Sell the club."

He looks shocked by the suggestion. I shrug. We both end up getting dressed. I don't like his silence. Garrett rarely has a lack of words. I am comforted when he stops me from leaving the office. Wrapping his hand in my hair, he pulls me forward to offer me his lips. "Be there for us, Thomas, that's all I ask. The rest will work itself out."

I kiss him, promising, "That's the plan," and hoping I can make it so.

"O cruel Jove, and thou, Fortune adverse…Fy on your might and werkes so diverse! Thus cowardly ye shul me never winne."

Geoffrey Chaucer, *Troilus and Criseyde Book IV*

CHAPTER 28

GARRETT

I know Thomas doesn't make promises lightly. So when he answers me saying, "That's my plan," I don't press him. He's a secret agent, working undercover, I doubt he could have promised me more than he has, but it sure would have been nice to hear him say 'I will be there.' I worry about the times he's away, knowing he is probably facing unimaginable danger. That fact was made even more real the night I operated on his brother. His tattoo will never be the same.

Thomas is scarred. I've never asked, but the quarter-sized scars that mar his perfect physique were bullet-made and he's riddled with them. I fear he won't come back to us, because if there wasn't danger to worry about he'd already have returned to us. I don't say these things to Kitten. She's too fragile to hear my fears, or maybe I just can't bear to voice my darkest worries aloud.

Walking beside him back to the play room, I accept the fact that I love him and something rips a little inside me. I've said the words before, I've even believed I felt the emotion, but I've never allowed him or Kitten to completely fill the empty place in my heart left by Tony. I think that may be changing. I think my desperation of late hasn't been because I feel he is taking over Celia, but because I'm so fearful of losing him.

If he doesn't come back, it will more than destroy the ménage, it will break whatever Kitten and I ever shared. I can't imagine what would be left of her if he broke her heart by not returning to us. She looks at him with dreamy adoration as he removes each of the needles. He looks at her with an equal intensity.

I'm glad there's no mirror because I would hate to see that I really am invisible.

She is still caged between pipe.

I think about being in this room with Dean and realize the reason I enjoy bringing him here again and again is because I don't feel invisible. He makes me feel invincible. He makes me feel God-like and that is heady stuff.

I once felt that way with Kitten, when it was just the two of us.

Moving to stand behind her, I bend forward, resting my chin on her shoulder. I try not to look at Thomas, but our eyes meet and it is his simple nod that lets me know that I am here. I'm part of this. His eyes burn through me, and I realize finally that he is looking at me with as much need as he looks at her. Just that makes me feel confident.

I kiss the back of Kitten's neck and rub my fingers lightly over her face. "Enjoying the endorphin rush, pet?"

"Yes, Master."

She is still looking at Thomas, watching him remove each needle. Over her shoulder I too can watch the process. The needle slides, he wipes away the pinprick of blood that follows.

I rub my hands down her back, enjoying the quick reveal of

gooseflesh.

Her scent is heavy in the air, the earthy fragrance of warm, needy pussy. I squat completely behind her, knowing as I reach between the raised dais of pipe supporting her thighs and ass, I will find her wet.

I slide my fingers between her labia, not surprised by the slickness I draw away. She gasps. Another needle slides free, Thomas wipes away the fresh blood, I sink two fingers deep. Her pussy contracts around the invasion as I rub my thumb over her clit.

"Oh!"

I leave a short trail of kisses down her spine, while her body adjusts to the presence of my fingers inside. "Relax."

I spread my fingers wide inside, a little light pressure opening her vagina—just enough for her to feel me moving inside her. Thomas keeps going about the business of removing his needle design. It is almost as if he is so focused on his task that he is oblivious to what I am doing, but that would be a lie. He knows what I'm doing, he knows exactly what I'm doing.

I thumb her clit, finding so much wetness. It is like a Slip 'n Slide, she is so wet. The feeling is magical, and I can only imagine she feels the same. Her hip muscles contract and I know it is because she wants to move against me, wants to press into my thumb, wants to establish a rhythm she can control, but that isn't happening. She is trapped by steel and not going anywhere.

Oh, the frustration of bondage. The pleasure. The agony. She is caught like a fly in a web, except her struggles are even more insignificant.

"Do you like that, Kitten?"

"Meow."

"No? Really?" I say sarcastically. "I can stop…if you want me to."

Her meow this time sounds desperate and I keep rubbing her clit. I push my fingers deeper, rolling them, thrusting them, finding all of her happy spots. I can tell because she is softly keening.

I want to fuck her, but worry there will be a repeat of my shriveling dick. More than wanting to fuck her, I want to top her.

"Quiet!" I say, and my voice echoes through the room. "Or do I need to gag you?"

She comes. Hard. The liquid evidence sliding around my fingers, hand and wrist. She is shuddering, gasping, and I am left surprised by the suddenness of her orgasm.

I withdraw and pinch her ass cheek. "Did I give you permission to come?"

She is crying when I stand to tower over her. She looks up at me with a mixture of pleasure and misery. "No, Master."

"Indeed you didn't." I see Thomas is removing the last needle. I know he isn't staying. I also know he will want to have some time alone with her. I lean forward and kiss her softly. "Next time. Don't. Come. Without. Permission."

"Yes, Master."

I leave them alone to finish the scene, telling myself it will be for the best if they have some time alone together, but I am kicking myself for going even before I get to my office. I imagine him holding her as she falls apart. The scene is so vivid I can feel the wetness of her tears as he kisses them away. I imagine the sweetness he whispers to her to calm her, promises and words of love. He is a harsh master, he's taken me to the edge and back again, and so I know from personal experience how intense the man is...but he is also tender. I have never met anyone more tender and compassionate when wrapped in the special intimacy following a scene.

And all I've been of late to Kitten is abrupt. I need to remember to tell her happy Valentine's Day, but imagine that it is already well past midnight. *Damn.* At least we shared a scene together as a ménage. We still have that.

"…an angry skipper makes an unhappy crew…"

Rudyard Kipling, *Captains Courageous*

CHAPTER 29

KITTEN

I've barely seen Master, to the point of being ridiculous. I know it's paranoid but in the week since our scene with Thomas on Valentine's Day, I feel like he's been avoiding me. If I felt things couldn't get any worse a month ago, I was wrong.

"Where are you?" I am so not impressed, I can't even begin to express my emotions as I leave a voicemail for Garrett. Again. I've been at the doctor's office for an hour. Alone. After Master insisting so vehemently I go to all of my scheduled appointments, even though he knows how I felt after the last one. I certainly don't want to be here *alone*. The doctor hates me; I can feel it. He might advertise that he is community-friendly, but I have my doubts.

I've obviously gained weight though the doctor's scales don't reflect it. My belly *is* getting big. The entire time he is measuring me, he is frowning. "Twenty weeks. You are halfway to term. How have you been feeling?"

I shrug, making a joke. "Like a pregnant woman?"

He doesn't laugh. The direction of his glance tells me why even before he accuses, "These bruises have been made since your last appointment."

"My partner took every safety precaution." I don't say my *other partner*. I'm not sure he's ready to know that I am in a relationship with two men.

"I was hoping Garrett would heed my advice," he interrupts. I am left opening and closing my mouth like a goldfish as he demands, "Would you be so selfish as to endanger your babies?" He looks at me like a specimen under a microscope. "Is your relationship consensual? Because if you are in an abusive relationship—"

Shocked by his tone, I insist, "I'm not abused."

His look is challenging, not comforting as he might have been trying for when he assures me, "If you feel you or your babies are in danger, there are people who can help you."

I laugh at him. "We are both talking about Garrett Lawrence, eminent Dominant in this part of the world, right? You do realize he gives 'Safe, Sane, and Consensual' lectures all over the country? He wouldn't harm me or my babies."

He looks at me pointedly, and I am immediately intimidated. "Then I expect him to respect my advice. No bondage or impact play for the remainder of this pregnancy. If you cannot address this issue with him, I will gladly do so for you."

I don't argue with him. I'm too afraid to. There is a voice screaming loudly in my brain, asking, "Or what?" not sarcastically, but fearfully. I do not want anyone looking at my relationship with my two men too closely. Is that irrational? Are all of my fears based around my fundamentalist religion upbringing? There are so many what if's...

The most horrifying being: what if some authority decided we were unfit to raise our children because of our lifestyle? I leave feeling more frustrated than I've ever been. Driving back to the office, I receive a text: *Where are you?*

"I could ask the same," I mutter to myself, turning on the radio.

The music drowns out my ringing phone. I know it will be Garrett since I didn't reply to his text. I debate not answering, but do. I don't even get out an appropriate, 'Hello,' before he is demanding in my ear, "You're late. I need you at the club. Now."

"Late? I—"

The call ends and I look at my phone's face, not believing he might have hung up. Irritated, I head to the club and my irritation turns to fury when the receptionist directs me to the conference room where Garrett and Morgana are interviewing job applicants.

Seeing I have arrived, he meets me in the hallway. "Where have you been?"

"I was at *our* doctor appointment."

It is obvious by his expression, he forgot. He takes my face between his hands. "I am so sorry. This is why this has to be done today. I can't do the work of three men. I'm neglecting you." One of his hands drops to my swelled abdomen. "I'm neglecting them."

He looks thoroughly remorseful, but I'm still irritated. I don't bring up the client he saw right before my appointment. I remind myself that he was just a client, not important. I do need to vent about Dr. Moran. I'm scared and worried.

"I need you to sit in on this."

"This?" I ask, thoroughly confused. He hires staff all the time without my input.

"I'm hiring two Dominants for The Attic."

"Two Dominants?" I repeat even though his meaning is

immediately clear. He's replacing Thomas and George. I can't believe it. What is he thinking? Surely to goodness Nikos won't need ongoing care for that much longer. "What happens when they return and their jobs are filled?"

"They'll be happy to have promotions."

"What are you talking about?" I say, realizing we are arguing in the middle of the lobby at the same time he does.

He leads me through the hallway to the conference room, but we don't go inside. "I made you a full partner to protect your interests when we formed the ménage, but I failed in making you aware of how things work. As it stands Thomas is my security manager, meaning he oversees Joel, Allen, and the entire security detail, roughly fifty employees. I have to replace him and not just temporarily."

"Thomas is coming back," I insist vehemently.

"Don't argue, just listen. You know and I know he isn't here. This month it is his brother, last month it was Eva, I don't even remember what the month before that entailed, but he wasn't here. I need a full-time security manager. That doesn't mean I won't still need him as my second. *Always.* That's why this isn't a demotion for him, I'm just moving him into a consultant position. I should have done it a year ago. My new security manager will report directly to him, the same as it is now, whether that is Joel, Allen or someone else."

I know he's right, because even without the brother-drama, there is always something else lately and Master has been covering. I try to mentally get on board with his decision even though I am emotionally destroyed. I feel really stupid asking because I should know but I ask anyway, "What does Allen do now?"

"He's our IT guy. All of our data security and building security systems are managed by him."

"Right." I've seen Allen, mostly after his shift, he'll come out to play with some of the regulars. He's a little scary for a computer geek, total Goth. He keeps to the large room in the basement, referred to by staff as The Lounge, even though it isn't a lounge at all. It's the data center. Neither him or the other two IT guys have wonderful people skills.

"And Joel is ex-military."

As if I wouldn't have figured that out all by myself. I'm tempted to add 'with a big, fat attitude,' but I don't. "You haven't decided yet?"

"No."

"Because neither are especially suited for the job or because Thomas does the job of five regular employees?"

Garrett laughs. "I knew I made you a partner for good reason, you catch on quick."

"You said 'or someone else'. You'd really hire outside of the *family?*"

Garrett lets out a heavy sigh.

"And when George returns, he's just going to find someone new, a stranger, running The Attic?"

"That one's easier. Morgana is already in charge of scheduling, I'm making hers a management position. For now, she'll report to me, once George returns full time, she'll report to him."

I try to imagine her overseeing the Dominant staff up there. She seems a little young and a little flighty, but lately it seems everyone seems a little young. And if she doesn't work out, George will deal with it when he returns. Personally, I don't think she's up to the task. Besides that, I just don't like her. I especially don't like the attention Garrett pays her. I know they've never been romantically involved but intimately? Maybe. I really don't want to know. I don't ask. I just accept that they are very closely bonded, just as Thomas and George are Garrett's Number One and Number Two.

He opens the door to the conference room, and I see that Morgana is already seated. I blush, glad she couldn't read my thoughts.

"Sit." He takes the center, Morgana on his left, me on his right, and the interviews begin.

If I thought to be bored, I was wrong. Morgana has already terrified the first two applicants but when the third enters she sits up straighter. He's young, at least younger than Garrett and I. It is then I realize Morgana is very young. I hadn't noticed before, owing the fact that it's so hard to see past her tough exterior the last thing I would have ever noticed about her was age.

Looking closer, early twenties.

The man facing us can't be much more than twenty-one himself. Stripped down to his underwear, as have been all the applicants, he doesn't fidget nervously. He is lithe, not overly muscular but obviously strong. His haircut marks him as military or ex-military.

Morgana passes us each a copy of Matthew Farris's resume, and the name Blaire Harrington glares at me from the third line under references. Likewise the telephone number for the reference is the same as the number for the cellphone Thomas provided for me to use as Blaire. *Okay, who in the hell are you?* Looking up, our gazes collide and a chill runs down my spine. Did Thomas send him, or is he one of the bad guys? I need to alert Garrett that there is a problem, but he is already asking questions about his experience.

"How long have you been in the scene?" I interrupt. Both Morgana and Garrett jerk at my rudeness.

"I've played privately for about six years. I'd say the last two or three I've played publically. Mostly in Europe. You'll see that I worked for a bit at a Fet Club called *Whips* in Paris."

I fire questions at him. "Submissive or Dominant?"

"Dominant."

"Are you straight, gay, bisexual?"

"You don't have to answer that," Garrett advises him.

"It could be seen as discrimination if he isn't hired," Morgana whispers, though by her dilated pupils I'd guess she's very interested in his answer.

The man smirks. "I don't mind. I'm straight as an arrow, but I'll top a gay or bisexual man if I'm asked to. I believe there's no intercourse between the professional Dominants and their clients, so I'm not certain why the question is relevant."

"It isn't," Garrett answers, giving me a look that demands my silence.

I'm trying to help. Can't he tell he's an imposter?

"But I—"

"Kitten. A word. *Outside.*"

In the hallway Garrett is none too happy. I should be embarrassed, but I'm not. I also have no idea how to explain my objections to the man without revealing the depth of my involvement in Thomas's current crisis management.

Master stares me down, then shakes his head. "I'm asking too much of you, too soon. Morgana and I will finish up. Wait for me in The Oasis."

I put my hand on his elbow to stop him as he turns to go back into the conference room. "I'm sorry."

He doesn't even look back.

I can't let this go and instead of going to The Oasis, I go to

Garrett's office where I keep my briefcase stashed while I'm here. Retrieving the cellphone Thomas gave me out of it, I dial him. He doesn't answer. *Damn it!* I text: *Matthew Farris?*

His response is immediate: *Hire him.*

I sigh heavily and dial again, knowing he won't answer. He doesn't want to talk to me. Does he give a damn that he's hurting my feelings? I try to not take it personally, trying to believe he is merely focusing on the problems at hand. His brother. Who tried to kill his brother. *And my protection.* I feel like an idiot, understanding only now that Matthew Farris is here to keep an eye on things. And I screwed things up by getting thrown out of the interview process. I ask the dead phone, "Shouldn't you have told me this before now?" *Damn it.* I have no idea how to position myself back into the process to get the man hired. This shouldn't be *my* problem! *God, what a shit day.*

Jackie catches me coming out of the office. "There you are."

I jerk, startled, and feel like I've been caught sneaking around.

"Are we going tonight?"

"Going?"

"Six p.m. The Primal Birth introduction class. Did you even talk to Garrett?"

"Oh, *that.*" I roll my eyes. "I talked, he didn't want to listen."

Jackie turns away, shaking her head. I think she looks even more disappointed in Garrett's behavior than me. She stops mid-stride. "I'd like to take you, if you think it will be all right for you to come with me."

I am close to tears, overwhelmed by *everything,* as I admit, "Jackie, right now, I'm alone in this pregnancy. I need help coping. Thomas is away. For all intent purposes, Garrett is too. If you are asking should I garner Master's permission? I think the better question would be, do I even have a Master? I would be very happy if you would take me."

She looks at me with pity, and I hate that worse than being abandoned by my men. Still, I am happy to be wrapped in her strong arms when she holds them out for a hug. "Anything you can talk about?"

A sob escapes my chest. "No."

She pats my back, and I press my nose into her ample bosom. She smells citrusy, like oranges or grapefruit mixed with a heavier spice. The scent is unexpected, but also somehow a perfect complement to her vibrancy.

Looking up at her, I tell her, "I bought the book advertised in the brochure you gave me and read it cover to cover. I want to thank you for opening my eyes to what this birth could be like."

She pulls away from me. "Let me guess, Garrett is being difficult?"

I nod, a fresh batch of tears welling up. "And the obstetrician he's making me see is a nightmare. I'm so afraid that after the birth he's going to have my babies taken away from me because of mine and Garrett's lifestyle. He hates us."

Several of Garrett's Dominants come out of the employees' lounge and walk by us. Jackie hurries me down the hallway toward the exit, asking, "What did the doctor say to make you feel that way?" rapidly followed by, "Does Garrett know your concerns?"

"This is what is hardest, to close the open hand because one loves."

Friedrich Nietzsche

CHAPTER 30

GARRETT

I'm excited to be finished hours earlier than I believed possible and hope to have a relaxing dinner with Kitten. The interviews went better than I'd ever hoped with our third candidate proving to be more than qualified for the position of security manager than just a mere Dom for The Attic. I hope he can straddle being both manager and additional help in The Attic as Thomas has for years because despite Kitten's obvious objection to him I hired him. I honestly think she just can't stand the thought of replacing Thomas, which I might be able to understand if he was still off the grid, but she's seen him several times. He's in the city. He's fine. I think it's fairly obvious that once everything is in order with his brother, he'll be rejoining us.

The thought is both a disappointment and a relief.

As much as I'd love to be Kitten's only Master, the three of us balance each other out well. We have the perfect ménage. I know this intellectually…emotionally, it's been tougher to accept. For a moment, right after Thomas had left with his brother, I'd allowed myself to imagine the possibility of what could be. Kitten and I raising a family together. I would be the twins' father, their *only* male parent. I can imagine the shock on my parents' faces. God, they don't even know about Celia's pregnancy yet. They'll have to be told. Even with Thomas back in the picture, they're going to be grandparents. I doubt they'll see it that way. There's plenty of time to break the news to them.

I regret being so harsh with Kitten the last few weeks. My only excuse is exhaustion. I hope to make it up to her with a nice dinner. We'll go out, someplace romantic. Someplace far away from Lewd Larry's. Hopefully she will be as happy as I am when I tell her I also hired four additional Dominants for the lower levels. Not finding her in The Oasis, I ask Hillary, our executive secretary, "Have you seen Kitten tonight?"

"Yes, Sir, she was here earlier." She takes a call coming in and holds up a finger as she answers questions. She mutes the call and points toward the employee exit. "She left with Jackie Sandburg about two hours ago."

"*She what?*" I look at the face of my cellphone and see that I have a missed text: *Went to Primal Birth class with Jackie.*

"Primal Birth class?" I thought we settled this, but then I remember wanting to sleep one day last week and saying anything to make that happen. *Damn it.*

I find the damn brochure in the middle of my desk right where she left it, right next to the book she asked me to read it in my spare time and the sticky note with the time and directions. At least it's a local address not too far away, and I hurry to meet them there. Pulling into the parking lot, I look toward the large glass-domed building and see her and Jackie standing in what appears to be the foyer. The interior lights brighten her face as they exit. The meeting must be over. I can't say I'm sorry I missed it.

Kitten looks radiant. Happy. Her smile is as wide as I've ever seen it. I don't park, opting to pull up to the curb instead. I step out of the car to watch their approach. Other couples are going to their vehicles as well. As soon as she sees me, Kitten's smile fades, and that really pisses me off. I walk around the car to meet them.

"Garrett," Jackie says. "Nice of you to join us."

"Jackie." I force a tight smile as I open the passenger door. "Kitten, get in the car. You can ride back to the club with me."

Kitten meets my gaze but doesn't say anything and I can't read her expression. Looking down at the ground, she kicks a pebble with her shoe. In a tone so soft I can barely hear her, she tells Jackie, "Thanks for bringing me. I'll call you tomorrow."

Jackie hugs her. "You need me...you call me sooner than that." To me, her best friend, she says nothing, making me feel like a supreme ass.

Kitten climbs into the car without another word. I close the door before facing Jackie. It isn't hard to figure out she is a woman with something on her mind.

"Our girl tells me you've forbidden her from seeking out a doula and pursuing a Primal Birth." She makes the statement lightly, but it feels like an accusation.

"Am I a horrible person because I want the babies born in the safety of a hospital?"

"Sterile. Unnatural. That's the introduction to the world you want to give the babies?"

I throw up my hands. "This is ridiculous. I do not even believe I am having this conversation again!"

"From what I gather, you haven't discussed it once."

"This is really none of your concern, Jackie."

"Um-hmm."

Frustrated, I demand, "What does that mean?"

She bobs her head side to side, challenging, "Your house, your rules, right? Did you ever think you might want to check with Thomas about how he feels about things? Because I'm pretty certain that he is the man who flew halfway around the world to make certain his wife gave birth on the sand of her homeland under a blazing sun."

"Kitten isn't Thomas's wife."

"Nope, she isn't, but last I heard the two of you agreed to share her equally and seeing that she carries his children, what does he say about all of this?"

I look away, not knowing what Kitten's told her. The official word at Lewd Larry's is that both he and George are on vacation. "When he returns, we'll discuss it."

Her eyes narrow. "What are you and Kitten hiding? There's too many tight lips about this man. Did he go back to his wife? Or did that blond bitch he showed up with a few weeks ago ruin everything for the three of you?"

"Nothing so dramatic," I lie. "Our ménage is fine, thank you for asking."

"Well, it should be interesting when he gets back. That's all I have to say. Interesting. Um-hmm." She kisses both of my cheeks before turning to walk to her car, and I try to not give her comments any thought. I do not want Thomas supporting this insanity.

Once I am buckled in beside Kitten and preparing to pull away from the curb, she says, "You're mad at me again."

I put the car back into park. "You left the club without asking permission."

"You were supposed to go *with me* to this meeting. It's on the calendar."

I really don't like her tone but then she looks at me, her eyes filled with tears, and although she doesn't say another word, I can read the accusation in the lines around her eyes. *You promised.*

I want to apologize, but don't want to appear weak. She's already trampling my authority. Trying to sound enthusiastic, I announce, "I hired Matthew Farris and four other Dominants. That should lighten the burden on me, give us more time together."

She doesn't comment.

"How would you like to skip the club tonight?"

She shakes her head. "You know I don't like being stuck at home alone."

I squeeze her fingers. "I'm saying I would like for us to spend an evening alone together. Name the restaurant, I'll take you anywhere you want to go."

"I already ate."

Leaning over, I kiss her cheek. "We could go home, snuggle on the sofa, watch a movie."

She nuzzles back, caressing my cheek with hers, whispering, "You could hurt me."

"Ah, no." Leaning back, I shift the car into drive and pull away from the curb. "Be happy with your servitude during your pregnancy, Kitten. There will be plenty of time for play after the babies are born."

"But the other night—"

"Doesn't change anything." Dead silence falls over the car as I leave the building's parking lot and pull into traffic. I can feel her simmering beside me. She doesn't have to say it out loud that Lord

Fyre would play with her for me to know what she's thinking.

Several miles later she demands, "You expect me to wait four months?"

Why does everything have to be an argument? I don't answer.

With a huff, she wraps herself into her arms. "Fine, let's go home, but I don't want to watch a movie. I want to tell you *all* about the Primal Birth class and how excited I am about creating a birthing nest and surrounding myself with people who will love and support my decision for a natural birth." She punctuates that she knows this is a thorny issue for me by adding, emphatically, "Outside, in nature."

I grind my teeth, trying very hard to not lose it. *Damn Jackie.*

"There is a woman I met tonight who sings birthing chants. I think I'm going to hire her to assist with my birth. She sang and drummed for us. It was the most wondrous thing."

At a red light I turn in my seat to make certain she sees in my glare that I am not wavering on this. "I am your master, you are my slave. I will not hear another word about any of this. Do. You. Understand?"

She doesn't answer. A second later she bursts into tears, and I don't have the mental or physical energy to do anything except drive us to the penthouse.

"All you need is confidence in yourself. There is no living thing that is not afraid when it faces danger. The true courage is in facing danger when you are afraid, and that kind of courage you have in plenty."

L. Frank Baum, *The Wizard of Oz*

CHAPTER 31

KITTEN

Time absolutely drags when you're miserable, and with Master sleeping in the guest bedroom each night I am nothing but miserable. I spend so much time alone, I hardly feel like I'm in a relationship, let alone a ménage.

Garrett is awake and has been for some time.

Thud.

The sound of a bar of soap hitting porcelain draws my thoughts to Master once more. Closing my eyes, I listen to the shower spray, imaging the water hitting his body. His skin will be flushed pink, he will smell of his scent: *Ocean Breeze: A Bay Spa Luxuriant.*

The furnace kicks on and air whistles through the vent. We're having an unusually cold winter, and I hate the thought of climbing out from under the quilt to go outside. If we hadn't had such a horrible last night, I might beg off. Lord knows my eyes are probably so puffy, I would be better off not going. No amount of makeup can cover up red-rimmed, cried out eyes.

Has it really been two weeks since I saw that horrible, judgmental obstetrician? The date on the calendar says it has because I'm supposed to see him again tomorrow and I don't want to go. It seems I've been counting each day with the dread of one on death row and the time has flown.

At least I have tonight. Maybe I can cause some havoc at the club. It's been a long time since I've sat in the middle of a table and given myself a tongue bath...

Maybe Jackie will be there, though since Valentine's Day and the appearance of a new man in her life it seems she's been spending less and less time at The Oasis.

Rolling over, I look at the small clock on the bedside table. Five-ten. The time when most of the city is battling rush hour traffic and I am just waking. Master has allowed me to sleep in. Maybe he has no intention of taking me to the club tonight.

Defeated, I flop back onto my back, feeling when I do so a bubble of hot liquid spill out of me. *Oh, no!* I didn't feel like I even had to pee, but one of the babies must have hit my bladder just perfectly.

Embarrassed, I hurry to the bathroom.

Garrett doesn't comment when I barge in and plop down on the toilet, it's been a normal enough occurrence of late. It takes a moment for me to realize the red stain on the inside of my thighs is blood.

"Master!" I scream and can't stop screaming. This is the worst of my fears realized.

He pushes open the glass door and sees immediately what is wrong.

"I'm bleeding! I'm not supposed to be bleeding."

He reacts, wrapping in a towel but not drying off. Dripping wet, he carries me back to bed, puts pillows under my knees and feet. "Try to relax. Lay here while I call the doctor."

How can I relax? Sobbing hysterically, I cry over and over, "God doesn't want me to be a mother." *Oh God, oh God, oh God.* I can't breathe, I can't think. There is no summoning a prayer. What would I say? What promise would I make?

"God!" I scream. "Don't do this!"

"To-day we love what to-morrow we hate; to-day we seek what to-morrow we shun; to-day we desire what to-morrow we fear."

Daniel Defoe, *Robinson Crusoe*

CHAPTER 32

GARRETT

"I'm going to take a look." Quickly I assess that she isn't hemorrhaging. Kissing her forehead, I explain, "There's only a little blood, so you need to calm down and try to relax." I kiss her forehead again. "I'm calling the doctor now."

I leave her alone in the bedroom. I speed dial the doctor on my cell and hurry through the penthouse to rouse Enrique. He is watching a talk show on the small television in his bedroom. "Kitten is in bed. Go stay with her while I call the doctor. Do not let her get out of bed."

Eyes wide, he doesn't ask questions, he just hurries to obey. I suck in a deep breath as my call is answered, then hurry to explain the situation. It turns out the woman answering the phone is only part of a physician's answering service. "If this is an emergency you should go to the nearest hospital."

"I need you to contact Doctor Moran and tell him to call me immediately."

"I'm sorry, that isn't possible. Doctor Moran is unavailable. The obstetrician on call—"

The noise from the bedroom is getting louder with Kitten taking the worst of her fears out on Enrique. I can hear him begging her to calm down and relax. Angry, I hang up on the answering service and call the lifestyle acquaintance who recommended his wife's obstetrician. He answers on the fourth ring. "John, Garrett. I need Doctor Moran's cell number. It's urgent I talk to him."

John informs me that the doctor doesn't give out his personal number.

"What?" If I was livid with the answering service I am moreso now.

"He should have one of his partners covering his calls. Did you leave a message with the service?"

I hang up on John. Rude? Sure. Do I care at the moment? No. I'm irate as I hurry back through the living room to the bedroom. Enrique is holding Kitten's hand and singing to her softly. For the moment she isn't screaming, which is a huge improvement.

Sitting on the edge of the bed, I run my hand over her stomach. "I want you to focus, Kitten. Tell me the last time you felt movement."

She is pale and scared but she meets my gaze. "When I woke up."

"Okay, that's good. That's been within the last hour. Have you felt them move since you returned to bed?"

Her face crumbles. "I don't know."

"Relax." I prod her baby bump lightly. "Does that hurt at all?"

"No," she answers, then adds with hope filling her voice, "One of them just moved."

"Good, that's good," I assure her. "Concentrate on feeling them while I make another phone call."

Closing her eyes, she rubs her hands over her belly. Enrique keeps singing softly. She is much calmer as I speed dial George. This time I don't leave the room, I only walk to the far side of it and look out the window while the phone is ringing. The sky is dark and rain is falling. Softly I explain the situation and am slightly annoyed when he repeats everything I explain, saying, "Celia's bleeding but has confirmed she can feel fetal movement. Her obstetrician is unavailable." I understand he was relaying the information when Thomas comes on the line.

"Do not try to transport her to the hospital yet. I'll have the obstetrician Lattie used come there immediately. It will be faster."

Twenty minutes later, Thomas and Dr. Wang are both standing in my bedroom. Thomas, Enrique and I step out of the room while he examines her. Enrique immediately moves a respectable distance away, close enough for him to hear us if we need anything but far enough that he doesn't hear our every word.

"I'm surprised you waited and we're not at a hospital right now."

"I guess I felt that if there is any chance she might not lose them the less she moves around the better."

I'm surprised when Thomas sits down hard, looking slightly pale.

"Are you all right?"

He nods but closes his eyes, and I realize if anything happens to the twins he's going to be absolutely devastated. It makes me wonder not for the first time how he is managing being away from his children. Home and family have always been the core of his universe.

We sit in silence, waiting, and it is the longest twenty minutes of my life. When the doctor appears, he doesn't look outwardly concerned. He smiles when both Thomas and I stand.

"She is fine for now. Both babies' hearts beat strong. I suspect a mild placental abruption. I think the best course of action is to wait and see how this progresses with complete bed rest. I do not believe that it will be the case, but if she would start bleeding heavily, arrange transportation to the hospital. I will put in an order for a mobile ultrasound immediately and based on their findings will reevaluate every other day. I will also have an obstetric nurse come by three times a day to monitor any changes. Does that seem satisfactory?"

Overwhelmed and relieved, I shake his hand. "Thank you, Doctor Wang."

Thomas sees him out but returns quickly and together we go in to sit with Kitten. She is lying back with her feet still propped up. She looks terrified, if not miserable. I am surprised when Thomas tells her he has to leave again but promises to return as soon as he can. She is heartbroken. After he leaves, I scoot onto the bed with her. "Is there anything I can do?"

She shakes her head and starts to cry. "This is my fault. I'm selfish and unworthy."

I quote statistics. "One in a hundred women experience placental bleeding at some point during their second or third trimester."

"Is that what is happening? My placenta is separating?" she asks frantically.

Crap. I said the wrong thing.

"Shh, I know it sounds scary, but as long as it is a tiny separation—which by the small amount of blood is the indication—it will clot and all will be fine. You will even be allowed out of bed in a few days."

"What if it isn't a small tear? What if my placenta really unattaches?"

"That would be more serious."

"The babies would die. They're too small."

I want to reassure her but knowing she is only twenty-two weeks and still underweight, I don't want to give her false hope. "That isn't going to happen."

"Can I use your phone? I want to call Jackie."

"What? No. You need to rest."

She remains adamant. "Please? I want her here. With me. She said she would come, day or night, if I needed her to."

With a heavy sigh, I relent and hand her the phone, knowing as soon as she starts recanting what has happened in minute by minute detail that I won't be needed for a while. I head for the kitchen to make her a cup of tea, using a selection of calming herbs, and am not surprised when the doorbell sounds. "Christ, Jackie." Except it isn't Jackie, as promised an ultrasound technician has arrived. It's almost eight and I really hadn't expected anyone until morning, but I'm glad he's here.

"When I speak of home, I speak of the place where—in default of a better—those I love are gathered together; and if that place were a gypsy's tent, or a barn, I should call it by the same good name notwithstanding."

Charles Dickens, *Nicholas Nickleby*

CHAPTER 33

THOMAS

Without thinking about it too much, I go to George's and corner my brother. "You are a problem. Doctor Psycho feels it would be unsafe for the Bay Area to release you into its midst, and I have promised you won't go around killing people if we allow you to live on your own."

He looks at me like I've lost my mind. Maybe I have.

"The question is, can you control yourself?"

"Yes," he answers cautiously.

"Even if some Joe gets in your face, waving a broken beer bottle?"

"I won't put myself in that situation."

"And if an armed extermination team comes hunting you?"

"There might be a few bodies left in my wake."

I slap his shoulder and congratulate him, calling over my shoulder to George, "He's completely rehabilitated. You've done a great job. We're leaving, and I know you are needed at Lewd Larry's. The place is yours to hold together until further notice."

George takes the news well, grumbling under his breath about lack of appreciation, but I can tell he's also biting at the bit to get to the club. An hour later, I'm pulling up to the artist's loft I bought him. "Don't make me regret this."

"I won't," he promises, beaming like a kid on Christmas morning. "What's happened? I was expecting to be Doctor Psycho's prisoner for many months to come."

"You have to stick to your therapy schedule." We stay in the car, heater blowing warm air on us. I don't want to go inside until we come to an understanding about a few things.

"Yeah, yeah," he whines. "Now answer the question."

"It's Celia. We had a scare today, thought she might lose the babies, and I realized as much as I feel responsible for you, my place is at her side."

Nikos looks concerned when he asks, "Is she all right?"

"For now. She's going to be required to have one-hundred percent bed rest, at least for a while. Garrett and I will take turns staying with her and taking care of his business."

Nikos nods. "Garrett being the man you share her with?"

"Yes. We're a committed ménage. After today, we'll be living together."

"I never meant to take you away from your family so long. Thank you."

I squeeze his thigh. "Thank you. Now, let's go inside. I want to get you settled so that I can get back to her."

Our car doors echo when we slam them closed, shattering the silence. Two dogs on opposite sides of the street react, further dissipating the quiet. I point out hidden security measures on approach, security cameras, pressure alerts that react to a change of weight on the sidewalk. No one will come near his front or back doors without his knowing well in advance.

"Self-destruct?" he asks.

"Of course. Once we're inside I'll show you all the bells and whistles."

After ushering him in, doubt is evident on his face. "I lived like a king before coming here. My apartment overlooked the beauty of Shanghai."

I almost laugh, but don't. I've brought him to a lost corner of the city, a gritty, rundown underbelly currently being reclaimed by artists and musicians. I've probably made a mistake, no doubt drugs are prevalent. Do I really expect him to abstain?

The loft seems little more than a derelict dump. Paint peels from the walls both outside and within, although the main room has been recently painted the color of a bruised plum, purple verging on black. There is a shit-green velvet sofa, obviously left behind because the back upholstery is torn and vomiting white stuffing.

He plops down in its center and I expect it to disintegrate under his weight. "I like bright light, clean lines, ultra chic. I like the best money can buy. Opulence. Luxury. My place in Shanghai had an indoor lap pool, a sauna, a hot tub for twenty."

With an approving pat on the seat cushion, he stands to inspect the rest of the space, moving to the kitchen area. He turns around and is back in the long, wide living area with its single sofa. He laughs. "My bedroom in Shanghai was bigger than this entire space."

I try to see the loft as he is seeing it. The kitchen is no more than a cubby corner where a mini-microwave sits on top of an apartment-sized refrigerator. There is a single sink that would have been better suited in a sixties era bathroom, as it is a pastel shade of pink with exposed pipes beneath. Opening a narrow door, which might be a pantry, he finds the toilet.

"It's sparse," I admit.

"My enemies will not look for me here," he tells me. "It's perfect."

Relieved, I lead him around the room, pointing out all of the state-of-the-art security measures he overlooked, including a bolt hole and hidden armory. He whistles at the display of weapons. "Now this, dear brother, is what I'm talking about. I could rule a small country with this much artillery."

"Yeah, well the plan is for you to not have to use it. Daniel is dead." Reaching into my jacket, I pull out his new documents: driver's license, passport, social security card, banking information, credit cards. You are now Joshua Lambert."

He takes the proffered documents.

"You grew up in Seattle, Washington. Your dossier is on this microchip, along with every detail you need to know about yourself."

This part he knows. We've both been so many people in our lifetime that becoming someone new is easy. Sometimes it's a relief. A do-over. Becoming Thomas was mine, I hope he sees becoming Joshua as much of a blessing.

"Pay very close attention, you do not leave this loft. In a few weeks, assuming all goes well, I'll loosen the leash a little, but for now, plan on being tightly reined."

"No problem."

"Of course, I will stop by every morning on my way home from the club and George will come by every evening on his way to work. I'll have food deliveries arranged…and *entertainment* if you want."

His lips twitch and I realize he is trying very hard to not laugh. It seems I have been his entertainment of late. He assures me, "Just food. For now."

I hug him. "By the way, we're not brothers."

He hugs me back. "I'll be a good boy, Ari. Trust me."

* * * *

Back at the penthouse, Sophia and Garrett are already in bed sleeping. Without undressing, I lay beside Kitten even though I'm not tired. I am torn by my responsibilities. Helping Nikos get resettled I worry that I have pushed him to do more than he is ready for, but if I hadn't and anything would have happened to make matters worse for Sophia and the babies, I'd have never forgiven myself.

Sophia kisses my shoulder and I realize I've wakened her. She asks, "Everything all right?"

"Everything is perfect now that I'm here. God, I've missed you." The bathroom light was left on to illuminate the room, and seeing her face she looks absolutely exhausted. "Are you okay? Any pain?"

"No pain and I haven't bled anymore."

"Good. That's very good. Try to sleep. I'll be here when you wake up."

She wraps her arm around me.

"Trying to sleep here," Garrett says with a sarcastic growl, before rolling away from us. He is snoring softly before his rollover is complete.

She snickers and whispers, "I'm glad you're here."

Echo of Redemption | Roxy Harte

I kiss her gently. "Are you eating enough?"

"Yes. Too much."

I smile, rubbing her swollen stomach. I know she's eating more than she was because the babies are growing. I slide down her body, kissing her stomach, whispering to my babies in Greek. I make promises to them I hope I can keep and am rewarded by feeling them move for the first time. She twists her fingers into my hair, saying, "I like when you talk to them."

I kiss my way back up her body, wrapping around her. "I wish I could make love to you."

That makes her blush and smile, but the worry she is feeling about our unborn babies doesn't leave her eyes.

"Everything is going to be fine," I tell her.

"An ultrasound technician came by while you were gone. The doctor will look at them in the morning but from what the tech said I suffered a fairly mild placental abruption. Master said that can be fairly common with twins in the second half of a pregnancy."

I am comforted that she is offering me assurances, but suddenly tears well up in her eyes. "I don't want to have a C-section. I know that Master would have never agreed to the Primal Birth in an outdoor setting, but I was at least hoping for a natural birth. I thought I still had time to talk him into a doula. None of that is going to happen now."

"Sh-h." I kiss away her tears. "Let's get through a few days, talk to the doctor, and find out what your options are going to be."

I hug her closer, knowing that isn't what she wanted to hear. It seems a long time before she is sound asleep. I stay beside her, stroking her when she whimpers. I offer her assurances even in her sleep. "Everything is going to be okay."

Hours later, I am glad when Garrett awakens. We sneak quietly from the room, allowing Kitten to sleep. He dresses, telling me he plans to go to the club tonight but he takes the time to catch up and discuss shared concerns, he drinking coffee, me tea. He says, "Thank you for bringing Doctor Wang to us, he seems capable."

"He practices both Eastern and Western medicine."

"Yes, well we've had a revolving door since you left. An ultrasound technician, a nurse, an herbalist and acupuncturist."

Garrett scowls when I chuckle.

"Did the acupuncturist do any harm? Or the herbalist?"

"No," he answers. "She actually seemed more relaxed after their sessions."

"Good. You know she's going to be devastated if she has to have a Caesarian birth. We need to do whatever we can over the next few days to make things easier for her. We need to alleviate her fears, not add to them."

Garrett stands and pours himself another cup of coffee. He lifts the tea pot asking, "More tea?" to which I decline before he returns to the table. Sitting, he sighs. "Jackie was here, and she brought a woman with her they met at the Primal Birth Center. It was quite *enlightening.* Incense. Candles. Chanting. It was all very New-Age-Hippy-Something."

I sniff the air. "I thought I smelled patchouli." Garrett rolls his eyes, and I smack his arm. "Lighten up. It was for Kitten's benefit, not yours."

He thinks he's won the battle. In his mind there is no doubt that she will have a C-section and that it will take place in a modern, sterile hospital. I don't even want to broker that subject now. I take a sip of lukewarm tea, trying to think of a safe subject.

"Will you be here all night?" he asks.

Something's up. "Yes."

"I need to go into the club, take care of some things. You will be fine here alone with her?"

I fake a chuckle, my suspicion rising. "We will be fine."

When he is gone, I phone Farris. "Keep an eye on Garrett for me. I want to know who he sees, every person he talks to, and if there is a single particular person he is spending more time with than the others."

"I don't have to watch him to tell you the answer to that one. One man. Dean Anderson. He's a client, real high roller. Pays Garrett for four hour time slots every time he comes in."

"Huh. How often does he come in?"

"Three times so far this week."

"Is he scheduled for tonight?"

"I can find out."

"Do that and I want to know everything there is to know about the man from the day he was born."

We disconnect. I'm not happy. The thought Garrett is involved with someone, not just work related is almost unbelievable because Garrett isn't that guy. He isn't a player. He loves and he loves hard. I just hope he comes to his senses as I did when faced with the opportunity for Eva to return to my life. It was tempting. She was my first love, and until I stood face to face with her in Lewd Larry's I'd believed I'd never loved a woman so deeply...but then I realized I loved Sophia and Garrett *more*. I chose the ménage because I considered what Sophia and Garrett mean to me and I realized *they are my family*.

And now Sophia carries my twins.

My chest swells with emotion as I watch her sleep. It will be many hours before she wakes and as I lie beside her, feeling the small babies move within her, I am filled with inconsolable grief for my other children.

"To let the brain work without sufficient material is like racing an engine. It racks itself to pieces."

Sir Arthur Conan Doyle, *The Adventures of the Devil's Foot*

CHAPTER 34

GARRETT

Driving to the club, two things are equally apparent: my dick is rock hard and my hands are sweating. I called Dean before I even pulled out of the parking garage, asking him to meet me at The Attic. I should not have a client on speed dial. It's my rule, no fraternizing with clients. By twisting facts, I allow myself to believe that I am not fraternizing—we have not had sex—still, I'm walking a very fine line. A very fine line indeed. That isn't why my palms are sweating.

I'm wracked with guilt.

Did I really just leave Kitten's bedside to meet a man I barely know? What is wrong with me? She could have lost the babies. She might still.

She needs me and yet I feel so powerless around her, especially with Thomas there. But I won't blame Thomas. I am the one at fault here. I admit that I am a horny mother-fucker who is thinking with his dick more than his brain of late. *I should be with her.*

I'm literally shaking when I arrive at the nightclub. Want and need feeding off guilt and loathing. It's a heady combination. I've sat in on lectures Doctor Psycho gives for our staff of Dominants, alerting them to red flags when dealing with clients, most of which are married and going behind their partner's back to have a BDSM experience. There is a certain level of sexual excitement generated by the mere act of sneaking around and the threat of getting caught. We are warned to avoid inappropriate contact between sessions. Innocent 'bumping into' the Dominant who led their session on numerous occasions in other areas of Lewd Larry's might be an indicator of obsession, a stalking mentality, or it might be as innocent as an infatuation. Any instance would need an immediate intervention by staff, usually George but sometimes Morgana or Lord Fyre. I rarely get involved in such issues.

My calling Dean more than crossed the line...

George would ask me if my reasons for wanting to top Dean more and more often stemmed from a fear of commitment, seeing that our ménage is being forced to evolve. We have been lovers, partners, but now, with the addition of babies, we are being forced into the role of family and our threesome definitely challenges the guidelines of what is considered normal—and I could argue that I've never worried about being seen as deviant, who cares, it's just a word—except in this instance it might mean we were unfit to keep our children. Is that why I'm running, because I fear a hypothetical fight with bureaucracy that might or might never happen?

I've never backed down from any label-defending fight before.

George would ask me if I'm struggling with low self-esteem, and as much as I want to argue 'No!' the truth is I feel powerful with Dean and weak with Kitten, and for the life of me I'm having a hard time putting all the pieces of the puzzle together as to why.

George would ask me if I'm unhappy at home and seeking chaos as a means to destroy the ménage, thus being given an *out*.

"Except, I don't want to destroy the ménage." *The three of us—no matter what.* That's what we agreed to. I roll up my sleeve, exposing the scar on my forearm. We have matching brands, and I realize now that this was Kitten's purpose when she came up with the idea. At the time she felt threatened by Eva, I doubt she ever suspected I might want to bring a fourth into our relationship. Is that what I want? A fourth?

I shake my head, realizing how totally inappropriate Dean is for the life we lead. He would add nothing to our strength and in the end weaken the bond I have with my other two. *I am a fool.*

Closing my eyes, I can see Dean's chiseled body. Perfection. I can smell his scent and taste the salt of his sweat and of his tears. With a labored sigh I leave my car and go inside. Heavy feet carry me to The Attic, where I find George. Thankfully, Dean hasn't arrived yet and I ask George to join me in his office. Aside from a curiously lifted brow, he doesn't comment, and leads me down the hall to where we'll be afforded privacy. He closes the door softly and still I jump when it clicks closed. "It's good to see you back."

He motions for me to sit in one of two heavily upholstered chairs and takes the other. "What's on your mind, Garrett?"

"An infraction of The Attic's rules. One of the Dominant's crossed the line and called a client at home in an attempt to begin a relationship."

He scoots forward on the edge of his seat, concern lining his face. "That's a serious accusation. You're certain?"

We both know there is usually no leniency in such circumstances and the punishment for the errant Dominant would be immediate termination. I answer with a curt nod.

"Which Dominant?" he asks.

I point at myself.

He slides back in his chair. "I see."

"I called him tonight with every intention of starting something outside the bounds of professionalism, and then on the drive here I decided that I am an absolute idiot."

He breathes a sigh of relief. "You haven't met with him for this purpose yet?"

"No."

"Good. And so now, are you asking permission or asking for an intervention?"

"An intervention. Definitely."

He slides forward again, clasping my knee. "You must not see him again. Not as a client. And especially not outside of the club environment."

I nod. "I agree."

"I'm assuming he's one of our regulars."

"A regular at The Attic, he is not a member of The Oasis. Whether he prowls the public areas?" I shrug, not knowing the answer to that. "I hate to lay this in your lap, but I need help walking away from this. My place is at home with Kitten and Thomas."

"I'll assist, but you must be accountable. You will have to face this man when he arrives."

"I'm sure he's already here by now."

George stands as do I, and together we leave the office. It is a long walk to the outer room which is reception and when I face him dread curls into a tight, painful ball in my guts. "Thank you for meeting me."

He smiles, expecting a session. Just as an hour ago I expected more than a session. I haven't done anything wrong and yet my palms are sweating, my heart pounding. I haven't felt this horrible since I jilted Ellen Kramer right before our wedding because I'd decided I was gay. *Oh God.* It's because I've led him on…led him on like I led her on…taking what I wanted. With Ellen it was normalcy, I didn't have to face being different; with Dean it was the power I felt topping him.

"We need to talk."

He looks confused. "Is something wrong, Sir? Did I do something wrong?"

"No," I answer as gently as I can. "You didn't do anything. I needed you to come down here tonight because I feel like when you were here last you might have left with the impression that our relationship was going to move outside of the professional parameters of Lewd Larry's…and I just wanted to make certain that you understood that isn't possible."

He gives me a crestfallen look but tells me he understands. *Damn it.*

I smile my perfect Lewd Larry's smile and wrap my arm around his shoulder. "I want you to meet someone. I'd like you to consider booking a session with Doctor Psycho. He's one of our most experienced and reputable Dominants."

I watch his face run the gamut from miserable to curious to excited in fewer seconds than it takes my brain to figure out that he isn't devastated by the sudden loss of *me.*

"Doctor Psycho?" He reaches out his hand. "It's an honor, Sir."

George doesn't take his hand. He gives him his classic domination glare.

"Oh! I apologize, Sir. I meant no disrespect. I-I—"

I leave Dean stumbling over his tongue and hurry away from the scene. I'm suddenly disappointed that I was so easily replaceable, but by the time I reach my car I'm laughing at myself. I could have really fucked up. Dean Anderson was a classic example of Dom Adoration. It didn't matter which Dom, any Dominant would do. I laugh harder, realizing he never saw *me* and that's perhaps the reason I felt so God-like being with him.

I think of Kitten's efforts to challenge me, forcing me to pull from a deep well inside myself to control her. She *sees* me. Human, not a God, and we're in this relationship, struggling together and against each other to figure out our power balance.

I smile, finally seeing past my failures. *God, I've been such an idiot.*

"They gave themselves up wholly to their sorrow."

Jane Austen, *Sense and Sensibility*

CHAPTER 35

THOMAS

I watch Sophia sleep from a chair near the window, though she awakens shortly after Garrett leaves and is understandably disappointed, but I am still surprised when she busts out in tears. "I never wanted to hurt the ménage. Master hasn't been the same since he found out I was pregnant. This is why I considered an abortion, to keep us from falling apart. Now, I might lose the babies anyway, and it won't matter if I've already lost him."

I join her on the bed, sitting down on top of the blankets. I pull them up to her chin, tucking her in. "I don't believe we've lost Garrett. I think he's had a lot on his mind."

She shudders, tears still sliding over her cheeks.

"You should go back to sleep. I can tell by looking at you that you aren't getting enough."

Petulantly, she argues, "I'm not tired."

She looks so vulnerable and afraid, not the woman of strength I've come to love. I'm worried about her. Of course, I'm concerned about the health of the babies and Garrett's peculiar behavior as well so I can hardly fault her for crumbling under the stress. Not to disregard my own behavior. Nikos has kept me away for too long. I kiss her cheek. "I'm sorry I was gone so long."

She barely acknowledges.

I pull the sheets and blankets away from her slowly, drawing them down her body in a teasing reveal. I cover her shoulders with kisses, gradually moving to her breasts. I kiss them only, not sucking her nipples though it is so tempting. I slide my hand down her stomach before drawing circles on her expanded belly.

"Do you wish me to pleasure you, Lord Fyre?"

"No." I slip my fingers between her thighs and feel her tense.

"I don't think—"

"Sh-h, relax." I interrupt her. "I have no intention of having sex with you until Doctor Wang feels it is safe." I slide my fingers through her damp folds. Showing her the fluid covering my fingers. "No blood. That's a very good sign."

She shifts nervously and our gazes touch.

"I don't think Doctor Wang would have any problem with me worshiping the vessel who is carrying my babies. Do you know how absolutely radiant you are? Or how powerfully sensual you look like this?" I rub my hands over the small swell of her womb. "I haven't told you 'thank you' yet. I know it is a terrifying journey you've embarked on, and until now I haven't been here to make you feel safe, or cherished. I am sorry for that." I kiss her...navel to toes...saying with each press of my lips, "Thank you."

* * * *

"I was going to wait until morning, but I brought you a present." I reach behind the bed for a large bag I placed there while she was sleeping. I remove a medium size box and hand it to her.

Readjusting pillows to sit up, she reads the label. "Smarter Baby?"

While she opens the box and investigates, pulling out headphones, a mini-microphone, a set of fetal speakers, and an elasticized wrap with pockets for the speakers, I explain, "You can play music or read a book to the babies and the speakers direct the sound inside."

She looks at me expectantly, not understanding.

"We had a set when Lattie was pregnant because I'd read studies had proven playing classical music to unborn babies helped to stimulate growth and enhance mental development. She enjoyed listening to the same music she was playing for the baby when she was exercising or doing housework. I thought it might be something fun for you to do while you're confined to bed."

She smiles but the expression doesn't extend to her eyes. Tears leak out when she explains, "I love the gift, I really do, I'm just so afraid I'm going to lose them."

"Please stop worrying." I take her hand and kiss her knuckles. "Do you trust me?"

She gasps. "Of course."

I take the remaining items out of the bag—a blindfold, several rolls of non-elasticized cotton bandage, thick cotton pads, and surgical scissors. "I want to do a scene with you."

She licks her lips, looking worried.

"You know that if I thought the babies were really in danger or if I thought I was going to put them at risk, I wouldn't even suggest doing a scene, right?"

She nods.

"Okay, so relax. Lay down."

She does and I uncover her. "I realized today that the scenes we do together are so intense that you are missing out on some of the simpler pleasures of bondage. What I want to do is allow you to relax completely, and we're going to accomplish that by depriving your senses."

I cover her eyes with the blindfold. Lifting her right hand I start tucking soft cotton pads between each finger and then using the bandage, bind her fingers together so that even the skin of her fingers doesn't touch. I wrap her hands, extending up her arms, not tightly, because I don't want to interfere with her circulation at all.

"I'm going to cover every inch of your skin, except for your nose and mouth, with bandage, so that you won't feel anything. You are going to be wrapped in a cocoon of cotton."

I wrap her left hand as I did the right.

"Okay so far?"

"Yes, Lord Fyre."

"Do you think you are going to enjoy this?"

She swallows and answers honestly, "I'm not sure."

She can't see my smile as I keep wrapping the bandage up her arm. When I finish, I set up the CD player and place fetal speakers next to her stomach, holding them in place by the included elasticized belt. I put the earphones over her ears but pull one away long enough to say, "You are going to hear what the babies are hearing. Just try to relax and enjoy the moment."

I lower the earpiece, press *PLAY*, and start wrapping her head.

Garrett comes in as I'm finishing the mummification, having wrapped her entire body. "Looks like I've missed the party."

"It's to help her relax."

He nods and pulls up a chair to sit closer to the bed. "I only wish I'd thought of it first. Did you put in ear plugs or can she hear us?"

"Headphones. They're listening to Mozart." I hand him the Smarter Baby box so that he can read all about the fetal speakers.

I can tell by the look on his face he thinks it was a good gift but he reads from the box, "In-utero fetal acoustic stimulation improves pregnancy outcomes," with skepticism.

I set a timer. "One hour?"

"Might be too long for a first mummification."

"We'll see how she responds. We can always cut her out early."

Garrett stands and tucks a pillow under each leg and under each arm. He nods at the improvement, then sits back down.

"You're home early," I say, not bothering to hide the slight accusatory tone that creeps in.

"I couldn't stay away from her. I was too worried."

I let it go. He's home, that's what matters.

"Oh, haggard mind, groping darkly through the past; incapable of detaching itself from the miserable present; dragging its heavy chain of care through imaginary feasts and revels, and scenes of awful pomp; seeking but a moment's rest among the long-forgotten haunts of childhood, and the resorts of yesterday; and dimly finding fear and horror everywhere!"

Charles Dickens, *Martin Chuzzlewit*

CHAPTER 36

KITTEN

As Lord Fyre wraps my arms and legs in cotton bandaging, I worry about how safe this is...considering...but in my heart I know we wouldn't be doing a scene if he was worried about me losing the babies...and I know how much he loves his children...he wouldn't take an unnecessary chance. He wants me to give birth, he wants my pregnancy to go to term so that the babies will be born healthy, which can only mean I was overreacting. *Oh God, that is so. I don't want to miscarry.* I console myself, knowing these things are true. Besides, it was only a little blood and the ultrasound technician said it was only a small tear.

With my hands and arms, feet and legs completely cushioned, I relax. *I'm fine. The babies are fine.*

He lifts my hips to slide the elasticized belt which holds the fetal speakers in place. It is cool and snug against my skin. "Feeling all right?"

"Yes, Lord Fyre."

He leans down to whisper in my ear, "I'm going to put the headphones over your ears and then wrap most of your head and face in the bandages. You will be able to breathe, and you will be able to say your safe word if you need to."

"I understand."

Mozart floods my head but only for a few seconds. He pulls one of the earpieces away to ask, "Too loud? Too soft?"

"Perfect. Is that what the babies are hearing?"

"Yes."

Smiling, I relax as he covers my ear and I am soothed with music. The sound seems to reverberate through my body, melding with my pulse.

The bandages make me feel cocooned. Safe. But as I relax, floating, it seems as if I am becoming both less than my body and more. I feel like I am one with my bed...the room...outside the room...maybe a fragmented part of the world. The universe.

I imagine my babies feeling so connected as well. One.

I imagine being cradled as one of the stars held in place within our galaxy.

I imagine being held in the arms of God, and it is so utterly peaceful. I do not fear fire and brimstone in this loving being's embrace. Nor do I fear for my babies' lives.

We're going to be okay. All of us.

"The world is full of obvious things which nobody by any chance ever observes."

Sir Arthur Conan Doyle, *The Hound of the Baskervilles*

CHAPTER 37

NIKOS

The bright sun of early morning beacons through the window. It's been months since I've felt its touch and I need to touch it, to feel it, no matter how unsafe it is for me to do so. My brother's voice is my conscience. *Stay inside.* Disregarding his order completely, I race out into the salt scented breeze.

I justify my hazardous behavior with the fact that in this part of town the sidewalks are almost empty this time of day. The sunshine as seen from my window is deceptive, the air cooler than I would have believed. I'm wearing only a black tank, and I think maybe I should have grabbed a jacket and just as quickly discard the idea. I want the sun beating down on my skin. Tipping back my face, I close my eyes and soak in so much light. My breath puffs out white.

A young child's scream makes me jump and look, but he is fine, he is playing. He and three others, chasing each other for no other reason than the joy of the chase as their mothers swap gossip on the corner. Their grounds for being out so early is evident as a yellow school bus pulls up to the curb.

Watching them makes me wish for the carefree days of my youth, and I remember there was a time before I'd ever held a gun in my hand, or a knife in my grip. There was a time before...before I'd ever killed anyone...that I'd known joy. It's a distant memory. It feels like someone else's memory.

I take off running, trying to jump back into the mind of the person I was then. I want to remember who I was and think like that person again. I want to be free, and joyful.

The pavement pounds beneath my feet. I haven't run in such a very long time. I used to like running, especially with Ari. God, there was a time when we could run for hours. We could run for days.

Here I am only three blocks away from where I started and already I am breathing hard. How did I ever run mile after mile for the hell of it? How did I get in such horrible shape?

My chest screams, making me remember the bullets, making me remember I had help in getting in this bad of shape.

I stop running, doubled over and clutching my chest, trying to remember how to breathe because it hurts too badly to do so without thinking. I back up against the brick wall of a building, not wanting anyone to sneak up behind me.

Inhale, exhale. *Mother-fucking God, that hurts.*

Inhale, exhale. *Okay, so running wasn't my brightest decision to date. Keep moving.* I start walking back to the loft. The three boys are no longer playing. They are watching the crazy man with tattoos almost die because he is an idiot.

I wave as I pass them and even though they are safe with their mothers on the opposite side of the street, they don't wave back.

My breathing finally calms and that's when I hear it, someone matching my footsteps, step for step. I don't turn around and look. I duck into an alley and take off running. I run three blocks before I even think about looking. I zig into every alley, changing directions again and again. I don't hear anyone behind me, but I'm too paranoid to look.

God, I'm an idiot. A lunatic. Whoever it was probably didn't even know me, probably didn't want anything to do with me. I collapse against a parked car's hood, trying once again to remember how to breathe.

I look up and realize I have no fucking idea where I am or how to get back to the loft. Brilliant. Just fucking brilliant.

I close my eyes and try to get a bearing for where I am based on where I ran from and start walking in the general direction I think is the right way to go. I open my eyes after a few steps, and the direction I chose still feels right.

I walk, clutching my chest and breathing. It hurts. Everything hurts.

It seems like hours pass before I actually reach a recognizable landmark. I've probably been walking in circles the entire time. Finally, I see my loft. Thank fucking God. Climbing the interior stairs is pure agony, and then I get a jolt of adrenaline seeing the front door is partly opened, knowing I not only locked I dead-bolted it with the key.

Reaching under my shirt, I unholster the Glock I wear behind my back. I'm on automatic-pilot now, doing what I'm trained to do. I might have been away from the action for more than a month, but it all comes back in less than a heartbeat. If I was afraid outside, where it was too open and I could identify a target, this, up close and personal, inside a closed quarter's environment was the cure. I feel the rapid flush of adrenaline, the happy speeding of my heart. I go in armed and ready, finger on the trigger, ready for Armageddon...and find my brother sprawled on my sofa.

"I told you not to go outside."

I lower my weapon and slide it back into its holster. It is only then I realize George is here as well. I've missed our session. He stands over a hot plate, waiting for a kettle to boil. He has brought with him a china set I haven't seen before, a teapot, cups and saucers decorated with a delicate floral pattern. Tea it seems is the answer to all problems as far as George is concerned.

My brother hasn't moved from the couch. It almost seems like he was napping before I arrived.

"I needed air."

He sits up quickly. "I needed time with my woman, but here I am. Waiting. Wondering if you are just stupid, or really incredibly stupid."

I sit down on the wood floor, excuses useless at this point. So are promises that I will do better, because we both know that I can't. I am who I am. "I should return to Shanghai."

Ari says, "You should probably be quiet while I decide what to do with you." Punctuated by the teakettle's whistle, I jump at the sound. *I do not fear my brother.* My wildly beating heart argues differently.

"Be comforted, dear soul! There is always light behind the clouds."

Louisa May Alcott

CHAPTER 38

KITTEN

Dr. Wang is enthusiastically optimistic that the bleeding episode I had was a singular event. After reviewing the ultrasound technician's report, he feels I will be perfectly safe to resume normal activities in another day or two. Master isn't easily convinced and I am left alone in the bedroom while they continue the discussion deep enough in the house for me to not overhear. *I am not a child.* My irritation grows when Dr. Wang doesn't return to the bedroom and hearing the front door opening and closing, I assume he's left.

I am surprised when Thomas comes in, making me smile despite my frustration.

"Are they arguing?"

Thomas understands immediately that I'm talking about Garrett and Dr. Wang. "They are having a deep discussion in the kitchen. So, what's up?"

"Doctor Wang says I'm fine."

"And?"

"Master wants me confined to bed for the duration of my pregnancy."

Thomas grimaces with great exaggeration, making me laugh.

I manage to ask, "Could you tell who was winning?"

"No, I didn't go near them. I wanted to steal a moment alone with you." Lifting my hand, he kisses the top. "I wouldn't worry. Doctor Wang's highly educated and very persuasive. I don't see you confined to bed more than you actually need to be. If anything he will be arranging for you to have a private Tai Chi session every day."

I squeeze his hand. "While we're alone, tell me something."

He lifts his eyebrow.

"Who are you? I mean, I know what you told Master about being a secret agent, but what does that mean and why doesn't what you've told us make sense in my head?"

He sits down with me and still holding my hand, rubs my arm with his free hand. After a long moment he manages to look me in the eye. "Sophia, you deserve to know the truth but to know everything there is to know could put you in danger."

I snort, irritably. "I've been under the threat of danger since the night your brother showed up here."

He nods, not looking away.

"You said your name is Ari? Demetres Aristotle Velouchiotis?"

"Yes, very good memory."

"It seems if you can trust me with the name you were given at birth, you could trust me with the truth?"

"The truth isn't pretty."

"I never imagined it would be."

We both look toward the sound when we hear the front door open and close. It is only a few minutes later that Garrett joins us, ending any chance for us to finish our conversation. I try to tell myself that it doesn't matter, but it does. I want to know who the father of my children is and there is so much I don't know.

"Kiss me though you make-believe. Kiss me, though I almost know you are kissing to deceive."

Alice Cary, *Make Believe* (1820-1871)

CHAPTER 39

NIKOS

Obviously, I didn't learn my lesson yesterday. Although I was exhausted and slept like the dead, midday finds me outside again, chasing sunbeams, running from my demons. Bare walls and empty spaces are my new enemy. The loft is too open, too big, even the shadows have shadows with a demon hiding in every one.

Today I jog. A nice slow pace to get me back into shape. By the amount of pain jabbing through my guts I am almost one hundred percent certain that the psycho doctor would say I am rushing things. Too bad, I can't stay inside another moment. Pain is just going to have to be today's new best friend. Tomorrow's too and every day until I can run for miles and miles without turning blue.

I realize the minute I am being followed and slow down, forcing whoever it is to pass me and reveal himself or detour to avoid detection. A slim woman sails past me. I listen but no one else is following.

The woman who passed me keeps to the sidewalk, I duck into an alley. Paranoid? Definitely. I double back to my loft, thinking I may never leave its confines again.

I'm safe here. No one is looking for me.

My breathing is slowed by the time I reach the top stair but my nerves are still on edge. I think about packing a bag, going back to Dr. Psycho's basement, but stepping through the threshold I realize I'm too late. *I'm not alone.* I go for the weapon strapped to my back and shove it under my assailant's chin in the same moment they shove their revolver under mine. We are wrapped as tightly as lovers, tightly enough to realize she too doubled back. The jogger.

Her breath is warm and sweet on my face. Without thought, my hand has twisted in her hair and is jerking her head back. The ball cap she is wearing falls off and long blond hair spills out. The gun she has pushed under my chin forces my head back as far as it will go. *Eva.*

She demands, "Pull the trigger, damn it. The last time I saw you, you had a fucking circular saw in your hand sawing my sternum in half."

"Yeah, I'm sorry about that." I think I even manage to look sincere. I look in her eyes, knowing *that* look; I've worn it myself for weeks. She would welcome death.

"Shoot!" she screams.

"You first."

That earns me a look and in an instant we both understand each other. We're out of options, out of reasons to live, and sick and tired of all the rest.

I suggest, "On the count of three, shall we?"

We count together, our voices echoing loud and desperate through the big empty space. "One...two...three."

Neither of us fires. She screams. "What in the fuck are you

waiting for?"

"I won't be the tool of your suicide," I shout back.

"What's with the bloody change of conscience?" She narrows her eyes, pushing her gun deeper into my flesh. "What happened to you, Daniel?"

"I don't go by that name anymore." I push beneath her chin with an equal amount of pressure. At this rate we may snap each other's necks.

"What would you like me to call you?"

"Joshua."

"Joshua? Seriously? I ought to blow your bloody head off," she threatens, but she lowers her weapon and despite my best poker face, I breathe a sigh of relief. I guess I honestly didn't want to die. Not now. Not yet.

"Do it. Please," I beg, stretching my arms wide, my gun hanging loose and useless in my right hand.

"And give you the luxury of bailing out of this shit pile? I don't think so." She looks hard at me, demanding an answer I don't understand the question to. "Henri didn't send you to finish the job did he?"

"No. I'm honestly just a guy at the wrong place, wrong time."

"When I saw you running yesterday, I thought the worst. I thought you'd been sent here to kill me. I'm really pissed at you, by the way. I thought we were friends," she says, poking her gun into my chest.

My mind flashes back to the moment I was holding that saw, preparing to cut her beating heart from her chest. Cobra's orders. I couldn't look on her as anything more than an assignment. Definitely couldn't dare recall the times I frequented a fetish nightclub called *Whips* or remember how pretty I always thought she was. If I had, I might have found myself wondering why I never fucked her. "You and I both know an agent never has friends. He only has the allies of the day."

Ignoring the weapon she has pointed at my heart, I make a move, stroking the back of her head. We both have guns cocked and ready, but I want to kiss her. Absurd? Sure. But it's been over a month since I've known a woman's touch...and she's here.

"What are you doing?"

I lick my lips and keep stroking her long blond hair. "I was just wondering why we never, you know."

She laughs. "You think you have a chance in hell of fucking me now?"

I waggle my eyebrows, moving closer. "You tell me."

She brings the gun to under my chin. "The only way I'd even consider letting you fuck me is if I have this gun to your head."

She doesn't trust me. That's okay, I don't trust myself. I kiss her, though it is more a ravishment. I feel like I am raping her with my tongue. I push my Glock into her temple. "You act like a woman with a price on her head."

She pushes her gun harder into my jaw, reminding me I am not the only one threatening death. She bites my cheek and starts to pull my t-shirt up by the tail with the hand not holding a gun. "There's one thing I want you to do before I kill you."

"Only one?" I tease. "And if there's still killing to be done, I'll be killing you, sweetheart, not the other way around."

I unbutton the front of her shirt, exposing her bra. "You wore black lace to kill me?"

She smiles against my lips. "I always wear black lace. Never know when it might be a tactical advantage."

I laugh into her open mouth, using the revolver to pull her head closer. I take what I want from her mouth, kissing her with savage intensity. If she notices my gun is no longer pointed directly at her brain she doesn't take the advantage to blow my brains out. Our teeth scrape, our tongues feud for control, and somehow, even armed, we both end up naked on the floor. True to her word she keeps her weapon aimed at my head. Should I have a hard time maintaining an erection? Probably. I'm not. If anything, the gun play, the danger, makes me even more aroused.

I roll onto my back, pulling her to straddle me. She breathes heavy, demanding, "Condom?"

I laugh. "Lady, you intend for us to kill each other, are we really going to not do this just because we don't have a condom between us?"

She slides down over my unsheathed dick, answering that question.

"God, Eva."

She rides me, slowly, killing me with the perfect rhythm of her hips. She says what I'm thinking, "We should have done this years ago."

* * * *

The room has grown dark and we're still tangled together when we both react to a creak on the staircase outside the door. Weapons aimed, crouching low, we're ready when six armed intruders enter. If they were hoping to have an advantage by surprising us, they were sadly mistaken. Killing them is too easy and we wait for a second wave, but nothing happens and soon sirens alert us to get out.

Dressing fast, we leave. I manage to trigger the self-destruct on the way out.

Eva drives, taking us west toward the bay, and I hope this wasn't a very elaborate ploy to set me up and get me away from the loft. She grabs my crotch and laughs, finding me hard as a rock. "You too? I always get horny as hell during gunfights."

"Only gunfights or will any fight do?"

We look at each other, knowing we both feel the same way. It is a huge aphrodisiac any time we walk away from death.

"Pull over."

She drives into a crowded parking lot, yet as we grab for each other, neither of us cares we're in a public place. An empty strip mall sprawls in front of us. She unzips my pants and my hard dick springs free. Climbing over the gear shift, she straddles me.

"I think the pants are going to have to come off, or this isn't going to work."

She looks at her legs, seeming to realize only then the predicament. Shifting, she shimmies, pulling down her pants enough to straddle me and impale herself. "Good enough?"

I grab her hips and force her down tighter. "Good enough."

Moving forward and back, she brings me quick, coming herself as I start to spurt. "God, oh God. Definitely good enough." Laughing, I echo her sentiment.

Too late, I realize we aren't alone in the parking lot. The car door opens, and she is jerked off my lap.

I react while they are still struggling, turning the key to the engine and pushing my left leg around the gear shift to hit the accelerator hard. I drive, watching their struggle with Eva in the rearview mirror. I'm outnumbered and there's no going back. Helpless to do anything, I watch them jab her with a hypodermic. They push her into a black SUV as I swerve out of the parking lot and into traffic. I drive for miles, not having a clue where I'm at or where I'm going.

Seeing her cellphone on the floorboard, I grab it and call Ari, saying only "Trouble."

"The bed is for lascivious toyings meet; there use all tricks and tread shame under feet."

Ovid, *Seeing Thou Art Fair*

CHAPTER 40

THOMAS

There is a hotel in the desert I sometimes use for emergencies. It isn't the kind of place one goes to for comfort or cleanliness but rather because it is off the beaten path. It isn't pretty and, having been built in the sixties, maybe earlier, has seen better days. It is a long, one-story row of small rooms, a place that should have been torn down in the name of progress two decades ago. Lucky for me it wasn't. I *own* room fourteen. It is the last room of the row and farthest from the street.

Nikos is already inside, waiting. I take my time going in, making certain I wasn't followed, he wasn't followed, or that there is even a solitary person I might deem out of place in a three mile radius.

When I finally decide to enter the room, I find him sitting on the bed watching Oprah, but as soon as I enter he turns the television off. I'm not happy and he knows it. A week hasn't even passed since I set him up with a new identity and already the loft is burned to the ground and SFFD is recovering bodies. "Tell me what happened and don't leave out a single detail."

His face doesn't betray any emotion. "Where would you like me to start?"

"How about from the moment the first bullet was fired."

"I was in bed. There were six of them. I killed them."

I nod. *That* at least matches my intel. "What aren't you telling me?"

His gaze never leaves mine. "There was a woman in my bed with me."

The look I give him must say it all because he starts spilling his guts. "She was following me and I evaded but then she was here and we both had our weapons drawn. Next thing you know, we're in bed fucking like bunnies in the springtime."

My mouth opens and closes before I start bellowing. "They sent a lead man and you decided it was a good idea to have sex?"

"Lead woman," he interrupts.

I lift my hand impatiently, and he shuts up. Shaking my head, I don't know whether to put a bullet through his head myself or if I want to try to figure this out. My Intel tells me no one is looking for him in the United States. Not a single solitary soul. So why the attack? And better question: who?

"She wasn't one of them."

"I know you aren't that naïve, brother."

"She shot at least three of them, and they had to tranquilize her to take her down."

I stare at him, not believing what I'm hearing. "What part of 'don't leave out a single detail' didn't you understand? You had a fucking woman with you and between the two of you six assailants were gunned down, but then backup arrived, tranqued *her*, and left *you?*"

"Not exactly." His shoulders slump and he lets out the breath he's been holding. I'm afraid to ask what he isn't telling me, and so I wait patiently for him to finish spilling his guts. It doesn't take long. "We took off at the speed of light after we confirmed all six were dead, I triggered the self-destruct, and we went off the main roads to regroup. The secondary team kind of took us by surprise."

"How in the fuck did they take you by surprise?" I grit out each word slowly, my jaw tight. None of this makes sense.

"Sex," he answers like he's surprised it happened. "The whole 'fucking like bunnies' thing. We were in the front seat of her car. Tight quarters to move around in—"

"You were fucking when they took *her*? And *you* managed to get away?" I pull my Browning and stick the barrel in the center of his forehead. "Are you an absolute moron?"

"Yes."

I cock the gun. "Tell me what you aren't telling me."

"The woman was Eva."

I spin away from him fast enough that I don't blow off his head. I slam the gun back into its holster under my arm and stomp across the room to put distance between us. Scrubbing my face with my hands, I try to make sense of it all, but only one name comes to mind. *Glorianna.* I will never forget the day we met. I was well hidden from my enemies on US soil. Every agency in every country that I had ever worked for thought me dead, but I had underestimated the cunningness of the clandestine agencies of the United States. It was this woman who found me. This woman who would have made my life a living hell had I not accepted her proposal. By becoming a guardian of US interests, a safe-keeper of her interests, I would have her protection. In the years since, I have had many instances to protect her, and she has honored her promise to protect me. She controls me. It isn't something I like to dwell on. The Guardians aren't recognized as a world power, their existence is the stuff of urban legends, but exist they do, and this woman controls their every move.

If I had to guess, I would say Glorianna discovered Eva was in the middle of her turf without permission.

"Damn it!" I punch a wall, but it doesn't help.

She asked me to bring her my brother. That was the assignment that took me to Paris in the first place. If she has Eva it will only be a matter of time before she knows about Nikos. So, this is it, I've done all I can do for him. *Fuck!*

Using the hotel's land line, I call Garrett at Lewd Larry's. My stomach sinks when he answers, because even though I have to make this phone call, I don't want to.

"Is Celia Brentwood near?" By using Kitten's real-life name I alert him that something is wrong. It is part of our ménage arrangement. If I leave the state or the country, I at least let them know I am going to be away. Before I would come and go, sometimes being gone for months with no word, only to return alive and well and ready for work—with no excuse for my absence. Garrett dealt with it and accepted my life as it was for more than a decade. Celia refused to adapt to the unknown. Now I use code to alleviate her fears.

"She's right here."

"Could you put it on speaker phone?"

"Hello?" She doesn't use my name, and I realize Garrett has alerted her that something is amiss. I smile, hearing her voice.

"Hi, sweetheart." My voice is force-filled with lightness. She translates sweetheart as *something is horribly wrong.*

I don't have to see her face to know the color has drained from it.

"I'm afraid I won't be home for dinner." *I'm leaving.* There isn't anything more I can tell her, and I've trained her to understand that this first call must be short and sweet. When I tell her, "I love you," it is not code, it is truth.

"I love you," she whispers.

I hang up before anything else can be said and hustle Nikos to my car before I change my mind about doing what I know I need to do. Driving down the road, I make a series of three phone calls, a sequenced code that will trigger an alert for Glorianna. Predictably she calls my cell a few moments later. "Do you have my package?"

"Yes."

"Good. Bring it to me."

"You know I can't do that, not without certain assurances."

"The contents of the package are insured for a huge sum, I will protect it with my life." She hangs up on me but I breathe a little easier, knowing my brother won't face eminent death. Facing him, I can tell by the look on his face that he thinks I just sold him out.

He shakes his head and buries his face in his hands. "A new life was too good to be true."

He is in a fragile mental state, George warned me as much. Keeping one hand on the wheel, I pull his hand away so that I can look into his eyes and see that he is crying.

"So, brother, blood of my blood, who did you sell me out to?"

I shake my head. "It isn't like that." *God, I hope it isn't like that.* "I work for her agency. Black ops. US based. She wants to meet with you. She has for several months. I'd hoped I could keep you hidden from her."

He sighs. "She has Eva and will force her to tell her the name of the man she was with."

"Yes." They've probably been following her for weeks.

"She said as much. She thought it was me."

"Wrong place, wrong time. Big mix up. You said they tranquilized her instead of executing her?"

"Yes," he answers, wrapping his fingers around his head, understanding filling his eyes. Eva is in a much worse predicament than he.

My jaw tightens. If Eva isn't dead already, I think she's praying she soon will be, but I won't tell him that. I can't take the chance he might run.

* * * *

Glorianna doesn't keep a poker face, leaving me surprised she ever attained the level of power she has. Shock. Dismay. Irritation. All directed at Nikos and she hasn't even said a word yet. For the moment we're sitting, a small desk separating us. Two guards block the door. We could be in any executive office, but this isn't any office, this is her office, Abigail Wainwright-Fuller, United States Senator.

She finally manages to comment, "You were a stronger force when you were identical." Standing, she walks around her desk to face Nikos. "Remove your shirt."

He doesn't stand. He pulls the tight black turtleneck he is wearing over his head and earns a gasp as the senator takes in the full depth of his body modification.

Silently, she returns to her seat. Disgusted, she demands, "Put it back on."

While Nikos pulls on his shirt, she directs her irritation at me. "You *could* be identical again."

I try to not let my distaste at her suggestion show. "No disrespect, but I think we both prefer to not be so."

Her secretary buzzes her intercom. "Henri Ulliel has arrived."

"Send him in."

Beside me, Nikos tenses. Both of us are surprised when Henri and Eva enter together. They are directed into chairs and neither look too happy about being here. Curious. Henri is perfectly coiffed, Eva on the other hand is definitely worse for wear, her face bruised.

Glorianna doesn't leave us in suspense. She seems pleased when she announces, "I have before me three of the world's most dangerous operatives." Looking at each of us, I feel the full weight of her assessment and believe the others do as well. "Henri Ulliel's intention is to take you three of you back to France." She measures our reaction, or rather lack thereof. "However, I do not believe that is in the best interest of the United—"

Henri stands, interrupting, "You agreed."

She lifts her hand in a gesture to silence him. "States. It seems the WODC has been left in a state of turmoil, following recent events, and something must be done to right affairs."

One of the guards steps forward and takes Henri by surprise, injecting him with a syringe. He jerks, eyes bulging, before dropping back into his seat.

"I'm afraid he won't survive the heart attack he suffers on US soil. The WODC cannot withstand the weight of more turmoil." She looks at Eva. "I've been watching you for years, and I can see why he'd name you his successor. As of this moment, you report to me."

Eva doesn't show any outward response but an air of tension circles the room. I don't believe any of us present are naïve enough to believe her refusal would face any result less than instant death. "Yes, ma'am."

"Your first directive is to accompany Henri Ulliel's body back to France and see to his state funeral." There is a moment of labored silence followed by Glorianna clapping her hands. "Go now. I'll be in contact."

Two men drag out Henri's body and without even a second glance Eva follows them.

Glorianna looks between myself and my brother. "Now, what to do with the two of you?"

I know the question was rhetorical but I can't remain quiet. "Allow Nikos to retire. I would be *in your debt*."

Nikos starts to interrupt but quiets when she looks at him hard. "Smart boy. Let your brother do this for you. You've earned a vacation."

"You will wait outside." She gestures at one of the remaining guards in the room to assist Nikos from the room. I feel his panic, as obviously does Glorianna. "Don't worry. I'll be finished with your brother momentarily. If I truly wanted you dead, don't you think you would have died in Shanghai?"

I feel like I've been kicked in the balls, realizing she has orchestrated everything from beginning to end. Nikos exits the room accompanied by both guards, leaving me alone with Glorianna.

Nodding at me, she asks, "What are you willing to give me for this favor?"

I did this to myself. *Damn.*

My silence is met by a direct order. "I need you. There are very few people I trust in this world. You are one of them. Consider the last few months a test. I couldn't respect a man who wasn't willing to die for his family, and you have proven you're more than willing."

I swallow hard, dreading the favor she is going to ask. A million scenarios circle through my brain as I consider the wildly fluctuating state of US-foreign affairs. The one post I don't consider is the one she gives me.

"Starting Monday morning you will be my personal assistant. I'll be announcing my bid for president."

My jaw drops. I never saw *that* coming.

"Twenty-four hours a day, seven days a week. In return, after your service to me and your country, you too will have your freedom."

I am astonished but not left entirely speechless. "You have bodyguards."

"I want you."

I don't miss her meaning.

"Is a few years service really asking too much when it guarantees both you and your brother retirement?"

"No, ma'am."

"Good. You have the weekend to get your affairs in order. Report to my Washington office Monday morning at seven a.m."

"Washington? DC?"

"That is where the job is."

"Yes, ma'am."

"Military haircut. Clean shaven."

I stand, trying hard to not show any reaction. Too late I realize my hands are fists. She meets me beside the door, giving me *that* look. She lusts me, pure and simple. I force myself to relax my hand before reaching to stroke her face. I whisper, "Glorianna," and my voice cracks with emotion I wouldn't even begin to be able to express. *Fuck, fuck, fuck.* There is no way out of this assignment without perilous consequences. Of course, I could kill her...but she knows and I know...I won't. We've shared a strange relationship for longer than I can remember. More than a decade. I aided her rise to a place of power and when I needed rescuing, she rescued me. She never asked for payment. She gave me a cushy cover story and few assignments.

"I'm not getting any younger, my sweet prince."

I take her face in my hands, hugging her cheeks with my palms as I gaze deeply in her eyes. *Why are you doing this?*

"She'll wait for you. I've seen in her eyes how deeply she loves you."

I go completely still, feeling threatened.

"She carries your twins."

I'm barely breathing.

"Of course your sons will go to all the right schools, become skilled just as you and Nikos became skilled."

My heart lodges high in my throat, choking me. I never believed she'd ever ask so much. I have Hektor and Nikkos, neither of which have been demanded into service.

"Twins have been and always will be a most valuable asset," she says with great exaggeration. "Congratulations, Aristotle."

I release her face to keep myself from breaking her neck. Without a word, I leave the office. There is a part of me that I never allow to react and that part is screaming in my brain so loudly that no other thought registers except that I must flee and take everyone I hold dear with me. The saner, less primal, part of me knows that there is no safe place on the planet I can run to.

My head is spinning as I am led down a long corridor to a very public lobby. My brother is being guarded by a Marine but is allowed to stand and exit the building with me. A taxi is waiting at the curb.

Nikos waits until we are safely ensconced in the back seat before asking, "What did she say?"

In Greek I lay out the bottom line.

"You aren't going," he insists.

"There isn't any other option."

"I can think of a few."

I look at him not believing his naïveté. "And have it *never* end? This is our way out of a profession from which no one retires." I don't mention her insinuation regarding my unborn children. The answer to that conundrum is best saved for another day. I stare out at the passing scenery, trying to figure out how in the hell I break the news of this latest disaster to Garrett and Sophia.

"You trust her to keep her word?" he asks.

"Yes." I don't look at him.

"And what do I do while you play secretary games?"

For a second the ocean comes into view and I am filled with melancholy for Greece. I want to pack up everyone I love and hideout in one of the rural towns of my youth. The taxi turns and I am again left with buildings to look at. I turn to face my brother. "You'll take over my assignment here. I'll get you settled in at Lewd Larry's, bartender not Dominant. Trust me, it's a fairly cushy place to work."

He shakes his head and crosses his arms. "No way. I want out. I'm not like you, I can't be a sleeper, waiting for months, maybe years for a job. I'll die of boredom. A bullet between my eyes would be better."

"No. It wouldn't. Damn it, Nikos, you survived Cobra, you can survive Lewd Larry's."

The taxi pulls up to the entrance of Garrett's building and I climb out. I wait for Nikos to join me but he makes no move to do so. I duck my head back in. "What are you doing?"

"You want me to go in with you?"

I shrug. "They're going to have to meet you. You're going to be working for them."

He shakes his head. "This is a horrible idea. Have you considered what you're going to do if they refuse to hire me?"

"I'll take your ass back to Glorianna and she can find you a job. So you better go in and make them fall head over heels in love with you."

With a heavy sigh he begrudgingly climbs out of the taxi and follows me through the opulent lobby. As we enter the elevator he demands, "I've been living in a dump and you come home to this every night?"

I roll my eyes. "You blew the roof off the tallest building in Shanghai and you think I would even dream of setting you up here? I don't think so."

He bobbles his head and repeats what I say mockingly, insisting, "Shanghai wasn't my fault."

The door is answered by Enrique whose eyes go wide when he sees Nikos. We push by him, leaving him gaping. Entering the living room, I see Sophia stretched out on one of the sofas, asleep. Garrett is staring out over the city, watching a glorious sunset.

"Gar?" I say softly, getting his attention.

He pivots on his heel and his expression goes from jubilant to angry in seconds, but he doesn't say a word.

I leave my brother standing between foyer and living room to embrace my lover. Hugging him, I whisper, "We need to talk."

He eyes Nikos over my shoulder.

Releasing him, I say, "May I introduce my brother?"

Nikos steps forward with his hand outstretched, a wide smile on his face. "I'm so glad to finally meet you. I want to thank you in person for saving my life."

Garrett shakes his hand, though by the look on his face he would have preferred to not have.

"I've heard so much about you...from Thomas and George. I think my brother is very blessed to have you as a friend, Mr. Lawrence."

Garrett takes a deep breath and releases Nikos's hand. "What do I call you?"

"Joshua. Joshua Lambert."

I hear Sophia gasp, though I can't see her through Garrett and my brother. When Garrett goes to her and joins her on the couch the blood has drained from her face. She is staring at Nikos like she's seen a ghost...or maybe a monster. In her mind I imagine that is exactly what she's conjured, a monster capable of ripping the ménage apart. My job will be to convince her to not take her anger and disappointment out on him after I leave.

"Enrique?" I call, and he steps into sight.

"Sir?"

"Could you show Joshua to the guest room and make sure he has fresh towels? I promised him he could freshen up before dinner."

Garrett and Sophia share a look and both of them are on the same page for the first time in a long time. Neither of them want Nikos under their roof a moment longer than necessary. Thankfully, Enrique doesn't question, he does what he is told, leading Nikos from the room.

"I can't believe you brought him here!"

I am shocked by the vehemence in Sophia's voice. Even Garrett gives her a harsh look for her honest reaction though given time he would have said the same thing. I kneel before her, taking her hands in mine.

She jerks them away. "I thought I might never see you again. When you called you scared the life out of me. And now here you are with him."

"When I phoned I wasn't sure I would have another opportunity. If I'd have known the way things were going to have turned out, I wouldn't have called."

"So, you're saying you were in danger…enough danger that you might have never had a chance to tell me you loved me again…and you called to say the words one more time?"

I nod and she slaps me.

"Damn you!"

I drop my face, knowing I deserve her outrage. I'm just surprised she hasn't cracked under the pressure before now. Garrett wraps her in his arms so that she can't move, and she struggles against him. "Kitten, please, calm down. It isn't good for you or the babies to be this upset."

"Did you hear what he said? He thought he might die. That's why he called. I told you that was why, and I was right. He could have died today."

He kisses her forehead, holding her tighter. "He isn't dead. He's here now."

Her face crumbles as she demands, "What about next time?"

I bury my face in her lap, hoping she will be able to forgive me when I give her the rest of the news. A sob escapes before I can stop it. I have never been asked to do something this emotionally difficult. I don't want to go on this assignment and if there was any way not to I wouldn't. My tears shock both Garrett and Sophia into silence.

I wrap my arms tightly around her folded legs, hugging her, holding on to her as all the loss I've experienced the last year hits me. She leans over me, hugging me back. "What is it, Ari? You're really scaring me now."

I sit back on my haunches and wipe my face. "I'm sorry. It's been a long day, and I'm afraid I don't have very good news."

"O blessed, blessed night! I am afeard. Being in night, all this is but a dream. Too flattering-sweet to be substantial."

William Shakespeare, *Romeo and Juliet*

CHAPTER 41

THOMAS

"Take her with you."

Garrett strides into the bedroom, finding me packing. I can't say his demand takes me by surprise, but I find it disappointing. I'd hoped he'd step back into the game. Since announcing her pregnancy, it seems he's been ready to walk away and allow us to be a happy couple, but neither Sophia or I want that. I answer, "That isn't an option," not even bothering to look up from the shirt I'm folding.

"She isn't happy with me. When you are away, she mopes for you constantly."

Grinding my jaw tight, I meet his gaze and silently count to ten. Then I count to twenty, knowing she is in the other room and the last thing she needs on the night of my departure, especially following the scare of a potential miscarriage, is the two of us butting heads. Under my glare, he flinches.

"Tell me what to do, damn it, because I'm out of ideas."

I carefully lay the folded shirt into my suitcase before walking to him. We've been in this power play before, the moment when time slows and the walls around us throb, waiting, matching the rhythm of our heartbeats. Usually, we end up beating the hell out of each other or fucking each other's brains out. Today we have time for neither. I step close, crowding him, but he doesn't step back. I caress his face. "Do you believe it would be any different for me should the situation be reversed? Do you not understand that she loves us both fully with the divided halves of herself?"

He snorts derisively. "You make her sound schizophrenic."

I hug his face between my palms, forcing him to meet my gaze. "We are all two halves of one whole, Gar. Light. Dark. Most of us fight to unite ourselves and find balance. She fights to keep hers separate."

He whispers, "I don't want you to leave. Not like this. Not knowing when or even if you will be able to come back for short visits or whether you will even be permitted to return for the birth of the babies."

I push my forehead against his. The emotion he is holding back is palpable. He's killing me. Sophia crying in the other room I can survive. But this? It's worse, harder to walk away from. "She will grieve. Mourn my absence with her as I did when you left."

A tear finally slides down his cheek and the force of need swelling the room breaks. I sigh, relieved, knowing he has accepted the fact that I am leaving and I'm not taking Sophia with me. I kiss him, his mouth warm and pliant beneath my lips.

He whispers against my mouth, "Don't go."

"Gar," I whisper, "I'm no happier about this than you. I'd give anything to make this assignment not so."

* * * *

Sophia has said nothing and that worries me more than Garrett's open grief. I think perhaps we should call George, but Garrett convinces me that the three of us should spend a final night in each other's arms and assures me that after I leave he will call George if it is deemed necessary.

After a quiet dinner, Nikos excuses himself and goes back to the guest bedroom. He feels horrible and I know he blames this mess on himself, but the honest truth is that I wouldn't even have the relationship I have with these two people I love so much if he hadn't taken my place a decade ago. I was only able to disappear because of his sacrifice.

Now, it's my turn.

We go to the bedroom agreeing on no penetration even though Dr. Wang has said he feels that all normal activities could be resumed. I'm not willing to take a chance, neither is Garrett. At this point it is fairly obvious that Kitten will have to be content with mere servitude as both Garrett and I share the agreement that no level of play is safe following the episode of bleeding.

Standing between us, she is almost unresponsive as we both kiss her. Garrett in front of her, kissing her lips, while I stand behind her kissing her nape. I bite softly, eliciting a moan, and she turns between us to kiss my mouth.

I am glad when Garrett takes it in stride and continues to caress her, rubbing her arms and breasts and belly through her clothing. I lose myself in her mouth, enjoying the sweetness of her kisses. She whispers, "I don't want you to leave."

"I know, baby, I know."

I pull her shirt over her head and kiss her skin as it's revealed. Garrett unsnaps her bra and draws it down her arms. I sit down on the bed and pull her forward to suck her nipples. She gasps and moans, so sensitive due to the pregnancy. I am not sure whether I am causing her pleasure or pain, but I don't stop.

Behind her Garrett is similarly tormenting her, alternating between biting her neck and sucking her earlobe. She exclaims, "God! Oh God."

I shimmy down her stretchy pants and help her to step free. Garrett drops to his knees and starts massaging her legs, rubbing his hands and lips over the backs of her thighs. She twists her fingers into my hair and forces me to meet her mouth, kissing me with need verging on desperation.

I drop back onto the bed, pulling her with me. Garrett moves onto the bed as well, helping me pull her into position. Rolling her beneath me, I crawl between her legs. I want her desperately but settle for licking her slick folds. Garrett climbs around so that he can kiss her lips while I worship her labia and clit. She moans softly. "Master, I want to suck you."

I am not surprised by her request, it is a frequent one asked of both of us. He maneuvers around to straddle her face. She takes his length into her mouth and makes soft happy sounds deep in her throat which makes my erection tighten painfully.

I don't stop licking her, not even when his mouth joins mine in the task.

Garrett and I share a kiss over her throbbing pussy, both of us smelling of her, before return to the task of helping her find pleasure. Our tongues collide and tangle more than once and I think that the sensation of both of us licking her does it for all of us.

Her orgasm starts, quickly followed by Garrett's. I take my own cock in hand, the touch barely necessary to find my own release. My orgasm is anticlimactic, one step closer to having to say goodbye.

It takes a moment for us to all rearrange so that we are lined up with our heads again on pillows. I am in the middle, making an immediate escape impossible, not that I want to go. That's the problem. My mind flies through a dozen different scenarios, all of them ending with me, Garrett, and Sophia lying under a hot sun on a foreign beach with icy frou-frou drinks in hand. I say for what seems like the hundredth time, "You both know I don't want to go."

Too soon it is time for me to go. I still have to get Nikos settled in at Lewd Larry's. I keep an emergency sleeping room there at The Attic and it was agreed by both Garrett and Sophia that they want him there. In part I think they believe that if he is there I will most certainly come back. Silly on their part, I wish I could make them see that they are all the draw I need. They are my family now as much as Nikos.

We are both quiet as Blake drives us to the club. I as lost in my thoughts as he is in his. Both of us worried about what direction our new roles will take us.

"They don't know that fucking the senator is part of the job description, do they?"

"No, and I'd like to keep it that way."

The night air is a cool, sensual caress on my face as I step from my car. A bass beat throbs in the air and we haven't even entered the building yet. It will be Nikos's first impression of his new place of employment, and what an impression the place is capable of making tonight. The Lewd Larry's crowd wraps around the block, waiting to get in.

"This is it?" he asks.

"This is it," I answer, looking up the side of the brick façade, four-story warehouse to a brilliant blue flickering neon sign that says it all: *Lewd Larry's Fetish Fantasy.*

I use my staff key to get us into a secondary entrance that leads onto the spacious dance floor, the heart of the casual observer's Lewd Larry's experience. Multi-level dance stages are outfitted with dance poles and surrounded by brass dance cages that offer eye candy in the form of barely clothed professional dancers. A club DJ on a raised dais is responsible for whipping the dance crowd into a frenzy, playing the hottest dance mixes and filling their minds with naughty ideas for what they might want to do in one of the secluded alcoves, should their partners be willing. A smokey haze fills the dance space and reflects a blaze of alternating colored lights. The overall mood is high class, mysterious, and very sensual.

"Welcome to Lewd Larry's."

"I get to work here?" he asks and I nod in answer, biting my tongue. This is actually the last thing I wanted, but at least he'll be safe here...and happy. I was. If anything, Lewd Larry's is distracting and entertaining. It's hard to be sad or melancholy within the closure of its fantasy world.

I find myself already on autopilot, making sure that security posts have everything under control as I gauge the throng for the evening's mood. The lower level Dominants work the crowd, deeming who is ready for admission into the more private arenas. It isn't easy to get an invite, but for those who receive invitations to the uppermost levels of Lewd's it is an eye opening experience. Assured the place has survived without me, I look at Nikos, finding his head tilted. He is close to drooling, something or someone has caught his attention. Not a real surprise *here.*

I follow the direction of his gaze to the descending glass elevator and the woman inside. *Morgana.* She stands close to the glass, watching the floor as she descends; I know it's because she is terrifyingly claustrophobic. To the casual observer she appears regal, not scared shitless. The red satin gloves that extend past her elbows, hides the fact her knuckles are turning white.

The glass reveals shapely legs encased in thigh-high black leather boots, five-inch heels; the girl has a thing for very expensive, very sexy footwear. Only four feet, nine inches, she's at a disadvantage as a female Domme, she needs all the height she can get. Flaming red hair cascades past her waist, hiding most of her barely there lace up the front corset and mind-fucking hip hugger hot pants, both in fire engine red. Tonight she is sporting a black leather harness with a flaming red, acrylic strap-on that would make most of the real penises in the room shrink with envy.

I tilt my head, seeing what he sees. Pale skin, very, very pale, I start imagining all the places her liberally sprinkled freckles hide and she's not even close enough to see the freckles. Having seen her completely naked before, it's not a forgettable memory, not that any man in their right mind would want to forget. I let out a long breath. It bothers me to think about her naked because we don't have the kind of relationship that leads to where the thought of her naked would take my brain. For some reason, it bothers me Nikos would think of Morgana in a sexual way, and by the tilt of his head and glazed eyes his brain has already gone on an X-rated journey.

"Your post is over there, bartending."

We both watch the sashay of her hips and bobbing rubber dildo bring Morgana closer.

"Fraternizing between employees is strictly prohibited."

He purses his lips, and I see that he's blowing a kiss to the woman in question.

She glares down her aristocratic nose at him, but because she is glaring means he has managed to catch her eye.

"It'd be worth getting fired to tie her up."

I laugh at him. "Morgana doesn't get tied up. Ever. She's hands off. I mean it. You are here under the good graces of Garrett Lawrence, the owner and my lover. Do not fuck things up by thinking with your dick."

"I could have her begging me to top her by the end of the night."

Morgana parts the crowd without even trying. She walks, people get out of her way.

"Oh God, I think I'm in love."

"Down boy." I hiss.

She smiles at me, still several feet away, heels clicking on the wooden floor, hot-pink prosthetic bobbing in time with her barely restrained DD-cup cleavage.

"I think I just came in my pants."

"Nikos." I growl in warning. Leave it to him to find trouble without even trying. "Morgana is off limits. I mean it."

"Fyre!" She squeals and jumps into my arms, throwing her arms around my neck and wrapping her legs around my waist, the hard dildo trapped between us.

I smirk, knowing this show is for my brother's benefit, being way over the top, even for Morgana. I wonder just what kind of impression she's trying to make on my brother.

"I am so glad you're here!" Her voice alludes to more going on, that perhaps needs said in private. Over the top drama is not Morgana's style, something is definitely up. "I thought you'd left forever, and Garrett wasn't sure when or if you were coming back!"

Nikos takes that particular moment to kick me in the back of my calf, and I set Morgana gently to the ground. He interrupts, "Hello! New guy needs an intro!"

Morgana steps back to inspect the new guy. Half-lowered lids don't reveal what she's thinking. She lifts her lip in distaste and snarls, "Tell me this isn't the new bartender."

"Oh, yeah! That's me, baby. *Your* new bartender. Why don't you tell me your favorite drink so that I can have it and a backrub ready for you at the end of your shift."

She turns to me with a snarl. "He isn't going to survive the night."

My brain snags on the freckle just above her upper lip on the left side, her cupid lips further setting off the paleness of her skin in a high cost, high slick shine of fire engine red lipstick. I manage to choke out, "How about showing the new mutt around?"

"Is he trained?"

I glare at Nikos, hoping he understands the consequences if he fails. "He can sit, heel, stay, and fetch adequately enough."

"As long as he follows directions."

"Ooh, baby. I'll follow you anywhere." He pants, then barks.

"Watch it, Fido. I have a single-tail with your name on in." Making a face of total disgust, she lifts her arm, his signal to lift his for her to rest her hand and forearm atop of, while she does the tour. In true Sir Galahad style, he bows regally before sliding his inked forearm beneath hers. Red satin and tattoos collide, then mold with an ease I didn't expect.

Morgana looks over her shoulder at me as she strides away, my brother lassoed and leashed by her mere magnetism. She winks at me, her darkly kohled and thickly mascaraed eye saying more than any words would have. She is going to eat him alive. God, I'm going to miss this place.

"I postpone death by living, by suffering, by error, by risking, by giving, by losing."

Anais Nin

CHAPTER 42

KITTEN

His text caught me by surprise: *Meet me at Louie's Barbershop, Chestnut St.*

My heart is pounding, my palms sweating, and I may throw up at any moment. Despite my promise to Master to the contrary, I do not tell him where I am going or that I am meeting Thomas. *What will I do if he asks me to go with him?* My heart flutters, one or both of the babies kicks. Nervously, I rub my hand over my ever expanding girth and climb from the car. He is waiting for me outside on the curb when I arrive and holds open his arms for me to walk into. He kisses my forehead. "Thank you for coming. I don't think I could have done this alone."

He holds my hand and opens the door to the barbershop. Scents of menthol and cologne war on the air, making my nervous stomach roll. Apprehensively, I squeeze his hand.

Fyre leans close to whisper, "It's a small world. I'll text you every day. E-mail. Phone calls. You won't have a chance to miss me."

"You plan to keep our ménage together long distance?"

There is a line of red leather upholstered chairs which look right at home in the very retro barbershop. Thomas pushes me down in one, then sits beside me while we wait his turn. He insists, "Yes, I do. I'll be in the United States. After the senator announces her bid for the White House, she'll go on the campaign trail and sooner or later that will lead us to her home state. I will manage to come home then, even if it is just for a little while."

"This sucks."

"Yes, it does, but the senator isn't heartless. I will do everything in my power to be home for the delivery," he promises, and I start to feel hope for the first time since he explained what had happened. He kisses me in the middle of my forehead. "Tell me you love me."

"You know I do."

The barber calls out to him, "You're up."

He says, "Tell me you're going to love me after I have a military cut and no beard."

Oh God. This is really happening.

"I love you."

It is too painful to watch as the scissors cut off several inches and that is before the clippers whirr on. Within minutes he has hair shorter than Garrett's and his face is smooth. The sight leaves me blinking back tears; not because he is ugly, far from it. With his military short locks and clean shaven face our nightmare is made real. He is leaving us. It hardly matters that he doesn't want to leave, or that we don't want him to go.

I remind myself he is a soldier and duty has called, feeling a sudden kinship to every woman who has stood in my place before…saying goodbye.

I remind myself he isn't going to a war zone and this moment could be so much worse if I believed I would never see him alive again.

He pulls me into his arms as the first tears fall over my cheeks, speaking softly in his native tongue. I don't understand a word except for the promise of love. Those words sound the same in any language.

I love you.

I love you.

I love you.

"I will come back to you, Sophia."

"I know," I answer, hoping we aren't lying to each other. "I'll be waiting."

* * * *

I sit behind the wheel of the car, frozen in place, watching the airport shuttle until it disappears. I don't start my engine because I know if I do I will chase after him. My heart is breaking and I have given up fighting tears. It is easier to hang over the steering wheel sobbing. A second later, I jump out of my skin, hearing a tap on my window. It is Master. He climbs into the passenger seat. His hair and jacket are damp.

Looking at the windshield, I realize it's starting to rain.

He says, "I thought I'd find you here."

"He text, I—" Shaking my head I stop myself mid-sentence. "I'm sorry, I should have told you where I was going, Master."

He smiles and kisses me. Water from his damp hair drips on my cheek. He wipes it away. "Sorry."

"It's okay," I tell him, meeting his gaze. "Well, it's finally happened. It seems we've both been waiting for this moment for a year and now it's here. He's gone." I blink back tears, feeling foolish and angry. I admit, "I'm scared."

"Do you love me?" he asks.

"Yes! Don't ever doubt that. I love you with all my heart."

"Are you *mine*?"

"Yes, Master," I answer, not understanding where this is going.

He lifts my arm and traces each symbol of the brand, saying, "Fire. Water. Ice."

"But—"

He silences me with two fingers pressed to my lips. "Thomas has promised he will come back, and I believe him."

I bite my lip to keep from saying the wrong thing.

"I think we have to trust him, or we have nothing. And while we wait for him to return to us, we have each other."

I close my eyes to keep from looking at him, my stomach sinking.

Lifting my chin, he waits for me to open my eyes and when I do tears glisten in his eyes. "I remember the first time I saw you and you were wearing another man's collar."

"I'm not sorry for the charade, if I hadn't lied I'd have never met you."

"Let me finish."

"Sorry, Master."

"I thought to myself you looked broken, so sad, but then Doug slapped your hip with the chain and there was a flash of lightning that shot through your eyes, and I knew you weren't a wounded sparrow at all but rather a mighty hawk. I fell in love with you in that moment because that woman, the woman who could express such passion and power with a glance, ignited a spark inside of me. I knew that with you I might find myself again. Do you understand?"

"I think so."

"I've never asked you before if you desired to be mine and right now, before we go further, I need to know. Do you want me to master you? Do you want to belong to Lord Ice? Forever?"

"You *are* my Master, Garrett Lawrence."

Lowering his mouth to my skin, he kisses the marking for water, and the barest touch of his soft lips to my scarred flesh makes me tremble. "I am one of your Masters, Kitten. Now, let's go *home*."

ABOUT ROXY HARTE

Roxy lives in southwestern Ohio in a small town bordered by fields and railroad tracks. She awakes to the honking of geese flying over head and falls asleep listening to her many wind chimes and the howling of coyotes and wrapped in the arms of her true love.

A wife, a mother of three daughters, and a grandmother to two granddaughters, she is grateful for the blessing of their lives entwining with hers. She is also thankful for her furry loves: Jazzi, Petey, Miss Kitty, and Blackie.

She has solid opinions, namely that life is too short to live with anything less than passion. There isn't room for negativity or unnecessary drama. Sunny days are meant for gardening, hiking, or relaxing in the sun. And a Renaissance Festival is always a welcome event.

She loves to hear from her readers, so consider dropping her a line to let her know your impression of The Chronicles of Surrender.

Roxy's Website:
http://www.roxyharte.com/
Reader email:
roxyharte@gmail.com

ABOUT THE CHRONICLES OF SURRENDER SERIES

Book 1: *Sacred Secrets*

Available in ebook and print from Lyrical Press

Book 2: *Sacred Revelations*

Available in ebook and print from Lyrical Press

Book 3: *Unholy Promises*

Available in ebook and print from Lyrical Press

Book 4: *Echo of Redemption*

Available in ebook from Lyrical Press

Book 5: *Cries of Penance*

Coming soon from Lyrical Press

WHERE REALITY
AND
FANTASY COLLIDE

Discover the convenience of Ebooks
Just click, buy and download - it's that easy!

From PDF to ePub, Lyrical offers
the latest formats in digital reading.

YOUR NEW FAVORITE AUTHOR
IS ONLY A CLICK AWAY!

GO GREEN!

Save a tree read an Ebook.

Don't know what an Ebook is? You're not alone.
Visit www.lyricalpress.com and discover
the wonders of digital reading

YOUR NEW FAVORITE AUTHOR
IS ONLY A CLICK AWAY!

LaVergne, TN USA
10 December 2010
208205LV00003B/54/P